ulia Justiss wrote her own ideas for Nancy Drew ˙ories in her third-grade notebook, and has been ˙riting ever since. After publishing poetry in ɔllege she turned to novels. Her Regency historical ances have won or been placed in contests by Romance Writers of America, *RT Book Reviews*, ˙tional Readers' Choice and the Daphne du Maurier ward. She lives with her husband in Texas. For news ad contests visit juliajustiss.com.

Discover more at millsandboon.co.uk.

THE EARL'S INCONVENIENT WIFE

Julia Justiss

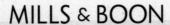
MILLS & BOON

First Published in Great Britain 2019
by Mills & Boon, an imprint of HarperCollins*Publishers*
1 London Bridge Street, London, SE1 9GF

© 2019 Janet Justiss

ISBN: 978-0-263-26894-2

Th   aper
          n.

To my fellow Zombie Bells,
for twenty-odd years of friendship, support and understanding. Along with brainstorming, fixing plot holes, figuring out muddled motivation, clarifying the Black Moment, and creating general hilarity. When the text bells start ringing, the muse starts singing!

Chapter One

London—early April, 1833

'You're certain you won't come with me?' Temperance Lattimar's twin sister asked as she looked up from the trunk into which she'd just laid the last tissue-wrapped gown. 'I know Bath isn't the centre of society it used to be, but there will be balls and musicales and soirées to attend. And, with luck, attend without whispers of Mama's latest escapade following us everywhere.'

Temperance jumped up from the window seat overlooking the tiny garden of Lord Vraux's Brook Street town house and walked over to give Prudence a hug. 'Much as I will miss you, darling Pru, I have no intention of leaving London. I won't let the rumour-mongers chase *me* away. But I do very much hope that Bath will treat you kindly—' *though I doubt it, London gossips being sure to keep their Bath counterparts updated about the latest scandal* '—and that you will find that gentleman to love you and give you the normal family you've always wanted.' Letting her sister go, Temper laughed. 'Although, growing up in *this* family, I'm not sure you'll recognise "normal" even if you find it.'

'You mean,' Prudence asked, irony—and anger—in her voice, 'not everyone grows up with a father who won't touch them, a mother with lovers tripping up and down the stairs every day and rumours that only their oldest brother is really the son of their father?'

'Remember when we were little—how much we enjoyed having all those handsome young men bring us hair ribbons and sweets?' Temper said, trying to tease her sister out of her pique.

Pru stopped folding the tissue paper she was inserting to cushion the gowns and sent Temper a look her twin had no trouble interpreting.

'I suppose it's only us, the lucky "Vraux Miscellany", who fit that sorry description,' Temper said, changing tack, torn between sympathy for the distress of her twin and a smouldering anger for the way society had treated their mother. 'Gregory, the anointed heir, then you and me and Christopher, the…add-ons. Heavens, what would Papa have done had Gregory not survived? He might have had to go near Mama again.'

'Maybe if he had, they'd have reconciled, whatever difficulty lay between them, and we would have ended up being a normal family.'

Temper sighed. 'Is there such a thing? Although, to be fair, you have to admit that Mama has fulfilled the promise she made to us on our sixteenth birthday. She's conducted herself with much more restraint these last six years.'

'Maybe so, but by then, the damage was already done,' Pru said bitterly. 'How wonderful, at your first event with your hair up and your skirts down, to walk into the drawing room and hear someone whisper, "There they are—the Scandal Sisters". Besides, as this latest incident shows, Mama's reputation is such that *she* doesn't have to do anything now to create a furore.'

'Not when there are always blockheaded men around to do it for her,' Temper said acidly. 'Well, nothing we can do about that.'

After helping her twin hold down the lid of the trunk and latch it, she gave Pru another hug. 'Done, then! Aunt Gussie collects you this morning, doesn't she? So take yourself off to Bath, find that worthy gentleman and create the warm, happy, *normal* family you so desire. No one could be more deserving of a happy ending than you, my sweet sister!'

'Thank you, Temper,' Pru said as her sister crossed to the door. 'I shall certainly try my hardest to make it so. But…are you still so determined not to marry? I know you've insisted that practically since we were sixteen, but…

Shock, his suffocating weight, searing pain… Sucking in a breath, Temper forced the awful memories away, delaying her reply until she could be sure her voice was steady. 'You really think I would give up my freedom, put myself legally and financially under the thumb of some man who can ignore me or beat me or spend my entire dowry without my being able to do a thing to prevent it?'

'I know we haven't been witness to a…very hopeful example, but not all marriages are disasters. Look at Christopher and Ellie.'

'They are fortunate.'

'Christopher's friends seem to be equally fortunate—Lyndlington with his Maggie, David Smith with his duchess, Ben Tawny with Lady Alyssa,' Pru pointed out.

Temper shifted uncomfortably. If she were truly honest, she had to admit a niggle of envy for the sort of radiant happiness her brother Christopher and his friends had found with the women they'd chosen as wives.

But the *possibility* of finding happiness in marriage wasn't worth the *certainty* of having to face a trauma she'd never been able to master—or the cost of revealing it to anyone else.

'Besides,' Pru pressed her point, 'it's the character of the husband that will determine how fairly and kindly the wife is treated. And we both know there are fair, kind, admirable men in London. Look at Gregory—or Gifford!'

Gifford Newell. Her brother's best friend and carousing buddy, who'd acted as another older brother, tease and friend since she was in leading strings. Although lately, something seemed to have shifted between them…some sort of wordless tension that telegraphed between them when they were together, edgy, exciting…and threatening.

She might be inexperienced, but, with a mother like theirs, Temper knew where that sort of tension led. And she wanted none of it.

'Very well, I grant you that there are some upstanding gentlemen in England, and some of them actually find the happy unions they deserve. I… I just don't think marriage is for me.' Squeezing her sister's hand, she crossed to the doorway. 'Don't forget to come say goodbye before you leave! Now, you'd better find where your maid has disappeared to with the rest of your bonnets before Aunt Gussie arrives. You know she hates to be kept waiting.'

Pru gave her a troubled look, but to Temper's relief did not question her any further. She kept very few secrets from her sister, but this one she simply couldn't share.

Tacitly accepting Temper's change of subject, Pru said, 'Of course I'll bid everyone goodbye. And you're correct, Aunt Gussie will be anxious to get started. Anyway, since you can't be presented this year, what do you mean to do in London?'

'Oh, I don't know,' Temper replied, looking back at her from the doorway. 'Maybe I'll create some scandals of my own!'

Trying to dispel the forlorn feeling caused by the imminent departure of the twin who had been her constant companion and confidante her entire life, Temper closed the door to the chamber they shared, then hesitated.

Maybe she should gather her cloak, find her maid and drag the long-suffering girl with her for a brisk walk in Hyde Park. With it being already mid-morning, it was too late to indulge in riding at a gallop and, as restless and out of sorts as she was this morning, she wouldn't be able to abide confining herself to a decorous trot. While she hesitated, considering, she heard the close of the hall door downstairs and a murmur of voices going into the front parlour.

One voice sounded like Christopher's. Delighted that the younger of her two brothers might be paying them a visit, Temper ran lightly down the stairs and into the room.

'Christopher, it is you!' she cried, spying her brother. 'But you didn't bring Ellie?'

'No, my wife's at her school this morning,' Christopher said, walking over to give her a hug. 'Newell caught me as we were leaving Parliament and, learning I meant to visit you and Gregory, insisted on tagging along.'

Belatedly, Temper turned to curtsy to the gentleman lounging at the mantel beside her older brother Gregory. 'Giff, sorry! I heard Christopher's voice, but not yours. How are you?'

'Very well, Temper. And you are looking beautiful, as always.'

The intensity of the appreciative look in the green eyes of her brother's friend sent a little frisson of...*something* through her. Temper squelched the feeling. What was wrong with her? This was *Giff*, whom she'd known for ever.

'Blonde, blue-eyed and wanton—the very image of Mama, right?' she retorted, hiding, as she often did, vulnerability behind a mask of bravado. 'I suppose you've heard all about the latest contretemps.'

'That was the main reason I came,' Christopher said, motioning her to a seat beside him on the sofa. 'To see if there was anything I could do. And to apologise.'

'Heavens, Christopher, you've nothing to apologise for! Ellie is a darling! We would have disowned you if you hadn't married her.'

Her brother smiled warmly. 'Of course *I* think so. I've been humbled and gratified by the support of my family and closest friends, but there's no hope that society will ever receive us. And wedding a woman who spent ten years as a courtesan wasn't very helpful to the marital prospects of my maiden twin sisters, who already had their mother's reputation to deal with.'

'Society's loss if they refuse to receive Ellie,' Temper said. 'To punish for ever a girl who was virtually sold by her father... Well, that's typical of our world, where gentlemen run everything! Which is why we need to elect women to Parliament!' She gave her brother and Newell a challenging look.

Rather than recoiling, as she rather expected, Christopher laughed. 'That's what Lyndlington's wife, Maggie, says. Since their daughter was born, she's becoming quite the militant.'

'Maybe I can join her efforts,' Temper replied. 'If you and the other Hellions in Parliament are so sincere about reforming society, you could start with the laws that make a married woman the virtual property of her husband.'

'Maybe we should. But the only earth-shaking matter I wanted to address today was to find out what had been decided about you and Pru,' Christopher replied. 'So Aunt Gussie agreed that, in the wake of the scandal, presenting you in London this year wouldn't be wise?'

'Temperance might prefer that you not discuss this with me present,' Newell cautioned, looking over at her. 'It is a family matter.'

'But you're practically family,' Temper replied and had to suppress again that strange sense of tension—as if some current arced in the air between them—when she met Gifford's gaze. If she ignored it, surely it would go away.

'I don't mind discussing "The Great Matter" with you present,' she continued, looking away from him. 'Since you *are* outside the family, you might have a more disinterested perspective.'

'The situation has improved a slight bit since last week,' Gregory said. 'It appears that Hallsworthy is going to recover after all, so Farnham should be able to return from the Continent.'

'Stupid men,' Temper muttered. 'It would have been better if they'd both shot true and put a ball through each of their wooden heads. Honestly, in this day and age, duelling over Mama's virtue! You'd think it was the era of powdered wigs and rouge! It's not as if she's ever spoken more than a few polite words to either of them.'

'Having them both dead would hardly have *reduced* the scandal,' Gregory observed.

'Perhaps not, but the population of London

would have been improved by the removal of two knuckleheads who've never done anything more useful in their lives than swill brandy, wager at cards and make fools of themselves over women!'

'Such a dim view you hold of the masculine gender,' Newell protested. 'Come now, you must admit not all men are self-indulgent, expensive fribbles.'

Fairness compelled her to admit he was right. 'Very well,' she conceded, 'I will allow that there still are a few men of honour and character in England, my brothers and you, Giff, included.'

'My point exactly,' he said, levelling those dangerous green eyes at her. 'I could also point out a number of the fairer sex who aren't exactly paragons of perfection.'

'Like the society dragons who won't accept Ellie? Yes, I'll admit that, too. But you, Giff, have to admit that though the ladies and their acid tongues may control who moves in society, it's women who are punished for any infraction of the rules, while men are…mostly exempt from them.'

'We concede,' Giff said. 'Life isn't fair.'

'Shall we move from the philosophical to the practical?' Gregory said briskly. 'As you may know, Christopher, since a presentation in London this Season would be…awkward at best, Aunt Gussie offered to take the girls to Bath. Where at least they could go out a bit in society, maybe even meet some eligible gentlemen.'

'I have no desire to wed some elderly widower and spend the rest of my husband's life feeding him potions and pushing his chair to the Pump Room,' Temper declared.

'And as you might suspect,' Gregory continued after Temper's interruption, 'practical Pru agreed, but intransigent Temper insists on remaining in London and brazening it out. Much as I love you, sis, I really would like to see you out of this house and settled in your own establishment.'

'Since I don't plan to marry, why must I even *have* a Season?' When none of the gentlemen bothered to reply to that, she sighed. 'Very well, but if I must have one, I'd rather have it straight away and not delay yet another year. Most females make their bows at sixteen and, what with one catastrophe or other occurring to forestall a presentation, Pru and I are pushing two-and-twenty, practically on the shelf! The Season will be a disaster, of course, but maybe after that, everyone will leave me alone and allow me to do what I wish.'

'Are you sure you want to press forward this year?' Gifford said. 'If you are cut by most of society, you will have few invitations to balls or entertainments or dinners. Wouldn't it be wiser to wait another year and try then, after this scandal has been buried under a host of new ones?'

'What's to say there won't be a new scandal next year?' Temper objected. 'Paying court to Mama's beauty is practically a…a rite of passage among the idiots coming down from university. Though she doesn't go about in society nearly as much as she used to, she's still as beautiful as ever. And as fascinating to gentlemen.'

'Perhaps even more so, since she doesn't encourage any of them,' Gifford acknowledged with a wry smile. 'The lure of the Beauty Unattainable.'

'The lure of knowing she hasn't always been "unattainable" and the arrogance that makes some man think *he* might be the one to succeed with her,' Temper corrected.

'Let's get back to the point,' Gregory said. 'I'd just as soon not wait to settle your future until next year, either. But if you insist on having your debut here, we shall need some eminently respectable female to sponsor you, since Aunt Gussie will be in Bath with Pru. Obviously, Mama can't do it.'

'Ellie is out, too, for equally obvious reasons,' Christopher said. 'But… I could ask Maggie. As the daughter of a marquess and wife of a viscount, she might have enough influence to manage it.'

'No, Christopher, I wouldn't want to ask her, even though she would agree. She's still fully occupied with the baby and, let's be honest, attempting to sponsor one of the "Scandal Sisters" won't enhance the social standing of whoever attempts it. Maggie is too important as a political hostess for Giles, helping him in his efforts to move the Reform bills forward, to risk diminishing her effectiveness, tarnishing her reputation by sponsoring me.'

'But society knows how close we are all, almost as close as family. They will understand the loyalty that would have her stand by you.'

'They might understand her loyalty, but they'd certainly question her judgement. No, if I press forward with this, I shall need a sponsor whose reputation is so unassailable that no one would dare oppose her.'

'How about Lady Sayleford?' Gifford suggested.

'Maggie's great-aunt?' Temper said, frowning. 'That connection is a bit remote, don't you think? I don't doubt that Maggie would take me on, but why should Lady Sayleford bother herself over the likes of me?'

'Maybe because I ask her.' Before Temper could sputter out a response, he grinned. 'She's my godmother. Didn't you know? My mother and her daughter were bosom friends.'

While Christopher and Gregory laughed, Temper shook her head. 'I didn't know, but I'm not surprised. Thick as a den of thieves, the Upper Ten Thousand.'

'You can't deny she has the social standing to carry it off,' Gifford said.

Temper smiled. 'If Lady Sayleford couldn't get her protégée admitted wherever she chose, London society as we know it would cease to exist. But even *she* would have to expend social capital to achieve it. I wouldn't want to ask it of her.'

'Knowing Lady Sayleford, she might see it as a challenge. She's never marched to anyone's tune, knows everything about everyone and has fingers in so many pies, no one dares to cross her.'

'I've never met her, but she sounds like a woman I'd admire,' Temper admitted.

'If you could secure her agreement, Lady Sayleford would be an excellent sponsor,' Gregory said, looking encouraged. 'If anyone can find an eligible *parti* to take this beloved termagant off my hands, it's the Dowager Countess.'

'Need I repeat, I have no intention of ending a Season, even one sponsored by the redoubtable Lady Sayleford, by marrying?'

When the gentleman once again ignored her comment, Christopher agreeing with Gregory that Lady Sayleford would make an excellent sponsor and asking Gifford again if he thought he could coax her into it, Temper slammed her hand on the table.

'Enough! Very well, I admit that Lady Sayleford has a better chance of foisting me on society than any other matron I can think of. But don't go making your plans yet, gentlemen. Let me at least approach Papa and see if I can convince him to release funds from my dowry for me to set up my own establishment—and get out of your house and hair, dear brother.'

The men exchanged dubious glances.

'If I can persuade him to release my dowry,' Temper persisted, 'you'll have no "situation" to discuss.'

'Yes, we would,' Gifford said. 'We'd be figuring out a way to rein you in before you organised an expedition to the Maghreb or India, like Lady Hester Stanhope.'

'Riding camels or wading in the Ganges.' With a beaming smile, Temper nodded. 'I like that prospect far better than wading through the swamp of a Season.'

'Well you might, but don't get your hopes up,' Christopher warned. 'You know Papa.'

Despite her bold assertion, Temper knew as well as Christopher how dim were her chances of success. 'I do,' she acknowledged with a sigh. 'I'll be lucky if he even acknowledges I've entered the room, much less deigns to talk with me. At least he's unlikely to bellow at me or throw things. With all the sabres and cutlasses and daggers he's in the process of cataloguing now, that's reassuring. Well, I'm off to pin him down and try my luck.'

'If I leave before you get finished, let me know what happens,' Christopher said. 'I'll be happy to return for another strategy session.' Planting a kiss on her forehead, he gave her a little push. 'You better go now, so you won't miss saying good-bye to Pru.'

'You're right,' Temper said, glancing at the mantel clock. 'Aunt Gussie could arrive at any minute. Very well—I'm off to the lion's den!' Blowing the others a kiss, she walked out—feeling Gifford Newell's gaze following her as almost like a burn on her shoulders.

Chapter Two

Gifford Myles Newell, younger son of the Earl of Fensworth, watched his best friend's sister walk gracefully out of the room. Just when had she changed from a bubbly, vivacious little girl into this stunning beauty?

A beauty, he had to admit, who raised most unbrotherly feelings in him. Sighing, he fought to suppress the arousal she seemed always to spark in him of late.

Unfortunately, one could not seduce the virginal sister of one's best friend, no matter how much her face and voluptuous figure reminded one of the most irresistible of Cyprians. And though she made an interesting and amusing companion—one never knew what she would say or do next, except one could count on it not being conventional—when he married, he would need a mature, elegant, serene lady to manage his household and preside with tact and diplomacy over the political dinners at which so much of the business of government was conducted. Not a hoyden who blurted out whatever she was thinking, heedless of the consequences.

Sadly, when he did marry, he'd probably have to give up the association that had enlivened his life since the day he'd met her when she was six. He chuckled, remembering the rock she'd tossed and he'd had to duck as he entered the back garden at Brook Street, her explaining as she apologised that she'd thought he was the bad man who'd just made her mama cry.

Her body might be the stuff of a man's erotic dreams, but she was still very much that impulsive, tempestuous child. A mature, elegant, serene wife would be a useful addition to his Parliamentary career, but he would miss the rough-and-tumble exchange of ideas, the sheer delight of talking with Temperance, never knowing where her lively mind or her unexpected reactions would take one next.

He wished the man who did end up wedding her good luck trying to control that fireball of uninhibited energy! Regardless of her childish protests that she never intended to marry, she almost inevitably would. There was no other occupation available for a gently bred female and he sincerely doubted her father, Lord Vraux, would release her dowry so his daughter could go trekking about the world, alone. How would she support herself, if she didn't marry?

She was too outspoken to become anyone's paid companion and no wife with eyes in her head would engage a woman who looked like Temperance Lattimar to instruct her children, unless her sons were very young and her husband a diplomat permanently posted at the back of beyond.

Fortunately, figuring out how to control Temperance Lattimar wouldn't be his problem. Until the day some other poor man assumed that responsibility—or until he bowed to the inevitable, gave in to his mother's ceaseless haranguing and found a wealthy wife to remove the burden of his upkeep from the family finances—he would simply enjoy the novelty of her company.

And keep his attraction to her firmly under control.

He looked up to find both Christopher and Gregory staring at him. Feeling his face heat, he said, 'She's still as much a handful as she was at six, isn't she?'

Gregory and Christopher both sighed. 'Pru will do what she must to fit in, but I'm uneasy about Temper,' Christopher said. 'That's one female who should have been born a man.'

Suppressing his body's instinctive protest at that heresy, Gifford said, 'I would love to see her on the floor of the house, ripping into the Tories who natter on about how disruptive to Caribbean commerce a slavery ban would be.'

'She would be magnificent,' Christopher agreed. 'But since female suffrage is unlikely to occur in her lifetime, we had better be thinking of some other options. I don't think she's going to have much luck squeezing any money out of Vraux.'

Knowing how much tension existed between Christopher and the legal, if not biological, father who had ignored him all his life, Gifford said, 'Probably not. But I'd love to be the parlour maid dusting outside the library door when she tries to talk him into letting her equip a caravan to journey to the pyramids!'

As it turned out, Christopher had left, but Gifford was just striding down the hallway towards the front door when Temper, with an exasperated expression, descended the stairs from the library that was Lord Vraux's private domain.

'I take it the response wasn't positive.'

She let out a frustrated huff. 'As I feared, he barely noticed I'd entered the room. You know how he is when he's in the midst of cataloguing his latest acquisitions! I stationed myself right in front of him and waved my hands until he finally looked at me, with that little frown he has when he's interrupted. In any event, he listened in silence and then motioned me away.'

Gifford knew from Gregory's descriptions how averse the baron was to being touched. Still, it must hurt his children that their father seemed unable to give—or receive—any sign of affection.

'Did he say…anything? Or just go back to cataloguing?'

She shook her head in disgust. 'He said I needed to have a Season so I could "get married and be protected". That women *need* to be protected. I couldn't help myself—I had to ask if that was why he'd married Mama. But he didn't respond, just returned his attention to the display table and picked up the next dagger.' She blew out a breath. 'Rather made me wish *I* could have picked up a dagger!'

Despite the baron's staggering wealth, which meant Gregory had never, as Giff had when they were at school together, gone hungry or had to get his clothes patched instead of ordering new ones, Gifford had always felt sorry for the Lattimar children. Possessed of a mother who, though loving, had made herself such a byword that her daughters' acceptance in society had been compromised, and a father who acted as if they didn't exist.

'I'm glad you didn't grab a dagger,' he said lightly, trying to ease her disappointment. 'The news that you'd stabbed your father, coming on top of the scandal of the duel, would further complicate your debut.'

She gave a wry chuckle. 'Thank you, Giff, for trying to cheer me up. I guess I shall be cursed with a Season after all. But I can't bear thinking about it right now, so please don't summon Gregory and call another strategy session just yet.'

She heaved another sigh. 'I'd rather have a shot of Gregory's brandy, but I'll settle for tea. Won't you take some with me?' she asked, waving him back towards the parlour. 'I haven't had a chance to talk with you since you took up your seat in Parliament.'

When had he ever been able to turn her down? Curiosity over what she might say always lured him in—as it did now, despite his unease over the physical response she sparked in him. 'I suppose I can spare a few more minutes.'

'Giff, a serious, sober parliamentarian,' she said in wondering tones as, after snagging a footman to send for tea, she led him back to the parlour. 'That's a notion that takes some getting used to! Wasn't it just last year that seeing you at this time of the morning would have meant you and Gregory were returning from your night's revels?'

Laughing, she gazed up at him, her glorious eyes teasing, her smiling mouth an invitation to dalliance. Sucking in a quick breath, he slammed his eyes shut. *This is your friend's little sister. You can't let yourself think this way about her.*

Maybe it would help if he didn't look right at her. Or sit close enough to smell the subtle jasmine scent that surrounded her, whispering of sultry climes and sin.

Seating himself a safe distance away, he protested, 'Not last year!'

'Well, maybe the year before. Gregory was just turned five-and-twenty when he inadvertently discovered what a muddle the estate books at Entremer were in and decided the heir must sort things out, since Papa obviously had little interest in doing so.'

'And you must admit, he's done an admirable job.'

'Who would have thought it? His most admirable achievement up to that point had been drinking three bottles of port in a night between entertaining three ladies. While in your company, as I remember, although he didn't divulge *your* totals.'

'How did you—?' Giff sputtered, feeling his face heat.

Temperance chuckled. 'Greg and Giff, what a pair, the two of you! When you staggered into our front hallway at eight in the morning, singing ribald songs, Gregory boasting of his prowess at the top of his lungs... In euphemisms, of course, but Pru and I knew very well what he was referring to.'

'Sometimes you girls are too perceptive,' Giff muttered.

'If we learned at an early age about dealings virginal maidens should have no knowledge of, that wasn't exactly our fault, was it?' she argued, an edge in her voice.

The footman returned with the tea tray and, for a moment, conversation ceased while she poured. Once they both had a cup of the steaming brew, she continued, 'I must say, I was rather surprised when Gregory told us you'd decided to stand for Parliament.'

'Young men must sow their wild oats, I suppose, but eventually one must consider how one intends to make his mark on the world. Especially we younger sons, who can't look forward to having an estate to run.' *Especially younger sons who've been virtually shut out by their family, all the attention of father and mother lavished on the son who would inherit*, he added silently, feeling a familiar slash of pain at that stark reality.

'Joining the Reform politicians is a choice I can admire! Are you finding the workings of Parliament as stimulating as you'd hoped?'

Gratification at her praise distracted him from both his pain and the smouldering anger her unfortunate situation so often sparked in him. Honest, direct and highly intelligent, Temper never flattered, and offered praise sparingly. Despite her youth, of all the females of his acquaintance, she was probably the one whose approval meant the most to him.

'I have to admit, I was dubious when Gregory and Christopher first urged me, but…it *is* stimulating.'

'You've found your calling, then.'

He smiled. 'I think I have. To stand on the floor of the House and realise that what you do there, calling for an end to slavery or for restricting the employment of children in factories, will better the lives of thousands, here and across England's possessions! It's both humbling and thrilling. Even if change doesn't go as far or happen as quickly as we'd like.'

'Yes, Christopher tells me that it will be difficult enough to hammer through the right of all men to vote, that I shouldn't look to see suffrage extended to women any time soon. Unless "women" are added as a class in the bill to end slavery,' she quipped.

He laughed, as he knew she intended him to. 'I'll grant you that married women are… economically disadvantaged. Although their circumstances are not nearly as dire, men with no control over fortune are restricted, too.'

'Your mama has been harassing you about money again?'

Surprised, he forgot his caution and looked at her. Luscious, lovely—and so perceptive. Looking quickly away, before her beauty could wind its seductive tendrils around his susceptible body, he quoted wryly, '"I thought a younger son debauching himself in the capital was expensive enough, but having one in Parliament has turned out to be even more costly".'

'Surely your mama realises you cannot sway the opinions of the brokers of power in a twice-turned coat and cracked boots. And from Christopher's experience, I know even bachelor members of Parliament must sometimes play host to entertainments at the inns or clubs where so many of the compromises are hammered out.'

Damping down his embarrassment that Temper had noticed how shabby his attire had sometimes become, when his quarter-day allowance came late—or not at all—Giff said, 'Quite true. Being a member of Lyndlington's "Hadley's Hellions" group, Christopher had the benefit of being included in the dinners Giles and Maggie gave. Alas, I have no such close connections to a political hostess.'

'Which is why your mama keeps pestering you to marry one. Or at least a girl with money.' His surprise must have shown on his face, for Temper said, 'She's bound to be wanting you to marry wealth—if only to remove the strain of your up-keep from the family purse. Although she may also want some grandchildren to dandle on her knee.'

Gifford tried to imagine such a picture and couldn't. Mama might be interested in the *heir's* children—but never his. 'I doubt that. She'd rather be rid of my expense so she can hang new reti-cules on her wrist and put more expensive gowns on her back!'

'I may occasionally be angry with Mama, but at least I know, infamous as she is, she loves us.'

Lady Vraux might be a fond mama, but the scandalous behaviour of her earlier years had caused irrevocable harm to her daughters. Gif-ford had trouble forgiving her for that sin.

'Even if I'm plagued with a Season,' Temper had continued, 'it's unlikely I'll become bosom friends with any pure young maidens. Watchful mamas will probably warn their girls to avoid me like a medieval scourge, lest a daughter's repu-tation become contaminated by mine. Are there any rich young ladies who have caught your eye?'

'Since, despite Mama's continual urging, I'm not yet ready to make the plunge into matrimony, I avoid gatherings where females of that ilk may be lurking.' He laughed. 'Not that I would be ac-counted a prime catch by any means.'

'Oh, I don't know! You're handsome, intelligent, well spoken, principled and from an excellent old family. All you lack is fortune and, for a girl with a large dowry, that would hardly be an impediment. If you're not ready to marry, you're probably wise to avoid places where some determined young miss might try to entrap you.' She grinned. 'Besides, though you may not be as… flagrant about your pursuits as in years past, I know for certain that when it comes to feminine company, you and Gregory still prefer ladies of easy virtue.'

'You really do have no maidenly modesty, do you?' he asked, half-amused, half-exasperated by her plain speaking.

'Growing up in this household? I would have to be blind and dumb to have attained my advanced age still retaining any. So, no *gently born* young ladies of interest at the moment. Should you like me to be on the lookout for likely prospects, if I manage to get invited to entertainments where virtuous young maidens gather?'

'Are you going to join my mother in haranguing? Not very sporting, when you profess yourself so opposed to marriage.'

'Not haranguing and our cases are quite different. As long as I can convince Papa to allow me some wealth of my own, marriage offers me no advantages. Whereas, for you, gaining a wealthy bride whose funds would free you from depending on the pittance your family grudgingly doles out would make your job in Parliament easier. Obtaining a hostess like Maggie, who is intelligent, charming and interested in politics, would be even more beneficial.'

The wives of Christopher and his friends were admirable, the couples did seem happy in their unions, and everything she said about ending his money worries and having a capable hostess was true. 'Perhaps,' he admitted. 'But I'm not ready to acquire the advantages of marriage yet.'

'Not ready to give up your ladies, you mean.'

'Let's return to your situation,' he said, having heard enough remarks about his predilection for the muslin company. 'I meant what I said about asking Lady Sayleford if she would sponsor you. She's truly as redoubtable as her reputation claims. If you must have a Season to bring your father around, she would be the best candidate to sponsor you. Anything I can do to help, you know I will, Temper.'

The amusement fled from her face, replaced by a sad little smile that touched his heart. 'I know, Giff. You've been good friend to all of us for as long as I can remember and I do thank you for it,' she said, reaching over to pat his hand.

It was meant to be a casual, friendly gesture. But her light touch resonated through his body with the impact of a passionate kiss. And produced the same result.

He froze, fighting the reaction. Unfortunately, Temper stilled as well, staring at her hand resting on his, her expression startled and uncertain.

And then, rosy colour suffusing her face, she snatched her hand back. 'Yes, ah, that would be, um, quite… I mean, if I must have a Season, I would appreciate your approaching Lady Sayleford.'

Her voice sounded as odd as her disjointed words. Which must mean that the touch that paralysed him had affected her, too. He wasn't sure whether to be satisfied or alarmed by the fact.

Maybe it was time to leave, before the randy part of him urged him to further explore that intriguing possibility. Setting down his teacup with a clatter, he said, 'I must be off. Shall I call on my godmother and see what I can arrange?'

If the moment *had* been as intense for her, it had passed, for the look she angled up at him was all laughing, mischievous child again. 'Yes, I suppose you must. Imagine—Temperance Lattimar gowned in white, making her debut among the virtuous maidens! That would set the cat among the pigeons, don't you think?'

'It should certainly be…interesting,' he allowed. 'I'll call again later after I've had a chance to chat with her. Thank you for tea and goodbye, Temper.'

'Goodbye, Giff.' She held out her hand to shake goodbye—as they had countless times before—and must have thought better of it, for she hastily retracted it. Not that he would have been foolish enough, after his disturbingly strong reaction to her previous touch, to offer her his hand.

No matter how much he'd like to touch that... and more.

Irritated by the simmer of attraction he was having such a hard time suppressing, Gifford strode out of the room. Trotting down the entry steps of Vraux House after the butler closed the door behind him, he blew out a breath.

He'd been sincere when he assured Temperance that he'd do whatever he could to help her. He truly wanted the best for her. But the attraction she exerted on him seemed to only be growing and doing this service meant he'd likely be seeing her more often than the occasional meeting when he dropped by to visit Gregory.

The prospect of seeing more of Temperance Lattimar was both alluring...and alarming.

Chapter Three

After watching Gifford Newell walk out, Temperance sat back on the sofa and poured herself another cup of tea.

Was she wise to let Giff help her? All she'd done was pat his hand and—oh, my! The bolt of attraction was so strong she'd been immobilised by it. So much that she forgot where she was and what she was doing, her brain wiped free of every thought except the wonder of what it might feel like to kiss him.

She didn't seem to be doing a very good job of ignoring the attraction. Perhaps she ought to regretfully acknowledge that a complication had arisen in what had previously been a care-free, straightforward friendship, and be on guard against it.

The last thing she should do was allow curiosity to lure her into exploring where those impulses might lead.

And then she had to laugh. It was highly unlikely that handsome, commanding, virile Gifford Newell, who probably had never seen her as anything but his best friend's troublesome little sister, would be interested in pursuing such feelings with *her*—even though she was quite certain he had felt the explosive force of that touch. Not when he already had long-standing and mutually satisfactory relations with ladies far more practised and alluring than she was.

Which was just as well. It would be unfair to invite him down a pathway she already knew she could never follow to its ultimate end. The mere thought of what that would entail sent a shudder of distaste through her.

Still, despite the uncomfortable, edgy feelings he roused in her, she enjoyed his company and counted him as one of the few people whose honesty and dependability she could count on. Though in the past he'd often exasperated her with his teasing, as she grew older, he'd begun to listen to her with an appreciation and understanding exceeded only by her sister's. She simply refused to give in and let this…irrational attraction she didn't seem able to suppress spoil a friendship she valued so dearly.

If she were forced to have a Season—and she didn't see how she was going to avoid it, however unpleasant the prospect—she really would prefer to get it over with. She'd vowed, when she turned fifteen and first discovered the implications of her close resemblance to her mother, never to let anyone see how much the censure and unearned criticism hurt. No, she intended to meet society's scorn with a public show of defiance—and weather it privately with fortitude. Though occasionally—if anger got the better of her, which it well might—she might be goaded into doing something truly outrageous, just to live down to society's expectations of her.

The delight of doing that wouldn't make enduring the rest of the ordeal any less unpleasant.

It really would be helpful to have Lady Sayleford guarding her back. Assuming, after meeting her and listening to Temper's frank avowal of how she intended to behave, that lady was willing to take her on.

Doing so, though, would mean having Gifford Newell act as her intermediary.

It wouldn't necessarily mean they'd see each other much more often than they did now, aside from the initial interview with Lady Sayleford, she reasoned. He'd just emphatically reaffirmed what she already knew—that, as he wasn't ready to take a wife, he had no intention of frequenting the sort of Marriage Mart entertainments she would be forced to endure. He would simply turn her over to his godmother and go back to his own pursuits.

She couldn't suppress a little sigh of regret. Despite the recent complication in their relationship, she knew with Gifford nearby, she would be safe—protected from the worst of the insults and scorn of those who disapproved of her and from any men who might seek to take advantage. And she truly would enjoy witnessing his reaction to all the Marriage Mart manoeuvring.

But since it was highly unlikely he would attend any of the entertainments she would be dragged to, she'd better work up the courage to face all those threats alone. After all, when Pru married, as she certainly would—what intelligent man could resist her darling sister?—Temper truly would be alone. Permanently.

For the first time, Temper faced that bleak prospect, not as some distant spectre, but as an event that would likely happen *soon*. She had to put a hand to her stomach to still the wave of bleakness and dismay that swept through her.

Wasn't gaining her independence what she wanted, though? She tried to rally herself. She'd still have Gregory and Christopher, Gifford's special friendship and could look forward to playing the proud aunt to Pru's eventual children. Doubtless somewhere in her family tree she could find some indigent female relation who would prove both congenial and willing to live with her.

As an independent woman, she'd be able to attend the lectures that interested her, visit the shops and galleries, and—her greatest ambition—work towards equipping herself to travel to the fascinating foreign places she'd read so much about. Foreign places where she could immerse herself in history and culture while she sought out treasures for her father. Where she could be herself, free of the stifling restrictions society imposed over women of her class. And, most important, having escaped the threating spectre of marriage, she might even manage some day to free herself from the dark shadows of her past.

All she need do to attain those goals was make it through one Season.

After ringing for the footman to collect the tea tray, she'd been about to go upstairs when a commotion at the front door announced the arrival of Aunt Gussie.

'Darling Temperance!' Lady Stoneway cried, handing her cloak over to a footman and coming over to hug her. 'How lovely you look!'

'You are looking in fine fettle, too, Aunt Gussie! The prospect of a sojourn in Bath obviously agrees with you.'

'I am looking forward to it,' her aunt allowed, joining Temperance to mount the stairs. 'Are you sure you won't come with us? Pru is going to miss your company—and your support—so very much! And I will, too.'

Dismissing a pang of longing, Temperance said firmly, 'No, I shall stay here. Not that I'm not grateful for your offer, but… I simply won't turn tail and flee, just because some idiots created a scandal that was not in any way Mama's fault.' *Nor am I interested in going where I might encounter a gentleman admirable enough that you and Pru would try to persuade me to marry him.*

Her aunt sighed. 'It is unfair, I admit. To your mama, as well as to you and Pru. But truly, my dear, in Bath we will have a fair chance of avoiding most of the scandal, finally allowing the two of you an opportunity to be courted, find a worthy gentleman to marry and settle down happily in your own households!'

'That's Pru's hope, not mine,' Temper reminded her aunt.

Lady Stoneway shook her head. 'Still dreaming of travel to some faraway place? I thought you would outgrow that foolish wish.'

'I haven't, for all that the wish might be foolish. However, though I couldn't convince Papa to allow me my dowry without having a Season, perhaps after it turns disastrous and he realises marriage to anyone save a fortune-hunting scoundrel is impossible, he will relent.' *For I'm highly unlikely, Papa, to encounter a true gentleman who wants to 'protect' me. Not if he knew the whole truth...*

'I'm not at all convinced it need be disastrous,' Lady Stoneway protested. 'So, you're going to wait for London next year after all?'

'Oh, no. As I told you when the scandal first broke, if I must debut, I intend to do so here, in London, just as we planned.'

Lady Stoneway stopped short, turning to look at Temper in astonishment. 'You intend to attempt a Season *this year*? In London?'

'Yes—if I can find a sponsor. But you mustn't even think of changing *your* plans! Pru is eager to marry and I fully agree her chances of finding a respectable partner will be far better in Bath. Whereas, since I don't wish to marry, it makes no difference to me that having a London Season now will likely produce...disappointing results. In fact, if it's truly bad, I might be able to convince Papa to let me abandon the effort after a month or so. But please, no more talk of that now. I haven't told Pru—she might feel obligated to change her plans and stay here to support me, which is the very last thing I want. She's been waiting so long for the kind husband and happy family she's always dreamed of! I don't want to delay her finding that even a day longer.'

'But who will sponsor you—?' her aunt began, before, at Temper's warning look, she cut the sentence short as Prudence ran out into the hallway to meet them.

'Welcome, Aunt Gussie! I'm all packed, so we may to leave as soon as you've rested and refreshed yourself.'

Giving Temperance a speaking glance, Lady Stoneway said, 'Ring for some tea and after that, I'll be ready. I've already instructed Overton to send some footmen up to collect your trunks. I suppose I should look in on my brother—though if he's in one of his collecting moods, he may not notice I'm in the room.'

'You could stop by, but he just got a new shipment of weapons and is fully engaged in cataloguing them,' Temper warned.

Lady Stoneway shook her head. 'I won't bother, then. Shall we have tea with your mother?'

Her smile fading, Pru shook her head. 'Knowing you would arrive at any moment, I've already bid her goodbye. Let's have tea in my room.'

'I'll fetch Gregory,' Temper said. 'We can have a pleasant family coze before you two head on your way.'

'I should like that!' Prudence said, coming over to link her arm with Temper's. 'I am going to miss you very much, dear sister.'

'And I, you,' Temper acknowledged with another pang. *Especially since, after your sojourn in Bath, I shall probably lose for ever my best and closest friend.* Shaking off that melancholy thought, she said, 'But how exciting, to send you off into the future! I hope this Season will end with you finding the man of your dreams.'

'I second that happy wish—for you *both*,' Lady Stoneway said, giving Temper a pointed glance as she ushered both girls into their bedchamber.

An hour later, after bidding the travellers goodbye, Temper walked back upstairs. Already the house seemed echoing and empty, now that the serene, optimistic spirit of her sister had left it.

Needing to stave off those unhappy thoughts, she decided to look in on her mama, who, she suspected, might be feeling a bit low. With a loyal maid who kept her appraised of everything happening in the household, she could not help but know that her precious daughter Pru, about to leave her house, most likely never to live in it again, had declined to invite her to her farewell tea.

Temperance could understand her sister's bitterness towards the mother whose profligate behaviour had spilled over to poison their lives. But she also understood how a woman's mere appearance led to assumptions, attack and uninvited abuse.

And knowing her papa, she could completely understand why a woman as vivacious, outgoing and passionate as her mother, denied affection and even basic interaction with her husband, would in desperation have sought it elsewhere.

After knocking lightly on the door, she walked in—to find her mama lounging on her sofa by the window, draped in one of her favourite diaphanous, lace-trimmed negligées. Temper had never seen the inside of a bordello, but she couldn't imagine even the loveliest denizen of such a place looking more beautiful and seductive than her mother.

Smiling at the picture Lady Vraux presented, she walked over to drop a kiss on that artful arrangement of blonde curls.

'Temperance!' her mother said in surprise, delight on her face as she turned from the window and saw her daughter—but not before Temper noticed the bleak expression the smile had chased away. 'I'd call for tea, but I expect by now you're awash in it. The travellers are off, I imagine.'

So she did know she'd been excluded, Temper thought with a wave of sympathy for her mama. Pru's resentment might be justly earned—but that wouldn't make the estrangement any less bitter for a mother who, Temper knew, truly loved her children.

'Gussie couldn't talk you into going with them?' Lady Vraux asked as she patted the sofa, inviting Temper to take a seat beside her.

Temper gave a dramatic shudder. 'To Bath? To drink the vile waters and be ogled by old men? I think not.'

'So what do you intend? I very much doubt Vraux will release your dowry. Christopher, then Gregory, stopped by to visit this morning and told me you intended to approach him.'

'I did and you are right. He won't release it to me.'

Lady Vraux rubbed Temper's hand. 'I'm sorry, my darling. If I had any money of my own, you'd be welcome to it.' She gave a bitter laugh. 'Unfortunately, I never had a feather to fly with, which is how I ended up married to Vraux in the first place.'

Her mother's family had been noble but penniless, Temper knew. The wealthy Lord Vraux's offer to settle the Portmans' debts in exchange for their Incomparable daughter's hand had been a bargain they would not let her refuse. No matter how cold, impersonal and unapproachable the character of the baron who'd made the offer.

'So you'll go forward with a Season?' Concern, regret and sadness succeeded the smile on her face. 'I would advise against it, my sweet. Not this year. Gussie is quite right in assessing your chances of success to be minimal after the Farnham-Hallsworthy fiasco.'

Dropping Temper's hand, she turned away. 'I…

I am sorry about that. You do know I did nothing to encourage them! I haven't taken a new lover for more than five years, just as I promised. And I was hopeful that Gussie, with her standing and influence, could smooth a path for the two of you despite…despite your unfortunate parentage.'

Temper gathered her mother's hand again. 'I know, Mama. I don't blame you for the idiocy of men.'

'Pru does, though.'

Temper was trying to find some palliative for that unfortunate truth when her mother continued, 'I've earned whatever infamy I bear, and as Miss Austen's Mary observes, "the loss of virtue in a female is irretrievable". But I hate that it continues to reflect upon you.'

'It doesn't matter for me. Unlike Pru, I have no desire to wed. But if Papa will not allow me to do anything else until I've had a Season, then I intend to get it over with. I expect it will be a noteworthy failure—indeed, I hope it is, the better to convince him a good marriage is impossible and get him to release my dowry.'

'There's no guarantee he will do so, even if your Season is unsuccessful,' her mother pointed out.

That was the one great flaw in her plan, she had to admit. 'True. But if I tell him I intend to journey to whatever place offers the treasure he is currently most interested in acquiring, so I may procure for him exactly what he wants, I might persuade him. You know he thinks of nothing but obtaining the latest object that catches his fancy.'

'That true enough,' Lady Vraux acknowledged. 'Coming at it from that direction, I suppose there is a *chance* you might persuade him.' After hesitating a moment, she said, 'Are you so sure you don't want to marry? Not to be indelicate, but you're not getting any younger, darling. When I was your age, Gregory was four, Christopher two, and I was *enceinte* with you! I know your father and I have hardly offered an encouraging example of the estate, but Christopher and Ellie seem happy enough, so you must see that contentment in marriage *is* possible. And marriage would offer you children. That is a joy I'd hate to see you deny yourself.'

For a moment, Temper was tempted to blurt out the dreadful truth she'd hidden from everyone for so long. But since revealing it would probably wound her mother more than it would bring Temper comfort, she bit back the words.

'I'll have Pru's brats to love,' she said instead. 'You know I've read every travel journal I could find since I was a girl! Travelling to exotic places—and finding treasures to bring back for Papa—is the only thing I've ever wanted to do. A dream of which a husband is unlikely to approve.

And once he got his greedy hands on my dowry, a dream I would no longer have the funds to pursue.'

'That is likely true. A lady with funds of her own to do what she wishes? I can't even imagine it.'

'Well, I can and I like the image very much. So, yes, I'll remain in London, debut if I can find a sponsor and brazen it out.'

'Gregory said that Gifford Newell offered to approach his godmother, Lady Sayleford, on your behalf. A formidable lady!' Lady Vraux shook her head, her eyes sparkling with amusement. 'The Dowager Countess's position is so unassailable, she even invites *me* to her entertainments. Then makes a point of ensuring all the disapproving society matrons see her chatting with me. She just might enjoy sticking her thumb in society's eye by sponsoring you. And under her care, you would be protected from the…disdain which I fear you might otherwise suffer.'

Temper wasn't about to increase her mother's worry by confessing she expected to meet with a lot of disdain, regardless of who sponsored her. She was too angry that, despite six years of impeccable behaviour where gentlemen were concerned, there was neither forgiveness nor tolerance for her mother. Whereas she knew for certain that a number of noble *men* conducted affairs in full

view of their wives and suffered no social consequences whatsoever.

'If Newell does secure you her sponsorship,'
her mother continued, 'I shall be very pleased to
see you immersed in all the activities of the Season. You needn't worry that I'll feel neglected. I
have Ellie and my friends. And who knows what
might happen? I will pray for your happiness and
success.'

'Then you will be praying for me to journey to
exotic places!'

Lady Vraux tapped Temper's cheek, her smile
bittersweet. 'There is no journey so exotic and
unexpected as a journey of the heart.'

If that journey led to marriage, it was one she
could never dare take, Temper thought sadly. But
before she could become mired in melancholy,
her mama said, 'If you do embark on a Season,
let me give you one more piece of advice. Never
show fear or weakness, or your enemies will fall
on you like rabid dogs. It's better to be scorned
than pitied.'

Rising, Temper leaned down to kiss her mama's cheek. 'That's a piece of advice I can embrace wholeheartedly!' After crossing the room,
she stopped in the doorway to look back at her
mother. 'Whatever society says or thinks, I am
proud to be your daughter, Mama.'

Lady Vraux took a shuddering breath, tears

glistening at the ends of her improbably long lashes. 'Your loyalty is precious, if ill advised. I would wish you to end your Season with more success than I did.'

'If I end it with the prospect of travel to foreign places, I shall be satisfied indeed.' Blowing her mother a kiss, determined to move towards the future *she* wanted, Temper walked out.

Chapter Four

Four days later, Lady Sayleford's butler ushered Gifford Newell and Temperance Lattimar into the Great Parlour of the Dowager Countess's imposing Grosvenor Square mansion. 'I'll tell the Countess you have arrived,' he intoned before bowing himself out.

'What a lovely room,' Temperance said, looking around the chamber, its delicate plaster decoration done up in pastel shades. 'Pure Robert Adams, isn't it?'

Was she remarking about decor to conceal her nervousness? Gifford wondered. He'd discovered an intriguing new side to Temperance Lattimar during their drive here this afternoon—that instead of behaving with her usual blunt exuberance, when she wished to, she could conceal her thoughts and feelings behind an impenetrable façade. Ever since he'd arrived at Vraux House to escort her to this interview, she'd been calm, composed—and for the first time since he'd known her, utterly unreadable.

'It is Adams,' he confirmed. 'Lady Sayleford was one of his first sponsors, engaging him to redecorate the public rooms of Sayleford House when she was just a young bride.'

'The symmetry, balance and delicacy of the mouldings are beautiful,' Temperance said. 'I'm so glad she didn't decide to change it out for the new Egyptian style.'

'Not a fan of crocodile legs and zebrawood carving?'

'Not unless I'm encountering them on the Nile!'

'Are you truly interested in furnishings and such?' he asked curiously. 'I never knew.'

'Of course I'm interested in furnishings—and architecture and sculpture and painting!' she retorted, giving him a look that questioned his intelligence. 'Why else would I be so interested in travelling to foreign places—or knowledgeable enough to promise Papa I could search out the treasures he seeks? It's not just the changing landscape abroad that fascinates. Just as interesting are the arts and artefacts that reveal so much about culture and character.'

'Little Temper—the scholar?' he teased.

'She certainly will be—once she has the chance,' she shot back. 'Since employment in the Foreign Office or in Parliament is currently denied her.'

Gifford was chuckling at that as she continued, 'Before the Countess arrives, let me thank you once again for arranging the interview. And let me apologise in advance, if my behaviour embarrasses you.'

Puzzled, he tilted his head at her. 'Why would it embarrass me?'

'Because, if I do have a Season, I must warn her I have no intention of behaving like a modest, accommodating young miss eager to attract a husband. I'm more interested in *dis*couraging suitors, so I may get through the Season and go my own way.'

Before he could respond to that, Harris returned to announce the Dowager Countess. Gifford and Temperance rose, the ladies exchanging curtsies while he bowed.

'Gifford, you rascal,' Lady Sayleford said as he came over to kiss her cheek. 'It's a sad thing when it takes an errand on behalf of a chit of a girl to get you to visit your poor godmother.'

'I admit it, I have been remiss,' he said. 'Parliament is busy.'

'I'm sure,' she murmured. 'Leaves only enough time to visit the doxies you favour—in company with this young lady's brother, I understand.'

To his chagrin, Temperance choked back a

giggle. 'You are just as well informed as Gifford promised, Countess.'

'So what is it you wish me to do for you, young lady?'

'It's rather what, if anything, *you* wish to do, Lady Sayleford. To be honest, I wouldn't have approached you at all, had Gifford not insisted. Being well informed, I'm sure you know about the latest scandal involving my mother.'

'Farnham and Hallsworthy,' the Countess said. 'Idiots.'

'Exactly,' Temperance agreed, her glorious smile breaking out. 'As you probably also know, my aunt, Lady Stoneway, has chosen not to present my sister and me in London this Season as planned and has taken Prudence to Bath instead.'

'And why you did not wish to accompany them?'

Gifford winced. Trust his godmother to dispense with the standard politenesses and probe directly to the point.

'Unlike my sister, I *don't* wish to marry, so there was no reason to accompany them to a place which would improve my chances of contracting a match. However, since Lord Vraux insists I must have a presentation, I'd rather follow our original plan and debut here, this Season. Once that's over, I hope to persuade him to release some funds so that I may do what I truly want to do.'

'Go exploring foreign places, like Lady Hester Stanhope? You really think you could persuade Vraux to fund that, simply because you fail to marry after your first Season?'

'It will be difficult, I grant. But if I can show him that no respectable gentleman will offer for me and vow to dedicate my explorations to tracking down whatever he's currently seeking, I might succeed. He's only ever been interested in *things*, after all.'

'Too sadly true. So, with Lady Stoneway off to Bath, you need a sponsor. Someone whose standing in society will make up for your mother's lack of it?'

Wincing at the remark, Giff braced himself for the furious defence of Lady Vraux that would likely spell an abrupt end to this interview. Instead, to his surprise, Temperance…smiled.

Granted, the smile was thin and he could almost see her head steaming from the fury she was holding in, but—hold it in she did.

Another revelation! Apparently, Temperance Lattimar could not only mask her feelings, she could withstand being goaded—which he was sure his godmother was doing deliberately, to see what sort of response Miss Lattimar could be prodded into producing.

She was certainly angry, for though her tone remained pleasant, the gaze she fixed on Lady

Sayleford was frigid. 'I'm sure I could turn up among my relations a matron more *respectable* than Mama to sponsor me. However, since only a woman of *unbounded* influence could force enough of society to receive a daughter of the infamous Lady Vraux that my father would consider my presentation adequate, I agreed to let Mr Newell approach you. Since sponsoring a daughter of the infamous Lady Vraux is likely to be thought poor judgement on the part of anyone foolish enough to attempt the task, it would be wise of you to steer clear of me. And now, I expect we have taken up enough of your valuable time.'

As Giff drew in a sharp breath, she started to rise—only to check as the Dowager Countess held out a hand. 'Please, sit, my dear,' she said in pleasant tones, as if Temperance's reply hadn't been a defiant rebuttal, however obliquely delivered. 'We haven't yet had our tea.'

As she spoke, the butler walked in with the tray, placing it on the table and pouring for them. Temperance sat in such absolute stillness, then took her cup with such measured precision, Giff had the vision of some wild beast from the Royal Menagerie immobilised by chains. How long could she restrain that anger? And would he be the unlucky victim of that storm when it did break?

After setting down her own cup, Lady Sayleford said, 'So, you think I should "steer clear of you", Miss Lattimar? Do you truly think I am in the habit of being guided by chits of two-and-twenty with no experience of the world and nothing but an outrageous reputation to boast of?'

Temperance's face paled and Giff felt his own anger rise. He'd brought Temper here to ask for help—not to have his imperious godmother subject her to the sort of set-down that had reduced matrons twice her age to tears.

Before Giff could intervene, Temperance set down her cup—and burst out laughing. 'Goodness, no, Countess!' she said when she'd controlled her mirth. 'I sincerely doubt you've ever been guided by anyone.'

Lady Sayleford smiled, as if Temper had passed some sort of test. Which, Giff supposed she just had—neither wilting under the Countess's pointed questioning, nor flying into a tantrum.

'You don't seem inclined to be guided, either,' the Countess observed. 'Certainly not by Lady Stoneway, who you must admit has only your best interests at heart.'

Temperance's amusement vanished as quickly as it had arisen. 'I do know that. But Mama has been treated outrageously for years. By Papa. By society. Lately, for things that are not at all her fault. I don't intend to hide away and act as if I believe they were.'

Lady Sayleford nodded. 'Your loyalty to your

mother is admirable and, as you may know, I value family loyalty highly. But you must admit that your mother was very foolish when she was younger and society is not forgiving.'

'Not of a woman,' Temperance said acerbically. 'Especially not one who is beautiful, charming and a magnet for the attention of every gentleman in the room.'

'They are much quicker to exile a Beauty than a wallflower, aren't they?' the Countess replied drily. 'I believe you do have enough backbone to last a Season. So, let me see… Vraux has pots of money. Angela, a niece of my late husband's, is a widow living in straitened circumstances, her son in the Royal Navy, her daughter married to some country nobody. To enjoy a Season in London, she would probably agree to serve as your chaperon. If your father will see her properly clothed and pay her expenses, I shall send for her.'

'Before you offer to help me, I must warn you that, even backed by your approval, I expect to meet with a considerable amount of disapproval. If goaded, I might be…irresistibly tempted to do something outrageous, just to live down to society's expectations. Which, of course, would further my goal of discouraging suitors.'

'It might encourage the unscrupulous, though. You're too intelligent to do anything stupid, I hope—something that might place you in actual danger. Men *can* be dangerous, especially to women they think invite their attentions. Sadly, my dear, with your looks and reputation, it wouldn't take much for them to make that assumption.'

Was it only his imagination, Giff wondered, or did Temperance once again turn pale? But then she shook her head, colour returning to her cheeks.

'I don't intend to encourage *any* man and I certainly wouldn't agree to meet one alone, if that's what you are warning against. If provoked, I might feel compelled to best some smirking gentleman in a race through Hyde Park—in front of a full complement of witnesses. Or I might accept a dare to drive a curricle down St James's Street past the gentlemen's clubs,' she added, chuckling when Giff groaned.

'You are indeed your mama,' Lady Sayleford said, her eyes lighting with amusement. 'But wiser and forewarned. I do hope, though,' she added, sobering, 'that you end up happier than she did.'

After a moment of silence, as if she were weighing whether or not to speak, Temperance said, 'She…she loved Christopher's father, didn't she? Sir Julian Cantrell? I've never asked her, not wanting to dredge up sad memories, and everyone else puts me off. I overheard Aunt Gussie telling Gregory that Sir Julian was the love of her life. That he loved her, too, enough that he was prepared to be shunned by society for marrying a divorced woman, only Papa refused to divorce her. I'm sure you know the truth. Won't you tell me?'

Lady Sayleford remained silent as well, so long that Giff thought she would refuse to answer. Finally, she said, 'I don't agree that it does a girl any good to have the truth withheld from her. It's not as if, growing up a member of the Vraux Miscellany, you have any maidenly innocence to protect!'

'That's true,' Temperance agreed with a wry grimace. 'So—you *will* tell me?'

Lady Sayleford sighed. 'After Vraux refused Felicia the divorce she pleaded for, I half-expected she and Cantrell would run away to America. But she loved Gregory and knew, if she fled, she would never see her firstborn again. She gave up Sir Julian instead. It nearly broke him, especially after he discovered she was carrying his child. By the way, I'm glad he was later able to reconcile with Christopher; a man should have a relationship with his own son, even if he can't claim the boy outright. It was only after Felicia lost Sir Julian that, once very circumspect, she became… careless of her reputation. She *must* have been devastated, else she would never have been taken in by your father.'

'Marsden Hightower?'

'Marsden Hightower,' Lady Sayleford confirmed with a curl of her lip. 'Rich, handsome, charming—and a cad of the highest order. He boasted of his conquest all over town, let slip lurid details of the rendezvous he persuaded her into—meeting him in some hostess's boudoir in the midst of ball, or in the shrubbery at some garden party! Details too deliciously scandalous not to become the talk of society—or to thoroughly offend the hostesses at whose events the purported dalliances had taken place. She was never forgiven—not that, being Felicia, she ever expressed remorse.'

'She would have confronted the rumours with her lips sealed and her head held high.'

Lady Sayleford nodded. 'And so she did. Despite the reputation she acquired, she never took a married man for a lover and she had countless opportunities to do so. A distinction I recognise and appreciate, even if many of society's harpies do not.'

'Is that why you still receive her, when most of the high sticklers will not?'

'I admire honour, as I admire courage. Especially honour and courage maintained when one is given no credit for possessing them.'

'Thank you for telling me the whole truth.'

Giff sat in shocked silence. He'd always accepted what rumour said about Lady Vraux, disdaining her as a selfish Beauty who took lovers to gratify her vanity with no thought to the harm her conduct would do her family. When Temperance told him his godmother invited the scandalous Lady Vraux to her home, he'd assumed the Countess did so on a whim, to demonstrate her mastery over society.

After hearing the truth, he realised with some chagrin that he, who prided himself on treating people as he found them rather than believing what rumour whispered, had done exactly that with Lady Vraux. He had to admit a grudging admiration for her courage—and for the courage of the daughter who had always believed in and passionately defended her.

Lady Sayleford gave Temperance a regretful look. 'Unfortunately, knowing the true origin of your mother's reputation doesn't change your present circumstances, my child.'

'No. But it does confirm what I've always known—that Mama is not the amoral, self-indulgent voluptuary society accuses her of being. But then, of what value to society is truth? It will believe what it wants, regardless.'

Lady Sayleford nodded. 'If you know that, you are well armed to begin a Season. I shall enjoy hearing about your escapades.'

Giff was smiling—until the meaning of that sentence penetrated. '*Hearing* about them?' he repeated. 'Won't you be *accompanying* her to social events?'

'To every frippery Marriage Mart entertainment that attracts silly young girls and nodcock young gents on the lookout for rich brides? Certainly not! I shall accept only those invitations that interest me, just as I do now. But I will introduce Miss Lattimar before I turn her over to Angela and make sure it's known that I will be watching to see how each member of society receives her.'

'Very well, I'm reassured,' Giff said, relaxing a bit.

'Besides, it's not *me* she needs to watch over her. In order to be truly protected, she'll need a *gentleman* standing guard. You, Gifford.'

Looking as alarmed as he felt, Temperance said, 'Lady Sayleford, is that truly necessary? Surely having a chaperon by my side every minute will afford sufficient protection! I never meant to embroil Giff in a social round he surely doesn't want—'

'Don't be argumentative, child,' Lady Sayleford said, cutting her off. 'It won't hurt Gifford to attend a few society functions. How else is he to find the rich bride a rising politician needs? Cyprians are well and good for pleasuring-seeking, but a career in government requires adequate funds and a suitable hostess.'

Her remarks were, of course, spot on, but that didn't mean Giff appreciated them—especially not in front of Temperance, who had recently preached from the same sermon. Feeling colour warming his face, he said, 'Thank you for the advice. But I'm not prepared to act upon it just yet, so don't be getting any ideas.'

Lady Sayleford smiled. 'What else has an old woman to do, but get ideas? My dear,' she continued, turning back to Temperance, 'do you think your father will agree to have Angela chaperon you?'

'If you approve of her, I don't see why he would object.'

'Just to make sure, I'll pen him a note. Tell him I'm grateful he's sparing my old bones as your sponsor by allowing my great-niece to act in my place. Vraux does like to keep things safe, even if he can't…care for them like normal folk. In any event, I'll sweeten the agreement by sending him a medieval mantelpiece Sayleford once outbid him for.'

'Oh, no, ma'am!' Temperance protested. 'I wouldn't want you to part with one of your husband's treasures!'

'Nonsense! I've been trying to dispose of the hideous thing for years. What better use to make of it than to dispatch it to someone who might actually appreciate it?'

Temperance laughed. 'My mother's reputation might be based on falsehoods, but yours is not. You *are* wise, as well as all-knowing!'

'There must be some benefit to growing old, other than the ability to interfere in other people's lives with impunity. But since I'm so wise, let me offer you one more bit of advice. Don't be blind, fixing yourself so narrowly on a single goal that you fail to see the alternatives that present themselves. As they always will. Now, I shall consult my calendar, but I think next week will do for an introductory tea. That will give me enough time to summon Angela. So drink up, Gifford. You've accomplished your purpose and it is time for me to rest.'

With that, they finished their tea, then stood as his godmother made her majestic departure.

Standing in the hall while the butler summoned their carriage, Temperance said, 'Lady Sayleford is amazing! I'd like to be her one day.' Then she shook her head, her expression rueful. 'But then, I'd have to be respectable to begin with.'

'You are less of a hoyden than you used to be,' Giff observed. 'I thought you displayed remarkable restraint today. I was initially afraid you might attack with nails and fists when she insulted your mother.'

'She was taking my measure, I think. And I'm not as thoughtless and impulsive as you seem to believe. At least, not all the time. For instance, I intend to keep my chaperon close by whenever there are gentlemen about, so I really don't think you need to attend social events to watch out for me. You'd probably be bored to flinders and hate every minute of it.'

'I hope to sidestep that fate—not because it would bore me, but I would rather avoid eligible young ladies for a while longer, despite my godmother's forceful advice.'

Conversation halted as, his tiger having brought his curricle to the entrance, they exited the house and mounted the carriage.

'If I thought you were going to be compelled to supervise me, I would never have asked for Lady Sayleford's sponsorship,' Temper continued after he'd set the horses moving.

Giff shook his head. 'Too late to withdraw now! If I know my godmother, by the time we reach Vraux House she will already have written to summon her great-niece.'

'I shall be happy enough to proceed, as long as we can convince her not to drag you into the bargain. No point going to market when you aren't ready to buy anything.' She sighed. 'I only wish *I* didn't have to spend time in the Marriage Mart, but since I must, I'll cheer myself with the hope that it might not be for long. With any luck, it will soon be evident that I attract only fortune hunters and fast young men looking to lure the "wanton" into the shrubbery.'

Giff didn't find that prospect very reassuring.

Neither type of man was likely to respect Temper—and the latter could, as his godmother had pointed out, actually pose a danger to her.

Maybe he ought to drop by a few of the entertainments she attended, just to make sure she was safe.

'It pains me that society will try to paint you in that light. When we both know that neither you—nor your mother, it turns out—possess such a character.'

'As I told your godmother, people will think what they want, regardless of the truth. But in this instance, I'm glad of it. It should require only a little push to have society confirm that I don't respect its rules, ensuring that no respectable gentleman will pay me his addresses.'

'Just as long as you are not targeted by the truly *dis*reputable.'

'As long as I have a chaperon clinging to my side, I hope I am! Everyone knows *disreputable* gentlemen are the most charming! Except for you, of course, Giff. You're respectable and—alluring.'

The change in her tone—from amusement to warmth of a different sort—pulled his gaze from the road to her. The yearning he read in her eyes fired his always-simmering attraction into full-on arousal.

Fierce, intelligent—and so beautiful. He had

an almost overwhelming urge to lean down and kiss her.

The curricle hit a bump, jolting him back to the job of controlling the horses. But his palms were sweating and his breathing uneven when he pulled up his team in front of Vraux House.

'You needn't see me in,' she said as his tiger jumped down and trotted over to help her out of the vehicle. 'I shall try not to be *too* outrageous, so hopefully your kindness in intervening to help me won't come back to haunt you.'

He looked at her full in the face this time, struck anew by her beauty—and the softened lips and molten gaze that confirmed the strong current of desire coursing through him was unmistakably mutual. For a long moment, they simply stared at each other.

She reached a hand out, as if to touch him, then drew it back again. 'Thank you, Giff,' she whispered, then turned away to let his tiger help her down.

Ridiculous, to feel an instant bolt of envy because that skinny, pock-faced boy was touching her—as he wanted to so fiercely and mustn't.

Fists clenched on the reins, Giff watched her walk into Vraux House—both regretting and hopeful that his part in the launching of Miss Temperance Lattimar's Season had just been completed.

Chapter Five

A week later, dressed to attend her introductory tea at Lady Sayleford's, Temper inspected herself in her looking glass. The afternoon gown, one of the new dresses she'd just acquired, was cut with the wide sleeves, narrow waist and belled skirts of the latest style, done up in a deep blue silk that enhanced her eyes. Not the virginal white of a timid debutante, but the colour suited her—both in looks and temperament.

Telling herself she had no need to be nervous, she was walking down the stairs to collect her cloak and have the butler summon her a hackney when the door opened and Gifford Newell walked in. He looked up, saw her—and stopped short.

She froze, transfixed by the intensity of his admiring gaze, for the first time glad that the exaggerated style emphasised the smallness of her waist while the low bodice exposed her neck and shoulders. Then, telling herself not to be ridiculous, she lifted her skirts and continued downwards, ignoring the accelerated beat of her heart and the queer fluttering in the pit of her stomach.

He was, she discovered when she looked up after descending the last step, still gazing at her. 'Exquisite!' he murmured. 'If being the most beautiful lady in the room means society will exile you, your Season will be over before it begins.'

She shouldn't feel such satisfaction at knowing he found her attractive—but she did. 'The colour is lovely, although I can't admire the style. These sleeves and skirts! Impossible to do anything useful wearing something so wide.'

'Of course not. As a society lady, you're supposed to be admired and have everything done for you.'

'In other words, be vacant-headed and decorative.' She sighed. 'Heaven help me survive this Season! You're looking handsome as always, Giff. Come to find Gregory?'

'No, I came to collect you. To escort you to Lady Sayleford's. I'm pleased to find you ready. My godmother detests tardiness.'

'You're escorting me?' she echoed. 'I thought the tea would be a ladies' affair.'

'So did I, but when Lady Sayleford commands, one complies. Unless one is prepared to move to the Outer Hebrides, which would be a rather inconvenient location for a sitting Member of Parliament.'

'I understand carrier pigeons can travel hundreds of miles in just a few hours,' she offered, smiling. 'But I agree, the Outer Hebrides would be inconvenient. Though if it is to be just ladies, I can't imagine why she would require you to escort me. Surely she knows I'm capable of taking a hackney from Vraux House to hers!'

'I long ago learned never to question my godmother's inscrutable ways,' Giff replied. 'Shall we go?'

'Yes. Hopefully once you've delivered me, she will release you back to your duties. As a sitting Member of Parliament.'

To her relief, Newell had brought his curricle, requiring him to keep his attention focused on his driving, rather than on her. With him otherwise occupied, she could sit beside him and enjoy the delicious frisson of attraction that sizzled between them without any chance of being tempted further down a road she had no business travelling.

The afternoon being busy and the traffic noisy, she made no attempt to converse as they made the transit. A short time later, he pulled up his team in front of Lady Sayleford's town house, his tiger springing down to help her out.

They walked in, Harris once again showing

them into the Grand Parlour where, this time, Lady Sayleford awaited them.

'Here I am, ma'am, as summoned,' Giff said as he bent to kiss his godmother's cheek after the ladies exchanged curtsies. 'Was that the extent of the service you wished me to render?'

'You think I would require you merely to deliver Miss Lattimar, who is entirely capable of making the arduous journey from Brook Street to Grosvenor Square on her own? No, I have other plans, which will put all your wit and charm to good use.'

Motioning them to a seat, she said, 'As you can see, you've been summoned before the other guests. I want you to meet my great-niece, Mrs Angela Moorsby, and instruct you, Gifford, on the role you must play. That first.'

'What, precisely, would you have me do?'

'I have invited a few of the most important society hostesses. After greeting them all, I wish to speak privately with each one. Your task, Gifford, will be to assist my niece in keeping the other ladies entertained, the conversation flowing brightly, so none are tempted—or able—to eavesdrop on my tête-à-tête.'

'What part am *I* to play?' Temper asked.

'You, my dear, will be sitting by me, so that each lady gets a...proper introduction.'

And with that explanation, which explained

nothing, I will have to be satisfied, Temper thought, suppressing a smile. Very well. She was quite prepared to recite her few lines while Lady Sayleford directed the overall action.

'I don't suppose I'm permitted to ask who, what or why?' Giff said, posing what, from the frown Lady Sayleford returned him, Temper knew had been a rhetorical question.

'Ah, here she is! Angela, allow me to present my godson, Gifford Myles Newell, and the young lady you are to chaperon, Miss Temperance Lattimar. Children, this is my great-niece, Mrs Angela Moorsby.'

Sucking in a breath in apprehension, Temper watched a small, plump woman cross the room, her rotund form garbed in a slightly out-of-fashion gown.

'Mr Newell, well met!' she said, curtsying to them, her pleasant face wreathed in a smile. 'And Miss Lattimar! So you are the angel of mercy who is enlivening my dull life by providing me a Season in London. And a complement of lovely new gowns, as well! Thank you! I intend to enjoy myself exceedingly—and, I promise you, to chaperon with a very light hand.'

Temper smiled back at the friendly gaze and open, honest countenance of Angela Moorsby, her fear of having to deal with an incompatible chaperon melting into an instant rapport.

And a sharp stab of guilt, to doom this pleasant, innocent lady to the criticism and censure she expected her presentation would heap on the head of her hapless chaperon. Looking over at Lady Sayleford, she said, 'Have you warned her what my Season will likely entail?'

'Oh, no, my child. I thought it better to allow you to do that.'

So you can listen to me explain one more time before giving final approval? Temper would not be at all surprised, should she express something to incur Lady Sayleford's disapproval, to have the offer of sponsorship revoked on the instant and the great-niece sent back to rural obscurity.

'Are you acquainted with the…circumstances of my family?' she asked Mrs Moorsby.

'Yes, Lady Sayleford related to me the…unusual nature of your upbringing and the reason why you are in need of a chaperon.'

'So you know society expects me to be ill behaved, amoral and capricious. Although I am none of those things, neither am I interested in marriage, so while my behaviour will give no credence to the first two traits, I am perfectly happy to play up the latter. In fact, I may take a few strategic actions to reinforce my reputation as an ungovernable woman no respectable gentleman would have as a wife. Acting as chaperon to such a creature may well be accompanied by…an unpleasantness that may make you wish you had remained in Portsmouth. Are you sure you want to take me on?'

'So that you can fulfil your father's requirement that you have a Season and go on to become a lady explorer? What a marvellous thing! If I hadn't grown so fond of my snug hearth and my comfortable little Portsmouth community, I would almost be tempted to go exploring again myself. I was never the Beauty you are, but I was rather adventuresome myself as a girl, marrying a merchant captain over my family's objections and going to sea with him.'

'How wonderful!' Temper declared, delighted. 'You must tell me about your travels!'

'Some other day, perhaps,' Mrs Moorsby replied.

She looked up to find Lady Sayleford smiling and was struck again by her shrewdness. *You sly old lady*, she thought. *You chose the perfect chaperon for me.*

'I've never held with mealy-mouthed females who haven't the wit to form their own opinion or who constantly look to some man for guidance.' Mrs Moorsby winked at her. 'My aunt warned that you will likely kick over the traces. I shall enjoy watching you.'

Temper smiled wryly. 'I hope it may prove entertaining. However, you may well have your judgement and your competence questioned, or find yourself pitied, when I prove to be…less than conformable.'

Mrs Moorsby shrugged. 'What do I care for the opinions of people I shall never see again, once the Season is over? As long as you enjoy shopping, theatre, concerts and—' she winked at Giff '—the company of handsome gentlemen, I'm sure we shall get on splendidly.'

Harris returned then, intoning, 'Lady Spencer-Woods, Mrs Dalworthy, Lady Wentwith and Mrs Dobbs-Henry.'

'You know what you are to do?' Lady Sayleford murmured as they all rose to greet the newcomers.

'Perfectly,' Mrs Moorsby said with a conspiratorial smile.

'Welcome, ladies,' the Countess said after the exchange of bows and curtsies. 'I wanted you to be the first to meet my protégée, Miss Temperance Lattimar, who makes her debut this Season. Her chaperon, Mrs Moorsby, and my godson, Mr Newell.'

The pleasant smiles of greeting on the faces of the newcomers froze as Lady Sayleford spoke. Four heads turned as one to fix surprised, then horrified, then offended gazes on Temperance.

Taking a deep breath, she straightened and gazed straight back, a smile fixed to her lips. *Is this how you do it, Mama?*

'Ah, here is Harris with our tea. Won't you be seated?'

Under the Countess's direction, Temper found herself on the sofa next to Lady Sayleford, Lady Spencer-Woods in a chair adjacent to them, while Giff and Mrs Moorsby sat with the other ladies in a grouping of chairs closer to the hearth.

After the initial shocked silence, with a murmur of voices and clink of cups emanating from the group near the fireplace, Lady Sayleford said, 'So, Elizabeth, I expect you will give your usual ball, now that Parliament is in session.' She turned to Temper. 'Lady Spencer-Woods's Opening Ball is the premier entertainment of the Early Season, attended by everyone of importance in society.' Looking back at her guest, she continued, 'You will certainly send Miss Lattimar and Mrs Moorsby a card.'

The guest shifted uncomfortably, shooting Temper a pained, faintly contemptuous glance, 'Really, Emily,' she said in a low voice, leaning forward as if speaking with the Countess alone, 'I know you are somehow…connected to her family, but this is outside of enough! You may amuse yourself, inviting the Vraux woman to your entertainments, but you cannot expect *me* to recognise a daughter of that…creature!'

Temper didn't need the Countess's subtle warning glance to know she must remain silent. *As if I weren't right here, listening to every word,* Temper thought, outrage filling her and the tea turning bitter on her tongue. *You must accustom yourself to hearing this and worse.* Was that what Lady Sayleford meant to teach her, by compelling her to witness this exchange?

'Leaving aside any commentary on Lady Vraux's character, the child is not her mother.'

Lady Spencer-Woods gave a thin smile. 'She might be worse.'

'I'll let that indictment of my judgement pass,' the Countess said mildly, but with a frigid look that saw her visitor's defiance collapse. 'It would please me mightily to have you send Miss Lattimar and her chaperon a card. And see that all your friends do, as well. However, if you wish to be…disobliging, I might suddenly recall a certain incident with a dancing master that happened in our debut Season.'

The matron paled. 'I hardly think society would be interested in…in a silly contretemps from so many years ago.'

'Oh, I don't know. When a lady is one of the premier arbiters of society, whose judgements about the character of young ladies have made or destroyed reputations and Seasons, I expect there might be exceptional interest in the story of a—'

'Never mind,' Lady Spencer-Woods interrupted, bright spots of colour blooming in her

cheeks. 'I don't think any further details are necessary.'

Not with a highly interested witness sitting in,
Temper thought. *Lady Sayleford, how clever you
are indeed.*

'For a woman, "incidents" are never truly past
and forgotten, are they? Even when one has lived
blamelessly for thirty years.'

'Felicia Lattimar has hardly lived "blamelessly"
for thirty years!'

'She might have, had her idiot of a husband paid
her any attention. And might have still, had that
cad Hightower not spread his malicious stories all
over town. In any event, you will invite Miss Lattimar to your ball—won't you? Ladies of power
and influence should present a united front.'

Lady Spencer-Woods held her hostess's un-
flinching stare for a moment, before dropping
her gaze. 'I suppose so.'

'Then we understand each other. Excellent.'

Lady Sayleford smiled serenely, as if she hadn't
just manoeuvred her outraged guest into check-
mate. 'You need do nothing more than receive
Miss Lattimar. I shall not hold you responsible
for her ultimate success, or lack of it. Unless, of
course, I learn you've said or done something disparaging to compromise it.'

'I shall not forget this, Emily,' Lady Spencer-
Woods said, looking back up at the Countess, her

expression a mixture of resentment and reluctant admiration.

'I don't expect you will. Now, I know you'd like to become better acquainted with Mrs Moorsby, who will be accompanying Miss Lattimar to all her entertainments.' She gestured towards the other group, a clear sign of dismissal. 'I shall look forward to seeing you at your ball.'

'I shall be delighted to welcome you. And your lovely protégée,' she added with a resigned glance at Temper. Then, unexpectedly, she laughed. 'Emily, what a trickster you are! One never knows what outrageous thing you will do. Have no fear, I shall play my part.'

'I never doubted it. I know just how...*ingenious* you can be, Elizabeth,' the Countess replied, amusement in her eyes as her guest's cheeks once again went rosy.

And so it went with each matron in turn. Lady Sayleford immediately demanded support for Temper, countered any objections about her and her mother, then moved in for the kill with a hint about some questionable event in the lady's past the Countess might just happen to recall, should her guest not prove accommodating.

After the guests took their leave, Temper turned to gaze in awe at her sponsor. 'You really do know everything about everyone!'

Lady Sayleford chuckled. 'The benefit of a long life spent building such a reputation for discretion, every bit of scandal finds its way to my ear.'

'Still, I regret that you had to play so many of the trumps you've kept close in hand. I hope giving them up—and the animosity you may have incurred for playing them now—won't come back to harm you.'

'You needn't worry, my dear. I have enough other trumps tucked away to be in no danger of losing whatever game I choose. Now you are privy to some of that knowledge, too.'

'And you made sure all those ladies knew it!'

'I don't intend to go everywhere with you. But they all know their secrets will. Shall we join the others?'

'How well you work your magic!' Mrs Moorsby said to the Countess as she made room for Temperance on the sofa beside her. 'After chatting with you, each lady came back to express her delight in making my acquaintance and her hope that my charge and I would be able to attend the entertainment she intended to give later in the Season. Bravo, Aunt Lilly!'

'One does one's possible,' Lady Sayleford said, a satisfied smile on her lips. 'The two of you did well, too, keeping your group from listening in—though, after each one finished her session, she must have known something similar was being said to the others and been agog to discover what lapse that lady had committed.'

'Have you made out a social schedule for us yet?' Mrs Moorsby asked.

'Not yet. We shall do that together, once the invitations begin to come in.'

'With Mr Newell present, as well? I imagine he has duties in Parliament, and we will want to make sure the entertainments we attend will not conflict.'

'Why would they?' Temper asked. 'Surely with you on hand to provide protection and assistance, Mr Newell's part is finished—and I sincerely thank him for his efforts!'

'Unless I'm mistaken, it's not at all finished,' Mrs Moorsby said. 'I may be your chaperon, but the Countess believes that Mr Newell should act as a sort of…guardian. Don't you, Aunt Lilly?'

The Countess nodded. 'You must admit, Miss Lattimar, that if some…unscrupulous man tried to take advantage, a female chaperon would be of limited assistance. Having everyone know there's a gentleman nearby, watching over you, will ensure that no blackguard makes such an attempt.'

'And while standing guard, Mr Newell shall have a chance to review the field of prospective brides,' Mrs Moorsby added.

'But wouldn't his being in my company compromise his reputation—limiting his chances of meeting eligible young ladies? For their mamas will surely want them to avoid me,' Temper countered.

Lady Sayleford waved a dismissive hand. 'If he were seen as a suitor, perhaps. But as my godson, delegated to look after the young lady I'm sponsoring, society should expect him to be in your company.'

Her chaperon's bright smile indicating how entirely unaware she was of the consternation this alteration in plan had just evoked, Mrs Moorsby stood up. 'I will leave you now to take my rest, but I understand we are to do some shopping later, Miss Lattimar. I shall look forward to it! A pleasure to meet you both.' After dipping them a curtsy, she walked from the room.

'Lady Sayleford, you cannot mean for Giff— Mr Newell to...to dance attendance on me at *every* social event I attend!' Temperance cried as soon as her chaperon exited. 'I would never have consented for him to consult you had I any notion you might require such a thing! You must release him from that obligation, or I shall—'

'What?' Lady Sayleford interrupted. 'Cancel your Season? Kick about the house in Brook Street for another year, or go bury yourself in the country at Entremer? Or do you think making a second attempt to convince your father to fund you will have better success than the first?'

Temper hesitated, torn. As Lady Sayleford was quite aware, none of those options was attractive. But to embroil Giff in a round of social activities he was sure to view as an outrageous imposition? As keenly aware as she was of her vulnerability, she couldn't repay his friendship by saddling him with that!

While she struggled to think of an equally safe and reasonable alternative, Lady Sayleford turned her attention to Giff. 'You did ask me to sponsor Miss Lattimar's Season, didn't you?'

He gave her a pained smile. 'Yes, but I didn't anticipate becoming quite so...involved in every event of it.'

'Gaining Miss Lattimar a sponsor was only part of the job. If you applied half the intelligence I know you possess to considering what will transpire once she actually embarks upon a Season, you must realise she can't be left with just a lone female for protection. You must know she is more vulnerable than an ordinary young miss. So, Gifford, do you truly wish to help Miss Lattimar? Or was your offer to intervene just a casual gesture taken without much thought, something you're prepared to back away from if implementing it will require additional time and effort from you?'

'Of course it wasn't casual or thoughtless,' he retorted, a touch of anger in his tone. 'I may not have anticipated that her having a Season would require additional time on *my* part, but I was—am—entirely committed to making that Season happen.'

'Very well. So, knowing the cost, you are willing to proceed?' With a wry smile, she added, 'Thereby proving the adage that "no good deed goes unpunished"?'

Gifford sighed. 'Let's proceed. I suppose you will instruct me on my additional duties as we move forward.'

'I shall, once our plans are made. But now I, too, must rest before the evening's activities. Manipulation is so wearying! Miss Lattimar, Angela will keep me informed of your progress with shopping and such, and inform you about which activities you are to attend.'

Temper couldn't help feeling that somehow, everything had gone awry. She wanted independence and a future lived on her own terms—but she'd never imagined seeking that goal would embroil Giff in a round of society functions he couldn't possibly wish to attend.

Accurately reading her expression, Lady Sayleford said, 'Don't look so regretful, my dear. Gifford may lose a few evenings with his doxies, but getting a closer look at the females available to become the wife he must *eventually* take will more than make up for it.'

'I only hope he finds it so,' Temper muttered.

'In any event,' she said briskly, 'it's a waste of emotion to regret the necessary. You wanted your chance and now you shall have it. What you do with it is up to you.'

Lady Sayleford stood and perforce Temperance and Gifford stood as well. As conflicted as she still felt, the Countess had made it unmistakably clear that the presentation would be done on her terms, or not at all. If Giff could stomach being part of it, she had little choice but to go along.

'If I cannot promise to appear to your credit,' she said with a sigh, 'at least I can promise to end the Season unharmed.'

Lady Sayleford nodded. 'I'm sure you will. Gifford will see to it.' Giving them a regal nod, she swept from the room.

Temper sank back on to the sofa. 'Giff, I'm so very sorry! You know I never meant to involve you in this escapade, but the Countess seems adamant about having some male to watch over me. I wish I could think of some alternative! And I truly don't want to wait another year. Are you sure you won't be furious if we go forward with this?'

Giff gave her a wry smile. 'I can't pretend to be delighted, either. But neither can I dispute the truth of what she said. Your reputation—however undeserved—does make you more vulnerable than the usual unmarried maiden. Even a respectable man knows he could probably get away with compromising you without having marry you and a borderline scoundrel… Well, *he* might feel free to try with you what he'd never dream of attempting with any other innocent miss. Now that I've thought about it, I have to admit I'd feel…uneasy about you proceeding with only Mrs Moorsby for protection. Since I'm responsible for involving Lady Sayleford—and her rules—in your presentation, it's only right that I see it through.'

'So…you won't resent me for ever?'

'If I'm angry at anyone, it should be at myself, for jumping into this without fully considering all the implications. It won't pain me too much to attend society soirées.' He smiled. 'It might even be amusing—especially if you discover a man who changes your mind about avoiding marriage.'

She shook her head. 'That man doesn't exist! In turn, I will try harder to get to know some of the young ladies. If I'm surrounded by a protective crowd of companions, you will be able to curtail the time you are forced to spend with marriage-minded females.' She grinned. 'Maybe I'll discover among them a lady who will change *your* mind about waiting to marry!'

Despite that teasing comment, Temper discovered as she finished her tea, she wasn't any more enthusiastic about the idea of Giff discovering a woman he'd like to marry than she was about the necessity of dragging him into her Season.

Shaking off that unsettling realisation, she said, 'I suppose I'm allowed to escort myself home now?'

Chuckling, he put down his own cup. 'No, better let me drive you. I wouldn't want to incur the Countess's displeasure before we've even got started.'

They walked out, pausing in the hall as they waited for the curricle to be brought around. 'I will insist to the Countess that we only attend evening entertainments, so that it doesn't cut into your duties with Parliament,' Temper promised.

'I doubt you'll be able to deflect her from accepting exactly the invitations she pleases, whenever they take place. I'll warn Christopher he may have to take notes for me.'

'Besides,' he added as he escorted her down the steps, 'what worries me more than missing Parliamentary sessions is the unmerciful ribbing I'm going to get from Gregory, once he discovers I managed to trap myself into escorting you for the Season!'

Chapter Six

A week later, Gifford Newell rode in the carriage with Lady Sayleford, Mrs Moorsby and Miss Lattimar to the first grand social event of the Season. Shifting uncomfortably on the backward-facing seat, which in the narrow confines of the carriage put him far too close to Temper, he tried to focus on the loquacious Mrs Moorsby.

'You mustn't be nervous about attending your first formal event, Miss Lattimar,' the chaperon was saying. 'I knew you were a Beauty, but the way those creations bring out the gold of your hair and emphasise the blue purity of your eyes? Frankly, I'll be amazed if any man can resist you!'

'She'll certainly create a stir,' Lady Sayleford predicted, giving Temper an approving glance.

'All of you ladies look dazzling tonight,' Giff observed, partly because it was true and mostly to try to distract himself from just how alluring Temper was.

It had been hard enough to control the wave of desire he'd felt, standing twenty feet away in the hall at Vraux House as she descended the stairway. He'd observed her in day dresses that showed off her narrow waist and voluptuous bosom, but that evening gown! The lacy confection not only bared her shoulders, the neckline swooped so low in front he could see the rising swells of her breasts…

His tongue had stuck to the roof of his suddenly dry mouth, making it impossible for him to return her greeting, while his mind was in turmoil, the body protesting the sacrilege of the evening cape the butler was draping over that glorious form, his brain applauding the masking of a vision that made his heart skip a beat and everything masculine in him leap to the alert.

He'd managed to mumble a few, probably nonsensical, words to her as he followed her out to the carriage, but he couldn't remember a syllable, too unsettled by the thrilling and dreadful knowledge that they would soon be crammed together on that narrow backward-facing seat.

He'd perched as far away from her as he could get. But that still left him sitting so close that she need move her slippered foot only an inch to touch his. Close enough that at any moment, the jouncing of carriage could bounce her hand from the seat on to his wrist…or worse, his thigh. Sat there with her jasmine perfume filling his senses, struggling to rein in an attraction even the knowledge that Lady Sayleford and Mrs Moorsby were both looking on couldn't extinguish.

Feeling sweat trickle down his brow, he looked over to see his godmother watching him, an ironic smile playing at her lips.

The wretch! That smile told him she knew exactly the agonies he was experiencing—and didn't regret inflicting them on him one little bit.

He wasn't sure whether she'd arranged this to remind him of the costs of involving her in Temper's Season, to test his mettle, or as a silent demonstration of the difficulties he'd brought upon himself by having always spent his time with females for whom there was no need to mask his physical response.

For there was no doubt, had Temper been a Cyprian, he'd have already pulled her close and sampled her lips…in heated anticipation of sampling much more.

When Mrs Moorsby leaned forward, continuing to chat to Temper as she straightened an errant ribbon in her charge's coiffure, Lady Sayleford murmured, 'You should be glad of the current style. Those wide skirts and ridiculous full sleeves give you almost eighteen inches of separation. The straight Empire gowns of former days would have clung right to her figure.'

The vivid image of Temper sliding up against him, clad only in a sliver of silk, burned itself into his brain before he could prevent it. Feeling another wave of heat wash through him, Giff grimaced.

'Well, my dear,' Lady Sayleford said as Temper's chaperon finished her task, 'are you ready for your first foray into the *ton*?'

'As I'll ever be, I suppose. Not…frightened, precisely, Lady Sayleford, though I do thank you for your concern. More like…resigned.'

'You should make up your mind to enjoy these events, not merely endure them,' Lady Sayleford advised. 'There's instruction and amusement to be had in every experience—no matter how initially difficult.' After a significant glance at Giff, she continued, 'Anticipate the unusual and intriguing, and you will find it.'

'Intriguing people, even among the *ton*?' Temper said sceptically.

'I'm a member of the *ton*, aren't I?' Lady Sayleford replied.

Temper laughed, her sober expression warming into a smile so full of merriment, Giff thought it must lift the spirits of anyone who witnessed it. 'You have me there. I shall just have to look for *other* intriguing and unusual members of the *ton*.'

The carriage began to slow to a halt, indicating they had reached the Portman Square home of Lady Spencer-Woods, for which Giff uttered a silent prayer of thanks. Little as he was looking forward to what he expected to be a boring event, Giff was heartily glad to hop out of the carriage and let the footman hand the ladies down after him.

Though viewing Temper again minus the concealing evening cloak was unlikely to relieve the state of arousal he'd suffered since collecting her, at least he could maintain some distance while he worked on the 'training himself to resist her' wisely suggested by his godmother.

The servants in the hall, busy collecting outer garments and directing guests up to the ballroom, paid them little notice. But as soon as they reached the landing on which guests waited for the butler to announce them, Giff noted the widening of eyes, sharp inhales of breath and inclining of heads to murmur to companions that signalled Miss Lattimar had been recognised.

She noticed it, too, her chin going up and a martial gleam appearing in her eyes. 'Apparently not everyone received the word that I'm to be accepted,' she murmured to Lady Sayleford.

'Those of lesser importance might not know it—yet,' his godmother replied. 'But everyone who matters does. The rest will discover it soon enough.'

'Or incur your wrath?' Temper suggested, a mischievous grin chasing away the militant look.

'Precisely. Newell, if you would?'

Giff offered his arm. Taking it, Lady Sayleford nodded regally to the handful of waiting groups as she bypassed them and proceeded to the head of the line, where the butler snapped to attention.

'Good evening, your ladyship! Who should I announce is in your party?'

'Mr Newell, Member of Parliament for Great Grimsby, Mrs Moorsby and my protégée, Miss Lattimar.'

As the butler announced their names, they walked into the ballroom towards the hostess, who stood at the head of a short receiving line. Looking over her shoulder to Temper, Lady Sayleford said, 'It's as important for the upper servants to become aware of your position as it is for *ton* hostesses.'

'How well I know it,' Temper replied ruefully. 'I've observed Overton keeping callers waiting for ever, if he doesn't think their consequence merits an immediate audience with Gregory.'

The Countess nodded. 'No one is more punctilious—or better informed—about a person's status than those who rule downstairs. Now, shall we greet our hostess?'

Lady Spencer-Woods met them with a wide, knowing smile. 'Lady Sayleford, so good to see you!' she said as the ladies exchanged curtsies.

'Mrs Moorsby, Mr Newell—and Miss Lattimar! How absolutely stunning you look!'

'Almost the image of my mother,' Temper replied sweetly. 'Although I could never hope to be as stunning as she is.'

Their hostess gaped at her, obviously at a loss how to reply, and Giff bit back a grin. Trust Temper to go straight to the attack.

'I'm sure you'll be quite stunning enough,' Lady Sayleford said drily. 'But come along, my dear, we mustn't keep the others in line waiting.'

Lady Sayleford led them into the ballroom, its floor so crowded with laughing, chattering groups that progress would have been slow even if the Countess had not paused every few feet to greet an acquaintance and introduce her niece, Giff and her new protégée. Though some—those 'who mattered', he supposed—returned the Countess's greeting without surprise, there were many who, upon her making the introductions, stood momentarily speechless.

The density of the crowd, the brevity of the introductions and the noise made it impossible for Miss Lattimar to do more than add a nod of greeting. His sense of anticipation growing, Giff wondered how the volatile Temper would weather the evident shock and disbelief her appearance had struck in many.

When they reached the chairs set up along the

wall on the far side of the ballroom—Lady Sayleford helpfully giving him some welcome distance by inserting Mrs Moorsby between him and Temper—he was finally able to relax and simply look forward to what she would say or do next.

She didn't disappoint. 'Fortunately, the throng was thick enough that no one was in danger of falling over from the shock of seeing me here.'

'Those who were surprised will recover quickly enough. We'll let the rest come to us,' Lady Sayleford said as she took her seat.

'Do you think anyone will?' Temper asked.

'Certainly,' his godmother replied. 'I timed our progress to be just long enough that word of our arrival should have percolated through most of the guests. My friends—and the curious—will certainly come by to look you over—'

'Your friends will be wondering what in the world you are doing,' Temper muttered.

'While the gentleman,' his godmother continued, 'once they catch a glimpse of you, will flock to make your acquaintance. Gifford's presence standing by will ensure no true blackguards dare present themselves.'

Almost at once, the influx began. Older gentlemen and ladies whose names he recognised as being particular friends of his godmother came first, their appraising expressions alive with expectation and curiosity as they looked Temper over—an inspection to which she managed to appear impervious. Following them were a select few matrons with marriageable daughters in tow and the society arbiters whom Lady Sayleford had invited to tea.

'What fun I shall have tonight, watching all the gentlemen buzz around Miss Lattimar,' Mrs Dobbs-Henry, last of the four, declared as she greeted them. 'Thank you, Lady Sayleford, for throwing down the gauntlet.'

'I may need a lance and shield to fend off the outraged matrons, once they recover from their shock,' Temper said wryly.

'They'll have to batter their way through the army of admirers first,' the lady responded. 'When the floor clears for dancing and they spy you here, you will be besieged!' Blowing a kiss to Lady Sayleford, she walked off.

As Mrs Dobbs-Henry predicted, once the crowd at the centre of the ballroom thinned, a stir ran around the room, gentlemen's heads coming up and turning in their direction. An ever-increasing stream began to approach them, making their bows to Lady Sayleford and begging her to introduce them to her charming protégée.

All were known to Giff, though some only by reputation. Several older peers he recognised from Parliament, one gentleman he vaguely remembered being a widower and a clutch of former university classmates he knew to be ladies' men who had at one time paid obligatory court to Temper's mother. As they bowed, he noted varying degrees of amazement at her beauty, universal admiration, curiosity—and the feral heat of males within scenting distance of a highly desirable female.

Much as he sympathised with the latter—suffering from the pull of that attraction himself—he also felt an unanticipated degree of hostility. Glad now that Lady Sayleford had detailed him to protect Temper, he had to bite his tongue to keep himself from warning them off—or inviting them outside, where he could punch that leering look off their faces. He might not be able to growl 'mine!', but he could certainly send them off with a ferocious 'not yours!'

Fortunately for his suddenly precarious hold over his temper, Lady Sayleford shooed each of the latter category away, telling them they might return later to claim a dance.

Maybe by then he would have his reactions fully under control.

The receiving line disbanded and the orchestra started tuning up. The guests took up places along the wall, waiting for the dancing to begin and leaving their party, for the moment, alone.

Mrs Moorsby looked around wonderingly, her eyes wide. 'I expected the ball would be impressive, but oh, my, how the reality exceeds my imagination! The sparkle of jewels reflecting the candlelight! The splendour of the ladies' gowns and the men so handsome in their evening attire! Is it not magnificent, Miss Lattimar?'

'Most impressive, even I must admit,' Temper conceded. But her guarded eyes and wary stance told him that though her chaperon might be expecting nothing but unqualified enjoyment, she was armouring herself for challenge and unpleasantness.

A wave of regret and anger shook him. By rights, Miss Temperance Lattimar, well-born daughter of a rich baron, should be gazing around her first ball with the same excitement and anticipation as her chaperon. He hated that air of coiled tension about her, hated even more knowing that she was right to be cautious.

While she replied to another of her chaperon's comments, Lady Sayleford murmured, 'Well done, Newell. From the thundercloud expression you offered every man who greeted her, they will know their conduct must stay in bounds.'

'Was it that obvious?' he replied, disconcerted to think his animosity had been evident.

'Patently, to me. But just enough to others that I'm sure the gentlemen took the point.'

'Protection is my job, isn't it?' he replied, reassured. One didn't wish to look like a jealous guard dog—even if one was performing that function.

But as he knew all too well, his godmother noticed a host of things ordinary people never observed.

'Yes. But men willing to brave my presence to get an introduction aren't the ones you need worry about. You must fend off the disreputable.'

'Fend off the disreputable?' Temper echoed, turning back to them. 'Oh, no, it's the *reputable* Newell must send away! I don't want to spend time with any gentlemen who might have honourable intentions! Besides, I predict Newell is going to be too preoccupied by matrons with young ladies in tow to be able to concern himself with *my* admirers.'

The low chuckle from Lady Sayleford alarmed him almost as much as Temper's words. 'I can't think what you mean,' he protested.

Temper grinned. 'Half the eminently respectable matrons at this affair may have nearly swooned at seeing me here, but you will note, a fair number were prepared to brave exposing their innocents to my wicked presence in order that Lady Sayleford might present *you* to their lambs.'

For once, he felt a wave of heat that was not desire. 'I'm sure you exaggerate.'

'Indeed, I do not! Did you not notice how they stationed their persons between me and their sweet innocent girls, offering me a greeting notable for its chilliness, while the tones they used when addressing you were warmly encouraging?'

While he frowned, trying to decide whether or not she was teasing, she laughed ruefully. 'I must apologise in advance! I fear your presence here means you will find yourself targeted by matchmaking mamas, whether or not you are ready for courting. You may be more in need of protection than I am! Unless you decide it's time to find that rich wife after all.'

A rich wife...like Temper? The idea of having a wife like *her* was becoming...less distasteful.

But there was, alas, only one Temper—and she was the little sister of his best friend. 'I'd have to be a great deal more financially pressed to be ready to resort to *that* option,' he retorted.

'I believe the Season shall prove interesting— for both of you,' Lady Sayleford interposed. 'Now, with the dancing about to begin, I'll bid you good-night.'

'You're *leaving*?' Giff said, aghast.

His godmother gave him a sweet smile in which he could discern no trace of either amusement or irony. 'I turn Miss Lattimar over to you. Well, what are you waiting for? The first set is forming.' She gave his arm a little push. 'Lead her into it before some other gentleman asks her.'

'An excellent idea,' Mrs Moorsby seconded. 'Quickly, now! Several are approaching.'

Well, if his godmother commanded... Besides, leading her into the first dance would underscore to all the men present that he was watching over her—and give himself more time to adjust to the unpleasant notion of having them hover all around her.

'You'll do me the honour?' he asked.

Temper gave him a tiny nod and laid her hand on his arm. Armoured against her as Gifford was trying to be, he still felt the sizzle of contact right through his sleeve. Looking down, he noted her surprise—ah, yes, she felt it, too!—and wariness in her expression. But then she smiled, the delight shining in those magnificent blue eyes warming him down to his toes.

'How pleasant, to open the ball with a friend, a man who will be neither scheming how best to manoeuvre me into the garden or calculating the size of my fortune,' she said as he walked her towards the other couples forming the set. 'Though I do apologise for Lady Sayleford corralling you. As it's hardly likely I'll be attacked in the middle of the ballroom with my chaperon looking on, after this dance you can escape to the card room.'

'Oh, no, standing guard is standing guard,' he said, meaning it—and no longer resenting the task quite so much. 'My godmother and Mrs Moorsby expect it.'

'I have to admit, I feel…easier, knowing you're nearby.'

That statement lit a little glow of satisfaction in

his chest, offsetting some of the other, more disturbing emotions. Like fierce protectiveness, an unwarranted sense of possession—and lust.

The numerous patterns of the dance didn't allow for much conversation, other than a mutual exchange of compliments over the excellence of their partner. Easily mastering the movements, Giff was glad his mama had insisted he learn to acquit himself respectably on the dance floor.

The patterns also allowed him to forget about conversing and simply enjoy what a lovely picture Temper made, gracefully going through the movements.

After the music ended, he offered his arm, bracing himself for the now-anticipated shock when she laid her hand on it.

'We'll see how many desert me, now that my champion has departed,' she murmured as he led her off the floor.

'I doubt many of the gentlemen will. Lady Sayleford gave you a very public seal of approval.'

Which meant he would have more than a few men to fend off, he realised, surprised again at the strength of his irritation at the idea of other men courting her, no matter how honourable their intentions.

Indeed, he could already see a fair number waiting beside Mrs Moorsby. And not just gentlemen—a few of the matrons to whom they had been introduced waited, too, their daughters in tow.

Hangers-on, positioning their girls where they might entice one of the throng of gentlemen sure to surround Temper? Giff speculated.

For the first time, Giff felt relieved that Temper espoused the ridiculous notion not to marry. She must, of course, eventually. But hopefully she wouldn't resign herself to that truth any time in the immediate future, which would make his task of fending off fortune hunters and the disreputable easier.

'And as you can see,' he continued, 'it's not just gentleman awaiting you. A few of the chaperons and their daughters want to further the acquaintance, too.'

She looked towards Mrs Moorsby, a surprised expression on her face. 'Perhaps there are some young ladies brave enough to risk my acquaintance after all.' She chuckled. 'I shall have to determine if any of them might make you a good wife.'

He looked down to utter a disparaging remark—and found her smiling up at him. 'Teasing me again, I see. You know I have no interest in being caught in the parson's mousetrap.'

'We shall just have to watch out for each other, then, won't we? Shall we brave the gauntlet?'

At his nod, she tightened her grip on his arm

and looked up—giving him a smile and a con-spiratorial wink, as if it were just the two of them setting off against the world.

Impossible not to smile back, beguiled by a wholly unexpected feeling of...camaraderie.

Once again, she'd surprised him. Not only had she shown him the little hoyden he'd known was now able to hold her tongue when necessary, she'd apparently risen to Lady Sayleford's challenge that she view the Season forced on her as an adventure. One she was inviting him to share. No longer as watchdog and innocent...but as allies.

Dismissing the contradictory emotions swirling in him, he told himself to simply enjoy the clever loveliness that was Temperance Lattimar walking beside him, her hand on his arm. No longer just his friend's little sister to protect, but...a comrade.

He resisted the rogue notion that he could be-come quite attached to such a partnership.

A moment later they reached Mrs Moorsby, her eyes merry as she indicated the small crowd sur-rounding her. 'A number of other gentlemen have asked that I present them to you. They were all,' she added in a tone whose irony would be lost on any but Temper and Giff, 'prevented by...other ob-ligations from begging that honour of Lady Say-leford before she departed.'

'Unwilling to face the scrutiny of the dragon,' Giff murmured to Temper.

'Before I do so,' Mrs Moorsby continued, 'you'll remember these ladies and their daughters? They would like you young people to become better acquainted. Lady Arnold with her nieces, Miss Avery and Miss Mary Avery, the Countess of Mannerling and her daughter, Lady Constance?'

'Yes, of course,' Temper said as the women once again exchanged curtsies. 'I should love to become better acquainted. Shall we do so between sets? Now, I believe we should accept the invitations of these kind gentlemen and dance!'

After murmurs of agreement, Mrs Moorsby introduced the waiting gentleman to all the ladies, after which the young people paired up, the rakish Lord Theo outmanoeuvring the other men to claim Temper's hand.

Ignoring a blatantly appealing look from Miss Avery, Giff said, 'As it's impossible to make a choice among so much beauty, I'll cede my place to you other gentlemen and keep Mrs Moorsby company.'

The young ladies and their escorts followed Temper and Lord Theo on to the floor, while several others remained beside Mrs Moorsby, chatting politely while they awaited their chance to squire the Beauty.

Depending on the other men waiting beside her

to make polite conversation with Mrs Moorsby, Giff turned his attention to the dancers.

Watching another man claim Temper was even more distasteful than he'd expected, he thought, frowning as Lord Theo pulled her rather closer than the movements of the dance required. Despite knowing she wasn't interested in marrying, she was too alluring, too beguiling—and, despite her upbringing, too innocent—to be trusted to rakes like Lord Theo. He wouldn't want her to be taken in by a dashing charmer—or compromised.

Fortunately, the dance wasn't a waltz. If Lord Theo had tried to hold her as scandalously close as *that* dance allowed, Giff might have found it necessary to intervene.

Just how had he let himself blunder into this aggravating situation?

At least there was one gentleman who had ceased to plague him over it, he thought, thanking Heaven for small favours.

As he'd awaited Temper in the hall of Vraux House tonight, he'd encountered Gregory departing to his evening entertainment at an exclusive establishment where the wine would be excellent, the play deep and the enjoyment afterward far more erotic than the delights available at a respectable society ball. A fact about which his friend had initially bedevilled him unmercifully.

At Giff's irritated response that Gregory ought

to be grateful to him for going above and beyond to get his troublesome sister off his hands, his friend sobered.

'I do appreciate it, more than you can imagine,' he responded. 'Had Lady Sayleford not roped you into watching over her, I would have felt compelled to do so myself. I value not just your kindness in stepping in to secure her sponsorship, but also the concern for Temper's safety that prompted you to forgo your own interests to protect her.'

Performing a brother's office, taking care of my baby sister, was the unspoken message.

Recalling it now, Giff sighed. He didn't regret—too much—giving up evenings accompanying Gregory in pursuit of easy, uncomplicated pleasure. He did wish his best friend's 'baby sister' weren't such a beautiful, alluring woman.

It wasn't just blackguards and bounders Giff had to ward off. As Lady Sayleford's trick with the carriage seating tonight had demonstrated with stark clarity, he needed to keep a tight grip over his own behaviour as well. Should Giff succumb to the desire Temper aroused, Gregory would consider it a betrayal of his trust.

He blew out a breath, relieved to be watching her from half a dance floor away, far from the temptation of her soft skin and sinful-thought-inducing scent.

He'd make sure he wasn't tortured by being seated beside her in the coach again. Even so, it was going to be a long Season.

Chapter Seven

While Gifford Newell remained beside Mrs Moorsby, Temper walked off with Lord Theo Collington, a man whom she hadn't needed Giff's warning frown to recognise as a charming rogue. She'd willingly offered Lord Theo her hand, curious to discover whether the Marquess of Childress's younger son would attempt to lure her into indiscretion, or intended to simply toy with her—and annoy Giff—by his attentions.

'At last, you rescue me from the doldrums of this interminable evening by granting me the hand of the most beautiful lady in the room,' he bent close to murmur in her ear.

Sidling away, she replied, 'If you find the evening is so interminable, I wonder that you have remained. Why not seek out more…entertaining company?'

'There may be company elsewhere more…

practised, but none so alluring…or delightfully innocent.'

She angled a glance up at him. 'Forgive me for doubting that it is *innocence*, rather than something more…earthy, that appeals to you.'

'Ah, but it is that mix of innocence with the sensual that is truly compelling.'

'An innocence of which you'd be happy to relieve me?'

Surprise—and heat—flared in his eyes. 'You are direct.'

'I have no use for polite subterfuge.'

'Then, yes, I admit I would quite happily tutor your innocence.'

'You being the most expert of instructors?'

He gave her a little bow. 'I do my poor best.'

'For as many as possible, I suspect. But alas, I have no desire to shock the company. Tonight, at any rate. So you might as well seek that "more practised" company elsewhere.'

She turned to walk off the floor, but he stayed her. 'How can I go, when it is so entertaining to banter words with you?'

'And annoy Mr Newell?'

That drew a genuine laugh. 'He does make it appear that, for the least infraction, it would be pistols at dawn.'

'Believe me, Lord Theo, were there to be an… infraction, it would be *my* hand holding the pistol. And without wishing to boast, I must inform you that my aim is true.'

'Is it, now? Is that something in the nature of a threat?'

'Consider it an…advisory. That I am neither the wanton some whisper the daughter of my mother must be, nor a helpless female dependent upon a male for protection.'

The caressing tone and flirtatious look gave way to an expression of genuine interest. 'Beautiful, alluring and ferocious—what a unique combination.'

'You find a dangerous woman alluring?'

'Indeed! What could be more alluring than danger, allied to passion?'

The heat was back in his gaze, yet for all the suggestiveness of his words, Temper found, surprisingly, that she didn't feel threatened. Just to make sure her instincts were correct, though, she added, 'You would not, of course, dream of using coercion to explore that passion.'

He drew back, a hand going dramatically to his throat. 'Coercion? Certainly not! A man of address need never resort to something so vulgar!'

'Since ladies generally fall at your feet most willingly?'

He shrugged. 'No more than you, would I wish to boast.'

Temper laughed, fairly sure now that she had

nothing to fear from Lord Theo. 'Perhaps we can continue our association. Both of us secure in talents of which we don't need to boast.'

He smiled, amusement dancing in his eyes. 'Perhaps we should. Until one or the other of us needs to demonstrate their talent? Passion persuades, but can sometimes lead to regret.'

'Only if it came with wedding lines attached.'

He shuddered. 'That *would* be a frightful outcome.'

'Then you may rest easy. I find that prospect of wedlock even more frightful than you do.'

He gave her a speculative look. 'Indeed? You don't wish to find a husband who would provide... protection for your explorations?'

The notion of falling into a life like her mother's chased away every bit of amusement. 'Certainly not,' she said grimly. 'The last thing I want is to be compelled by an indifferent spouse into "explorations" that lead only to loneliness, disillusionment and notoriety. So as I told you, I have *no* interest in marriage.'

He chuckled. 'A lady who means what she says? That would truly be an amazing creature.'

'No more singular than a gentleman who tells a lady what *he* truly thinks. Instead of paying compliments to a female he finds unattractive, or whispering words of devotion to a woman he merely wishes to bed.'

Surprise once again widened his eyes. 'You are most astonishingly frank.'

'You may rest easy. The dance will soon end, relieving you of my odd company.'

'On the contrary! I would have more of your "odd" company.'

'Another pretty speech, Lord Theo?'

'Not at all, Miss Lattimar. In this instance, I am following your lead and saying exactly what I mean.'

She turned an assessing gaze on him, which he met steadily. Unable to find a trace of deception in it, she gave a reluctant smile. 'Perhaps you *are* being honest. And if you intend neither to compromise me nor marry me, we might be friends after all.'

'I'll start with "friends".' As he twirled her under his arm in the dance's final figure, he added in a murmur, 'Until a desire for intimacy becomes mutual.'

Another tease—or a challenge for her to try to resist him? Amused, she shook her head at him as she took his arm to return to her chaperon. 'Alas, fond hopes are so often disappointed.'

Lord Theo returned her to Mrs Moorsby, where an earnest young man immediately stepped forward. 'Your chaperon has promised you will grant me the next dance.'

A bit taken aback by his insistence, she raised

her brows at Mrs Moorsby, who said, 'Temperance, allow me to present Lord Solsworth, who was most persuasive that I recommend him as an agreeable partner for the next dance.'

Ignoring the glowering looks of the other gentlemen waiting around them, Lord Solsworth held out his arm. 'You will honour me, Miss Lattimar?'

With a little shrug to the others, Temper said, 'With such a recommendation, what can I do but agree?'

Giving her new partner a rapid inspection as he led her to the floor, Temper decided he was handsome, determined—and perhaps even younger than she was. Indifferent about the success of her Season, unlike most young ladies about to debut, she hadn't bothered to discover the names and titles of all the eligible bachelors, but given the deference shown him by the other gentleman, her partner must be highly born. 'Are you still at university, Lord Solsworth?' she asked after they'd taken their places.

'Yes, but I get to town often,' he said. 'I assist my father in the Lords and hope to stand for a seat in Parliament myself soon. To gain some experience, against the day I must eventually step into his shoes.'

The heir then, probably with his own courtesy title, who would take over a place in the Lords after he inherited. 'Is your father a reformer?'

'Lud, no!' he said with a laugh. 'Almost reactionary! He don't know it yet, but if I get that seat in the House, we shall probably cancel each other out. I very much approve of the goals of the reformers, especially Ashley-Cooper's to restrict the working hours of children in the mills. But here I am, prosing on about politics, when what I wish to say is that you are the most beautiful creature I have ever beheld! It's a wonder beyond describing to have the privilege of escorting you.'

Indeed, the ardent gaze he fixed on her as she moved away from him, performing the next figure of the dance, supported his claim of dazzled admiration.

'Thank you for your kind words,' she said when she returned to him, 'but any beauty of form I possess owes nothing to me. It is a gift of nature.'

'Such beauty of form could not help but be allied to beauty of character.'

She laughed shortly. 'I think you will find many here to dispute that claim.'

'Because of your mother? I think it monstrously unjust that *you* be judged based on *her* actions!'

'You would be my champion against the malicious?' she asked, thinking him surprisingly naive, but also touched by his gallantry. 'Even knowing nothing of my character? You might find me unworthy of such defence.'

'That, I could never believe.'

Temper ought to say something outrageous to deflect his obvious infatuation, but she found herself reluctant to hurt him—and malign her own character—by uttering some cutting rejoinder. He was obviously the highly eligible son of some peer and, if he was at this gathering, must be at least marginally interested in marriage.

Which made him exactly the sort of gentleman of whom Vraux would approve and therefore one she should discourage, if she meant to end the Season unwed. But how to disillusion him without being cruel?

'I doubt I could live up to the high expectations you seem to have of me,' she said, hoping candour might produce the same result as cruelty. 'It's probably better that we part before I disappoint you.'

'Indeed, not! I am sure knowing you better will only confirm my initial impressions of your excellence.'

Temper wasn't sure how to assess Solsworth's attentions. He seemed too young and idealistic to have ulterior designs on her person and perhaps too young to be seriously considering marriage. Even so, as a highly eligible *parti* of whom her father and society would approve, she should redouble her efforts to discourage him.

She was debating how best to do that when, as

the dance ended, a matron in a large turban and an indignant expression stormed over to them.

'Sidney!' she cried. 'I sent you over to dance with Miss Avery! Not with this…*creature*.' Looking down her nose at Temper, the lady continued, 'Mrs Spencer-Woods's standards are certainly slipping, if she's invited the likes of *you*. I may have to cut the connection.'

'Mama, please!' her partner protested, his face going scarlet.

After an initial shock at the suddenness of the attack, Temper schooled her face to a polite mask, inwardly kicking herself for having been caught off guard. After all, wasn't this the sort of reception she had expected tonight?

'I'll pass along your disapproval to my sponsor, Lady Sayleford,' she said in dulcet tones. 'As we haven't been introduced, I can't bid you good evening, Mrs…' She let the phrase trail off, watching the bloom of fury on the woman's cheeks at her insulting neglect to address the mother of a titled man as 'my lady'. 'So I will simply say goodbye. Thank you for the dance, Lord Solsworth.'

Turning her back on them both, she walked back to Mrs Moorsby.

No need for any further worry about how to discourage Solsworth. His harridan of a mother would make sure in future that her precious son kept well away from the scarlet woman.

More shaken than she'd like to admit by the encounter, as she reached her party, she angled her face away from Giff's searching gaze.

'Was Lady Agremont unpleasant?' he demanded.

'Is that who she was? She didn't bother with an introduction before dragging her son away from my contaminating presence.'

Giff muttered a curse. 'Her husband, the Marquess of Agremont, is one of the highest sticklers in the Lords. I'm surprised her darling only son and heir had the courage to dance with you.'

'Apparently he was so struck by my beauty, he was willing to risk his mother's wrath.' Temper laughed ruefully. 'What an innocent! He seemed convinced my physical loveliness must be accompanied by beauty of character. I'm sure his mother is about to disabuse him of that misconception.'

'She could have been more polite about reclaiming him,' Mrs Moorsby said indignantly. 'Even if she does disapprove of you—most unjustly, as she knows *nothing* about you beyond your name—she could have waited to convey her opinion until after her son escorted you off the floor.'

'I suppose I'm lucky to have suffered only one unpleasant encounter thus far,' Temper said, suddenly tired of the event. 'All I want is to escape the Season with a whole skin and get on with doing what *I* want.'

As the dance floor emptied at the conclusion of the last set, the other ladies and gentleman who had been standing beside Mrs Moorsby began to drift back. After refusing the several gentlemen who petitioned her for the next dance, with Giff and Mrs Moorsby engaged in conversation by several of the bystanders, she glanced behind her. Confirming that the curtained windows created a quiet alcove where she might be alone with her own thoughts for a moment, she was about to slip back there when a hand at her sleeve stayed her retreat.

She recognised the person restraining her to be one of the young ladies she'd met earlier. A young lady who had, she realised, been an onlooker when Lady Agremont verbally assaulted her.

'If you are not going to dance, would you like to chat?' the girl asked.

And dig out all the gritty details about her public dressing-down? Her anger flaring, Temper snapped, 'Miss Henley, isn't it? Didn't you just hear that I'm not a proper person to know? I wonder you dare approach me without your chaperon for protection!'

She immediately regretted her sharpness, for poor Miss Henley had done nothing to deserve her wrath. Before she could apologise, however, the girl laughed.

'Oh, Mama never worries about me,' Miss Henley said, appearing not the least bit upset by Temper's rudeness. 'She could hardly wait to perform all the introductions so she might go off on the arm of one of her gallants.'

Tall, angular, with a long, plain face and nondescript brown hair done in ringlets, Miss Henley had no claims to beauty. But her merry laugh and friendly smile made Temper even more ashamed of her sharpness, while the girl's unexpected comment made her curious to know more.

'Your mama sees no need to protect you?'

'Not really. As she never tires of reminding me, I'm neither pretty enough to tempt a rake, nor rich enough to tempt a fortune hunter.'

Miss Henley's tone was matter of fact, stating the truth as she saw it with no hint of self-pity. Inherently honest herself, Temper wouldn't offer her false protests about her loveliness. But she could admire such a level-headed acceptance of reality.

'How delightful to meet someone who dares to speak the truth, without recourse to flattery or false modesty. Your mama does not value you as she ought.'

Miss Henley chuckled again. 'No, she doesn't. But to be fair, we are chalk and cheese. She's a Beauty, as was my older sister, who thrilled her by making a brilliant match with a duke's youngest son. Whereas she despairs of finding even an acceptable match for me. Although I have to admit, it is amusing, watching the gentlemen try to walk the fine line between being attentive enough to be polite without according me enough attention to raise expectations.'

Easily able to visualise such exchanges, Temper had to smile. 'You are very plain spoken.'

'Yes, one of my many faults. Despite my lack of looks and modest dowry, I'm very choosy, you see, and Papa, though he ignores me most of the time, is not such a bully as to force me into a union I don't want. Since I have a small inheritance from an aunt, he'll not be saddled with my upkeep, should I fail to marry.'

'What a blessing to have independent means! I, too, have enough to live on that I need not marry.'

'But you're so lovely! I'm sure you could have any gentleman you fancied.'

Temper grimaced. 'I don't fancy one. I'd much rather remain single and pursue my own interests.'

'How fascinating! Won't you tell me more? I should love to know how you've acquired a dubious reputation before you were even out. And about your famous mama, of course. Oh, forgive me!' she added, clapping a hand to her mouth. 'My mother would say I am being vulgarly intrusive! If it seems so, I do apologise—but I *am* curious. My life is very dull, you see. I've never been anywhere or done anything interesting.'

'No apologies necessary. You are very forthright—but I like that,' Temper said, her positive first impression of Miss Henley reinforced. 'I'd love to talk at length—but it's far too busy here.' Out of the corner of her eye she could see Giff, having bid goodbye to the lady who'd been occupying him, glancing around for her. Several of her previously dismissed swains were also sidling closer, probably to renew their requests for a dance. 'Do you ride?'

'I do, but tomorrow I promised Mama to wait until the Promenade Hour.' Miss Henley made a face. 'It will mean being restricted to a trot at best, but at least I won't have to sit with her in the barouche. She claims going to the Park is supposed to be for me to display myself to potential beaux, but it's really Mama who loves stopping to chat with friends, or to take some favoured gentlemen up in her carriage. But if you rode with me—and shooed away the gentlemen who would certainly beg to accompany you—we might manage a good coze without anyone interrupting us.'

'Yes, let's do that,' Temper said.

Miss Henley smiled. 'Mama will scold at first, saying that I will show to disadvantage beside an Incomparable like you, but I will counter by telling her that as an Incomparable inevitably gathers an admiring crowd around her, I will have an opportunity to impress the gentlemen waiting to claim your attention. Unlikely, of course, but that view of it will content her.'

'You really are the most complete hand!' Temper said with a laugh. 'Do you manage everyone around you so deftly?'

Miss Henley shrugged. 'As a female, one must learn how to manoeuvre people with subtlety. It's the only way to get to do what you want.'

'Perhaps you can teach me some of your tricks! Until tomorrow, then!'

The girls exchanged curtsies, Miss Henley pressing Temper's hand before slipping past her. As she turned back towards the ballroom, Temper discovered that Giff's progress towards her had been arrested by Miss Avery.

Unaccountably annoyed, Temper absently accepted the offer of the first man to reach her and walked with him on to the dance floor, her gaze straying back to Giff and his persistent admirer.

She was too far away to hear their conversation, but after a few moments' chat, shaking his head and smiling, Giff bowed—an obvious dismissal. Temper saw an expression of pique cross the young lady's face before she smiled as well and gave her hand to a different gentleman.

Though she hadn't any right to be, Temper felt…pleased that Giff had politely turned away the girl's efforts to lure him into a dance. She would want dear Giff to find a companionable wife and there was something about Miss Avery she just couldn't like.

If he were going to do her the favour of watching out for her, she ought to reciprocate by actually evaluating the eligible ladies for him, as she'd flippantly offered, thinning out from those who tried to attach him any she felt would not make him an admirable partner.

Going through the steps with *her* current partner, a callow young man too shy to talk, allowed Temper to look back across the ballroom to where Newell stood beside Mrs Moorsby. She suppressed a little niggle of regret that Giff—who'd turned out to be an excellent partner—hadn't invited her to take the floor with him again this evening.

Of course, he'd been practically coerced into doing so the first time by Lady Sayleford. And it was best that she not put herself so tantalisingly close to him—a fact that unexpectedly disturbing carriage ride had revealed.

Having accompanied her brother and Giff numerous times over the years, she'd taken the seat beside him without a thought—and immediately known it to be a mistake. Unable to think of a way to ask Lady Sayleford to alter the arrangement without the request appearing very odd, she'd suffered through—the sensual tension between them, she thought ruefully, unfortunately mutual.

Dancing with him had been just as fraught,

though, thank heavens, the first dance had not been a waltz. It was dizzying enough just walking out on to the floor with her hand on his arm, feeling the tingle of connection all the way up to her shoulder when he clasped her hand to turn her through the figures of the dance. To have his arm around her waist, her hand on his shoulder as the waltz required, so close she could feel the heat emanating from his body, catch the faint scent of his shaving soap… A wave of warmth rippled through her at the thought.

So much for her optimistic hopes that whatever strange effect he was having on her would diminish with time…or become easier to ignore. How, in the space of a few short months, had he changed from her brother's best friend, who'd bedevilled, teased—and encouraged—her since she was in short skirts, into this dynamic individual whose physical presence now seemed to cast some sort of spell over her, making her want to draw close to him?

A spell more difficult to resist because this was *Giff*, a friend she'd known for years, one of the few men she trusted implicitly.

She was beginning to understand why, denied intimacy with her father, her mother had been drawn by another man's physical appeal. But though she might be tempted, she didn't have the protection against misfortune of a married woman, whose child from another liaison might be covered up as long as her spouse, knowingly or not, accepted the child. As Temper's father had.

Nor could she allow herself just a taste of passion with Giff. However willingly she might lure him, if he considered that he'd compromised her, honourable Giff would insist on marriage. With her brother being his best friend, even something as simple as a kiss might be enough to make him feel obligated to offer for her.

And marrying him would mean disaster. As friends, she and Giff had always worked together well, but as a wife, she would destroy him—his career and his peace. She might, given the attraction between them, manage more than just that simple kiss. But even with Giff, attempting something more intimate would risk having the ugly memories surge up and over the barrier she'd constructed to contain them.

Besides, if she were to wed him, she would have to reveal the truth of what had happened that summer afternoon so many years ago. Almost as awful as the event itself would be watching Giff's expression change from shock, to disgust, to revulsion as she confessed it. The idea of telling him the whole, and thereby forfeiting for ever his respect and friendship, was unthinkable.

No, she couldn't risk it.

Acting upon the edgy, unwanted, but impossible-to-ignore attraction between them was simply impossible, she concluded with a sigh. No matter how difficult she was finding it to recapture the uncomplicated friendship they used to share.

Chapter Eight

A few hours later, Gifford escorted his ladies into the carriage for the ride home. Mrs Moorsby, clearly unused to late evenings, soon nodded off in her corner. This time, Temper sat across from him, occupying the seat beside her chaperon left vacant by Lady Sayleford's early departure, leaving Giff mercifully alone on the backward-facing bench.

Inclining her head at her dozing chaperon, Temper said softly, 'Her first *ton* evening might have been a bit too stimulating, but I think she enjoyed it.'

'I'm sure she did. How did you find *your* first ton evening?'

'Not as dull as I feared. And Lady Sayleford did her work well. Aside from that one unpleasant encounter, I was treated kindly.'

'I'm glad.' Recalling the outraged Lady Agremont, he laughed shortly. 'The Marquess's wife is likely to have an unpleasant encounter of her own, once my godmother hears how she treated you.'

Temper smiled ruefully. 'You're probably right. I can almost feel for Lady Agremont.'

Trying to keep his voice casual, he continued, 'You never lacked for partners. Did you meet anyone of particular interest?'

She laughed shortly. 'Most were attentive, but forgettable. Lord Solsworth was the most bedazzled, although I expect his disapproving mother will make short work of that infatuation.'

Giff hesitated. Temper hadn't mentioned the man who was his chief worry. Choosing his words with care, he continued, 'What did you think of Lord Theo? I hope you didn't find him *too* charming, for I have to warn you, he's a rogue through and through. I wouldn't have you…taken in.'

The smile that comment produced was not reassuring. 'Ah, Lord Theo. You need not worry about him, Giff. He's no more interested in marriage than I am. And if it comes to seduction, I've told him I shoot straight.'

Giff stared, not sure at first that he'd heard her correctly, then had to laugh. 'Did you indeed? Did he believe you?'

She chuckled. 'I think so. Or at least, he gave the warning enough credence that I don't think he will put it to the test.'

'That would be a blessing.'

'So might his friendship be—if his continuing attentions solidify my reputation as a "fast" female no prudent man would consider marrying. I'll be spared the attentions of honourable men and, relying on you to chase away the dishonourable, I may be able to convince Papa to end this farce of a Season sooner rather than later. And I find Lord Theo…interesting.'

'That kind of interest could lead to compromise!'

'Oh, I don't think he'd try to take me against my will.' She grinned. 'I have it on his own authority that he abhors the idea of coercion. Not that I would mind being compromised by him, since neither of us has any desire to marry. A small scandal might help me end this waste of a Season more quickly.'

'That might suit you, but what about a scandal's effect on Lady Sayleford and Mrs Moorsby?'

'Maybe a *very* small one?' She sighed. 'Though I don't want to appear proper and conformable, neither do I wish to repay the kindness of Mrs Moorsby, Lady Sayleford—and your own—by embarrassing all of you. I will *try* to avoid scandal—but I won't be surprised if it finds me.'

'I shall have to work harder at my job, to make sure it does not,' he said emphatically.

'Dear Giff, still trying to protect me,' she said, the warmth of her smile causing a curious tightness in his chest. 'And what a thankless task! I apologise again for catching you up in my battles.'

'I don't mind, truly. I'm as eager as Gregory to see you settled and happy.'

She gave him a grim smile. 'Then you'll have to choose between "settled" and "happy", because I could not be both. Enough! I survived my first evening with only one minor incident and met a potential friend in the engaging Miss Henley, with whom I shall ride tomorrow. During the Promenade Hour, unfortunately, but she has promised to accompany her mother then.'

'Miss… Henley?' he repeated, trying—and failing—to attach a face to the name.

Temper gave him a deprecating glance. 'She's not a Beauty, so men overlook her and her mother doesn't value her. Despite all that, she seems to have turned into an interesting and independent young lady. I'd like to know her better.'

He sighed. 'Tomorrow, during the Promenade Hour? I suppose I can be free to accompany you.'

'I don't mean to ruin your afternoon!' she protested. 'Surely I will be safe enough, riding in the Park amid a throng of the *ton*, with a groom and Mrs Moorsby to accompany me.'

'But Mrs Moorsby doesn't ride,' Giff pointed out.

'Damn—drat and blast!' Temper said, her

cheeks reddening. 'I completely forgot. I suppose I could send Miss Henley a note, crying off—'

'No, I promised Godmother I would see the Season through and I mean to do so. Although I would appreciate it if, hereafter, you remember to ride in the morning.'

'Leaving afternoons and a few evenings free for your Parliamentary work.' She sighed. 'Once again, I apologise for embroiling you in the social Season. I shall hope to be discredited sooner rather than later, so that Papa releases *me* from its toils as well!'

The carriage slowed, indicating they had reached the Vraux town house. 'I'll climb down quietly, so as not to disturb Mrs Moorsby,' Temper told him.

'Very well, but I'll see you to the door—and don't even try to tell me it isn't necessary. A gentleman never leaves a lady standing on the kerb like an abandoned parcel!'

She was chuckling at the description as the footman handed her down, Giff resisting the urge to perform that courtesy himself. Better he refrain as much as possible from subjecting himself to the intoxicating effect of her touch, since courtesy required that he offer his arm while she climbed the entry steps.

Ah, and sweet temptation it was, the feel of her hand clasping him. How much more dizzying would it be were she to wrap those slender hands around his shoulders, lean that tempting body against his?

Beating back those thoughts, he pulled his arm away as soon as they reached the landing and summoned up a smile. 'I'm glad you enjoyed your first evening—somewhat. Shall I stop by to collect you tomorrow afternoon?'

She sighed. 'I suppose you must. And I can't even promise you a good gallop as a reward for giving up your afternoon!'

With her head angled up at him, lamplight playing over the gold of her hair, outlining her nose and full, soft lips against the night gloom, his mind jumped to the sort of gallop that would truly be a reward. 'Perhaps another time…for the gallop,' he said disjointedly, trying to rein his thoughts back into line.

'Yes, another time. Until tomorrow, then.' With a smile, she disappeared behind the door the butler had opened for her.

He stood for a moment on the landing, letting his erratic pulse settle. It was too late to back out on his offer to help with her Season. He'd simply have to find a way to better control not just his actions, but his mind as well. He couldn't end every encounter where some act of courtesy required him to touch her by thinking of kissing… and more.

No matter how much he regretted it, kissing her was forbidden.

* * *

The following afternoon, Temper rode to the park with Giff, her groom trailing behind. 'I'm rather glad we are not going to gallop,' she told him, glad also that she was meeting Miss Henley and would send him off. The disturbing effect he'd had on her dressed in evening clothes hadn't abated a jot now that he was dressed for riding. And her foolish pulse had sped, making her light-headed for a moment as he handed her up into the saddle before they set out.

'Glad you can't gallop?' he repeated. 'Are you ill? Should I summon a physician?'

She made a face at him. 'I won't mind so much riding a job horse if we're to be limited to a decorous trot. Although this beast seems acceptable, there's no way he could match my Arion at the gallop and I would be sure to miss him.'

Giff tilted his head, seeming to have just noticed she wasn't riding her usual gelding. Was he as distracted by her presence as she was by his?

'Where is Arion?'

'He picked up a stone in his shoe yesterday. Nothing serious, Huggins said, but he thought it best that the bruised hoof be rested for a time.'

'Probably also knowing you'd be hard-pressed to refrain from a gallop if you rode Arion,' Giff observed with a grin.

'You slander me!' she protested. 'I would never do anything to put Arion at risk.'

'And for your safety, too,' Giff continued, his face a careful blank. 'With a sore hoof, he might suddenly stumble or rear up, and land you on your ear.'

'Me, land on my ear?' she echoed indignantly. 'You know I'm never unseated! Surely you've seen me ride often enough…' She let the sentence trail off as he burst out laughing. 'Wretch! You deserve some vile punishment for maligning me so!'

'I beg pardon!' he said, holding up his hand. 'But I couldn't resist. Your eyes blaze such blue fire when you're angry.'

She grinned back, her irritation evaporating in the welcome warmth of their familiar camaraderie. This was the Giff she knew—teasing, cajoling and amusing.

'I concede,' he continued. 'I *have* seen you ride often enough to know you maintain perfect control of your mount, even one as spirited as Arion, and even dressed in the ridiculous full skirts fashion now decrees.'

'I should hope so. Though I admit, I would much prefer a gallop in the open countryside in a pair of Greg's old breeches.'

His face tensed and he swallowed hard. 'I'd rather not envision that.'

With her limbs fully outlined by the worn, clinging calfskin and thin linen shirt? The idea of Giff watching her in such revealing attire flooded her with warmth of a different sort, reviving the strong undercurrent of sensual tension his teasing had momentarily suppressed.

She dared a quick glance at him at him, but could read nothing from his inscrutable expression. Did he feel the same odd mix of ease and discomfort, attraction and the need to repress it? And sadness, for the loss of what had once been such a simple, straightforward friendship?

But she had to be encouraged that they'd managed to recapture their old ease, even if briefly. She'd just have to figure out more ways to make that happen—and keep the disturbing sensual connection buried.

For once, she welcomed the concealment of voluminous skirts and wide sleeves. And knowing that she would soon be meeting her friend in the park and distancing herself from his both engaging and disturbing company.

'Once we find Miss Henley, you can safely take yourself off—else you might be corralled into talking with Lady Henley. Apparently she is usually accompanied by a coterie of gallants. You'll want to escape before she adds you to their number.'

'Thank you for the warning! I shall take myself off swiftly—but remain in the vicinity, in case you have need of me.'

'I should be able to handle cuts and slights on my own, but it does give me more…confidence to know that you are nearby. Able to come to my rescue if I *should* be assaulted in Hyde Park in broad daylight.'

If he had been nearby to rescue her that day long ago…would she still be as set upon living her life unwed?

A street urchin darted out in front of her, pulling her attention back to controlling her horse. The increasingly crowded streets then demanded that they ride single file, Giff leading the way to clear a path, the groom bringing up the rear.

Passing through the entry gates, they found the carriageway already crowded with riders and vehicles. Though they could once again ride side by side, progress was dawdling and they'd made almost a complete transit down Rotten Row before Temper spotted her new friend, mounted on a grey hack beside a smart black landau.

'That's Miss Henley and her mama over there!'

Giff gazed in the direction of her pointing finger and nodded. 'I'm to stay for the introductions and then take my leave?'

'I'd appreciate it if you remain nearby, as offered, and waylay anyone who seems bent on interrupting us. I can't ask any truly intrusive questions with a crowd around to overhear.'

He chuckled. 'Are you sure you wish to ask intrusive questions? You might frighten Miss Henley into nipping this potential friendship in the bud.'

'I've already discovered that she prizes plain speaking. If I can say what I truly mean and *don't* frighten her off, she might become a true friend.' Feeling a wave of sadness as she voiced the words, she added, 'With Pru off getting herself married, soon I shall need a friend to talk with.'

'I know you must miss her. It wouldn't be like confiding in the sister you grew up with, but remember, you'll always have me.'

She looked up at him sharply, some nameless something passing in their gazes. 'I hope so,' she said softly before forcing herself to look away.

She'd have him as a friend—until he married. Which he must do, probably sooner rather than later, given his Parliamentary ambitions and slender purse. She mustn't let herself rely on him too much. Better that she concentrate on planning the travels that would take her beyond the restrictions of England, out into the wider world.

A prospect that seemed suddenly a little lonelier and less appealing than it had in all the dreams she'd spun growing up.

Suppressing that disturbing notion, she spurred her mount and rode over to intercept her friend.

Chapter Nine

After greetings all around and introductions to the two older gentlemen who were accompanying Lady Henley, Temper gave Giff a significant nod.

Returning a quick wink, he said, 'I'll just let the young ladies chat, while I catch up with some friends. If you'll excuse me, ladies and gentlemen?'

As he rode away, Temper turned to her companion. 'Shall we try a trot, Miss Henley? With your permission, of course, Lady Henley.'

'Go on, girls, enjoy yourselves,' she said with an indulgent look.

Smiling at Temper, Miss Henley signalled her mount forward. 'I doubt we can manage a trot in this throng, but we can try!'

'Only until we're far enough away to speak without being overheard,' Temper added in an undertone.

'Let us be off, then!'

It truly being difficult to ride with any speed through the crowd of horses, carriages and pedestrians, the two girls soon slowed their mounts to a walk.

'Now we may ask each other as many "vulgarly intrusive" questions as we please before the world catches up with us again,' Temper said.

'Excellent! I should ask first, for there is truly nothing interesting about me. I've spent most of my life buried in Hampshire and possess no talents other than an aptitude for riding and a penchant for reading. Despite the fact that you could have any man you wanted, you told me you would rather go adventuring than marry?'

'I don't know that I could have any man I chose—assuming I wished to choose one.'

'Ah, yes. Your curious reputation. You exactly resemble your mother, I've heard.'

'I'm nearly her twin. So of course, in the eyes of society, I must share her profligate tendencies. Thereby making me a female no responsible man would dare to marry,' Temper said, trying to keep the bitterness from her tone. 'Then there's my brother Christopher, who married a former courtesan last year, putting the family further beyond the pale. So it's fortunate that I have no desire to wed.'

'Have *you* actually done anything…profligate?' Miss Henley asked.

'Not yet,' Temper replied with a laugh. 'But society is just waiting for me to do something scandalous. Which is so annoying, I may lose my temper, and find a way to behave very badly, just to live down to their expectations.'

Instead of looking alarmed by that prospect, Miss Henley laughed. 'What nonsense, that you are being judged before you've done anything at all! Another example of how ridiculous society is. If you do decide to do something scandalous, may I join you? I'm not pretty enough to catch the attention of a scoundrel, but a whiff of scandal might make me more interesting to the gentlemen.'

'You wouldn't want to be compromised into having to marry a scoundrel!' Temper protested.

'No. But it might be deliciously wicked to ride or dance with one. Until he finds out I'm not daring at all. I suppose I shall end my days living in some little London town house, with an elderly relation to give me consequence and a pug dog at my feet.'

'You mustn't settle for anything so dreary! Come adventuring with me! I've wanted to explore foreign lands since I was a girl and have read every travel journal I could find by individuals who have travelled to India, Russia, the Far East. My father collects weapons and antiquities.

I hope to travel with his commission, acquiring things for him.'

'It sounds marvellously exciting, though I'm not sure I'm brave enough to accompany you! I should very much like you to call me your friend, though. Know that you can count on me to be yours, whatever shocking thing you might do!'

In Miss Henley's avowal Temper could find no trace of insincerity. A wave of warmth and gratitude swept over her. Perhaps she *had* found a friend who could partially fill the void left by Pru's departure. Miss Henley seemed to possess the same sunny, optimistic disposition that made her twin so lovable.

'Thank you,' Temper said at last. 'I should like very much to call *you* my friend as well.'

'Good! I'm glad we settled it, for I fear we're about to be overtaken by some of your admirers. See the ones, over there, waving at you?'

'Drat,' Temper muttered, noting that there were indeed some gentlemen picking their way through the riders and carriages, headed towards them. 'I shall be lucky to recall any names.'

Miss Henley gave her a surprised look. 'Do you not know them all?'

'I actually know almost none of the men who were presented to me last night,' Temper said. 'My mother, you remember, isn't received by many in society and I'm acquainted only with the handful of gentlemen who are my brothers' closest friends. I'm ashamed to admit that I had so little interest in society, I never even thought to discover the identity of its occupants. Lady Sayleford would know everything about everyone, of course, but I'd rather not ask her.'

Miss Henley shuddered. 'I should think not! My mother wouldn't let me step near a drawing room until I could recite from memory the names of every society hostess, every aristocrat of note and every unmarried gentleman in London. I can coach you, if you like.'

'Thank you, that would be most helpful!' And a perfect opportunity to obtain an honest assessment of any member of society she needed to know more about—without having to ask Giff or Lady Sayleford.

'Are there any particular beaux you had in mind?'

'Lord Theo?'

'Ah, a charmer, but one who prefers the amusement of married ladies with indulgent spouses. A younger son who receives a generous allowance from his family, he has no pressing need to marry. Which means, although everyone who is anyone attends Lady Spencer-Woods's Opening Ball, you're unlikely to see him at any of the Marriage Mart events. He's not dangerous, though—I've never heard of him trying to seduce an innocent and Mama would surely have warned me against him if he had.' She smiled, her eyes merry. 'He would make an excellent flirt, though, if you wish to keep fast company.'

'I just might. Your account confirms my impressions of him. Now, what about Lord Solsworth?'

'You mean the biggest catch in London?' she said and laughed when Temper groaned. 'Despite the fact that Lady Agremont would be a horror of a mother-in-law, I can't tell you how many ladies have set their caps for him! But he's young yet to marry, nor has he ever shown a particle of interest in any lady. Which made the rapt attention he showered on you last night so notable.' She giggled. 'The spectacle of her son bedazzled by a lady of questionable reputation must have given his mama palpitations! Which is probably why she dressed you down so rudely.'

'Perhaps that will put an end to his interest— I hope. I don't want to be pursued by anyone my father might expect me to marry!'

Temper was on the point of asking about her tongue-tied dance partner of the previous evening when they rounded the corner to see Giff, who'd ridden ahead of them, drawn up by Lady Henley's carriage—with the Misses Avery on horseback beside him. Temper couldn't prevent an instinctive recoil of distaste.

'Do you know the Avery girls?' she asked, trying to keep her voice neutral. 'Isn't it unusual to have two sisters presented at once?'

'Yes, that's another story. The girls are being sponsored by their mother's sister, their own mother having passed away two years ago. And presented together, rather than one at a time, Mama said, because their father, Viscount Chilford, plans to remarry and they don't wish to still be at home after he does.'

'I can understand that. It would be hard, watching someone else take your mother's place.' Temper frowned, suddenly making the connection. 'Viscount Chilford?' she repeated. 'He's Ben Tawny's father, isn't he?'

'Why, yes. You know the Viscount?'

'No, but his son Ben is one of my brother Christopher's closest friends! They were at Oxford together. Ben virtually lived at Vraux House after he and Christopher were elected to Parliament, until he married Lady Alyssa.'

'Oh, yes, now I remember Papa mentioning them—Hadley's Hellions, your brother's political group is called, isn't it? Lady Alyssa is an artist?'

'Yes. She's off on one of her sketching expeditions at the moment, but I'd be delighted to present you to her when she returns. And to the other wives of Christopher's close friends. All are unusual—Lady Maggie's been a political hostess for years, assisting her father before she married Lyndlington, and though Faith is a Dowager Duchess, she prefers to be known simply as "Mrs David Smith".'

'The whole group made marriages that were... out of the ordinary. I would love to make their acquaintances—ladies who are actually *doing* something! And I must make you known to my closest school friends, too. Not that we are exceptional in any way, except that we are all fortunate to possess a large enough competence that we will not be forced to wed.' She grinned. 'We call ourselves "the Splendid Spinsters".'

'I should like to meet them. If none of you is desperate to marry, in our world, that makes you exceptional,' Temper retorted.

Just then one of the pursuing riders caught up with them. Though sorry to have her informative tête-à-tête with Miss Henley brought to an end, Temper was relieved to recognise the gentlemen, without requiring any prompting.

'Lord Theo, good afternoon,' she said, nodding. 'Miss Henley, I believe you have met this gentleman. I've been delighted to discover, Lord Theo, that Miss Henley is another of those singular females who says what she thinks and does not hold with flattery.'

'Another forthright lady who disdains flattery and says what she thinks?' Lord Theo said with a smile. 'I must add you with Miss Lattimar to the list of females whom I shall seek out to dance and converse with.'

'And what a very long list that must be,' said a coquettish voice from the direction of the Henley carriage, which they had nearly overtaken. Temper looked over to discover the speaker was Miss Avery, who had turned in the saddle to give the Marquess's son a flirtatious glance as Temper's group approached.

Temper felt herself stiffen again. Had the girl eyes in the back of her head—or just an ear tuned to pick up the sound of any gentleman's voice? Must she claim the attention of every man who came within speaking distance?

'You mustn't credit anything Lord Theo tells you, Miss Henley,' Miss Avery continued in a playful tone that grated on Temper's nerves. 'He is the most shameless flirt!'

'I protest, Miss Avery, you are unfair,' Lord Theo replied—giving no sign, Temper was pleased to note, that he felt inclined to respond to the girl's overtures, despite the fact that even Temper had to admit Miss Avery was quite pretty. 'How could one not wish to make himself agreeable to charming females? But I'm afraid another appointment claims my attention and I must go. Ladies.' Giving them a short bow, he turned his mount and rode off.

After casting another smile in the direction of Lord Theo's retreating figure, Miss Avery turned to Miss Henley. 'If you would allow me to offer a word of advice? Though he is exceedingly charming, Lord Theo has quite a sad reputation as a rogue. As you do not possess the…ah…*striking* form and great fortune Miss Lattimar does, your behaviour—and your choice of companions— must be more circumspect.'

Furious, Temper had no trouble interpreting the veiled innuendo. 'You mean she would be wiser to avoid his company—and mine.'

'Your large dowry and acknowledged beauty may continue to make you acceptable—to some gentlemen—regardless of your conduct, Miss Lattimar,' Miss Avery replied coolly. 'But I should hate to see poor Miss Henley pulled along by you into some…indiscretion.'

Though Temper could have cheerfully throttled the Avery chit for her demeaning attitude towards Miss Henley, her new friend seemed neither upset nor cowed. 'I thank you for your concern, Miss Avery. However, my lacklustre reputation might be *enhanced* by a bit of scandal.'

'Oh!' Miss Avery replied. 'I meant no offence. Only to protect you, as your mama—' she cast a significant glance at the carriage, where Lady Henley was laughing at some sally made by one of her escorts '—seems to frequently be too… preoccupied to offer guidance.'

'And just what would you consider "scandalous", Miss Avery?' Temper asked though clenched teeth.

'With you, Miss Lattimar, I can hardly dare imagine! I don't expect you would go as far as to actually…*consort* with gentlemen, as your mother does. But being such an excellent rider, you might decide to show off your form and figure—riding past the gentlemen's clubs on St James's Street, perhaps?'

Though Temper admitted she'd taken a dislike to the girl the moment they'd met, having limited herself to exchanging only innocuous comments with Miss Avery, she wasn't sure why the girl was being so unpleasant.

With a minute shake of the head to silence Miss Henley, who by the annoyed expression on her face was about to intervene with some plain speaking, Temper said, 'I must make sure to add riding down St James's Street to the list of enjoyments I wish to experience before I quit London. Miss Henley, thank you for the ride. Mr Newell,' she called to Giff, interrupting the conversation of the group around Lady Henley, 'are you not due back at Parliament soon for a meeting?'

Giff took one look at what Temper could feel was the heightened colour on her cheeks and made a show of checking his pocket watch. 'Goodness, you are right! I must hurry to escort you home, else I shall be late. Lady Henley, gentlemen, young ladies, you must excuse us. You are ready, Miss Lattimar?'

'More than ready,' she snapped, barely waiting for him to make his farewells before signalling her mount to a trot.

Giff had to spur his horse to catch up. 'Why the hurry?' he asked as he drew even with her. 'And what happened to put you in such a fury?'

Temper had to damp down her anger to reply in an level tone. 'Miss Avery—whose offensive remarks irritated me so much, I feared I would not be able to remain civil if I had to suffer her presence a moment longer! I certainly hope you haven't taken a liking to her, for I find her to be the most annoying, wasp-tongued female I've yet encountered! I could understand, even forgive, her animosity to me—perhaps, with my large dowry, she sees me as a rival for gentlemen's attention. But she has no reason to be so dismissive of Miss Henley!'

Giff looked surprised. 'Miss Avery, wasp-tongued? She seemed pleasant enough to me— if putting herself forward a bit too much for my taste. She's very pretty, I'll allow, but a gentleman likes to think *he's* the one making the overtures—

no matter how cleverly the lady manoeuvres him into it.'

'I hope you won't be making any overtures to her!'

'Believe me, I have no plans to.'

Feeling better now that she'd vented her anger—and discovered Giff had no liking for the girl—Temper said, 'I'm sorry to have pulled you away so abruptly. Though I wager you are not all that disappointed to end a meaningless social encounter and return to Parliament, where you can turn your hand to something important.'

'There actually is a meeting this afternoon. With any luck, I shall catch the last part of it.'

'Concerning one of your reform bills? Christopher told me two of great interest may come to a vote this session. One banning slavery, the other looking to limit the hours children can work in factories.'

'Yes, and both are dear to my heart,' Giff said, his eyes lighting with enthusiasm. 'Especially the factory bill. I took part in some of the inspections done by the committee gathering information for the proposed bill and the plight of some of those children is dreadful!'

'Those poor babes. Bravo to you and the reformers for being determined to help them.'

Giff nodded. 'We try to do what's right. Englishmen may need cloth—but they don't need to obtain it over the exhausted bodies of innocent children.'

Listening to the passion of his words, Temper felt a surge of pride in the work he and other reformers were doing. Lady Sayleford—and her sister, Pru—were right. There *were* gentlemen in London who were both honourable and compelling.

In fact, she felt a renewed pang of guilt for getting Giff tangled up in her Season, forcing him to dance attendance on her and taking him away from business that truly mattered. Though she would sorely miss his company, if he were to suspend his escort, Temper realised. She was enjoying even more than she'd anticipated having the companionship they'd experienced off and on through the years become an almost daily event.

Still, conscience prompted her to ask, 'Are you sure you don't want to dispense with this escort nonsense and concentrate on Parliament? I feel I'm wasting your time, dragging you to meaningless society events.'

'You are an important work, too,' he said, smiling.

She felt a ridiculous little spurt of pleasure that he would think her important and quickly squelched it. 'I have a sponsor and a chaperon to guide me through something whose greatest threat to my security is probably boredom. Those factory children have just a few visionaries like you trying to provide them far more essential protections. I really ought to insist that you give up on my Season.'

'What, you'd urge me to jump ship and have Lady Sayleford hunt me down, like a press gang searching out deserters? It's more than worth missing a few meetings to avoid incurring her wrath. Besides, we don't expect either bill to be ready for a vote before summer. And there's a special treat for tonight—one you will actually be enthusiastic about.'

'A social event I'll be enthusiastic about?' she asked dubiously.

'Lady Sayleford sent me a note, informing me we're to attend the theatre tonight.'

'Truly?' Temper cried, the promised treat wiping away the last vestiges of her irritation. 'I've been so looking forward to attending! Finally, something about this obligatory Season I can actually enjoy.'

'I thought you'd be excited. Well, here we are, back at Vraux House. Go select your prettiest evening dress. I'll join the ladies in Grosvenor Square and pick you up this evening.'

'Thank you, Giff, for sending me off with something you knew would brighten my day,' Temper said as she jumped down from the saddle and turned her horse over to the groom. 'It's daylight and Overton has already opened the door for me, you needn't dismount. This stray package can complete her delivery unaccompanied.'

'Just this once,' he said, chuckling. 'I'll see you tonight.'

The theatre! she thought with delight as she climbed the stairs. She didn't even care which play they were to see. She'd always loved amateur theatricals and couldn't wait to attend her first professional London production.

Not that most of theatregoers would be there to watch the performance. Haymarket, Convent Garden and Drury Lane were second only to the Promenade Hour in Hyde Park as the place the members of the *ton* frequented to see, be seen and gossip.

She only hoped Miss Avery wouldn't appear there, too, to mar her enjoyment.

Chapter Ten

A‌s he ushered the ladies to their box later that evening, Giff had to smile. Temper had certainly followed his advice. Wearing a gown of deep gold silk embroidered with little silver stars that sparkled like the diamonds at her ears and throat, her face vibrant with excitement in the bright gaslight, she was magnificent.

She'd been enveloped in her satin evening cloak when he'd called for her at Vraux House. But even he, armoured as he tried to be against her beauty, had caught his breath when she removed her cloak and he beheld her in that gown.

Good thing he was going to stand guard tonight. Sitting on display beside Lady Sayleford and Mrs Moorsby in their box, Temper was going to draw male eyes like shavings to a magnet. They would be thronged with gentlemen wanting to meet her.

Despite Temper's scepticism, he thought it

likely that some lucky man among all those competing for her attention this Season would succeed in piquing her interest—and earning her affection. Though she was still Temper, impulsive, difficult to manage, quick to say exactly what she thought, she had matured, he noted. She'd shown an ability to control her volatile temper and could even sometimes mask her feelings. He also appreciated her genuine concern for his Parliamentary work.

But though she hadn't created any fireworks among the *ton* yet, he didn't expect that period of tranquillity to last. She'd never be a conventional lady, an obedient, conformable wife—or the serene, diplomatic hostess a politician needed at his dinner table.

Still, he had to fight the possessive feeling that assailed him whenever another gentleman claimed her as a partner for a dance—or a ride, he thought, remembering her laughing with Lord Theo in the park this afternoon.

Of course he felt…protective. He was her brother's best friend, had watched her grow up. It would be hard to let her go to someone else, but eventually he must steel himself to watch that happen. He swallowed hard against the sinking feeling that thought evoked.

As for the passion she stirred so readily—well, the little girl he had watched grow up was now a desirable woman and he wouldn't be male if he didn't find her alluring. As long as he didn't act on the passion she inspired, the attraction he couldn't suppress wouldn't be a betrayal of her trust—or Gregory's.

He heard the ripple of murmurs moving like a wave though the audience as the ladies took their seats, saw a hundred pairs of eyes turn towards their box. Yes, he would play the watchdog, keep the ne'er-do-wells away and make sure, when she did give her hand and heart, they went to a man worthy of her.

Bleak as that prospect appeared.

'Well, child, is it everything you had imagined?' Lady Sayleford's voice broke into his thoughts.

'Yes, ma'am, it's wonderful!' Temper said, her voice awed as she gazed around the theatre. 'The beautiful domed ceiling, the rich red velvet of the curtains, the vast array of gaslights! Thank you so much for bringing me tonight. I can't wait for the performance to begin.'

'The melodrama to follow may be a bit silly, but I think you'll enjoy the play. The present actors don't rival Kean, Kemble or Siddons in their day, but are competent enough.'

Although the murmur of voices scarcely lessened, actors took the stage and the play began. 'Don't let anyone into the box until intermission,' Lady Sayleford told Giff. 'I want Miss Lattimar to be able to enjoy the performance before she is pestered by gentlemen's attentions.'

And so, one eye on the stage and one on the door to the box, Giff alternated between glimpsing the action onstage, warding off strolling gentlemen who mimed their request to enter—and watching Temper. He couldn't help but smile at her rapt expression as she followed the action of the play, her eyes shining, her lips curved in a half-smile of delight. No feigned boredom for her, or indulging in gossip with her chaperon about the notables in the boxes around them—just complete, enthusiastic enjoyment, displayed as openly as the child she'd once been.

No, she'd never be moulded into displaying fashionable manners. And he was glad of it.

At length, the interval arrived and Giff could no longer refuse the press of visitors demanding entrance. First to push his way inside was Lord Theo. Despite an instinctive resistance to him, Giff had no good reason to bar the man from entering.

'You may put away the dagger, Newell,' Lord Theo said sotto voce. 'I mean her no harm.'

'See that you do not,' Giff said curtly, further aggravated by the man's amused chuckle as he passed by him, a uniformed gentleman in tow.

'Ladies, how magnificent you look! You are enjoying the performance? Lady Sayleford, would you allow me to present this officer?' At her nod, he continued, 'Let me make known to you Lieutenant James Masters, of the Queen's Royal Second Foot, presently back from India on leave. Lieutenant, Lady Sayleford, Miss Lattimar and Mrs Moorsby.'

After bows and nods were exchanged, Lord Theo turned to Temper. 'Having heard you have a desire to travel to foreign places, I thought you would find Lieutenant Masters's conversation of interest.'

'Indeed, I would!' Temper said, her eyes lighting with enthusiasm. 'How kind of you to bring him by.'

'Lady Sayleford, would you tell me and Mrs Moorsby about other versions of this play you have seen performed…perhaps by the great Kemble himself? While those two chat about overseas adventures.'

'Certainly. Miss Lattimar, you may use this opportunity to ask the Lieutenant all the question you like.'

Giving Temper a wink, Lord Theo helped rearrange the chairs, taking a seat beside the Dowager Countess while Lieutenant Masters claimed one beside Temper. Giff, moving his chair to the rear of the box, settled back to keep watch. Though officers in his Majesty's army were usually gentlemen, he'd make sure this newcomer knew how to behave around a lady.

A necessary caution. Because he couldn't count on Temper, enthralled to speak with someone who'd actually been to one of the foreign lands she dreamed of exploring, to display any reserve at all.

'Welcome back to England, Lieutenant! I'm sure you must be pleased to be home among family and friends,' she was saying.

'Indeed, ma'am. A welcome break from the heat and dust!'

'Would you be so kind as to tell me more about your life in India? I would so much like to visit the country! My brother found me a copy of Godfrey Charles Mundy's *Pen and Pencil Sketches*, made during his time as ADC to Lord Combermere. Such enthralling scenery, and such charming glimpses into the life—"*Dak* travelling" and "Tiger's attack on the Elephant".'

'Mundy published his journal? I hadn't heard of it.' He gave her a wry smile. 'If it's an accurate picture of the place, it should tell of monsoons, vipers and attacks by dacoits. Not something, I think, to interest such a beautiful lady. Lord Theo warned me you were enchanting, but the reality far exceeds his description. How delighted I am to make your acquaintance! I hope I shall see more of you while I'm home on leave.'

Giff read the disappointment in Temper's eyes

and suppressed a grin. He needn't worry about the lieutenant or his intentions. Most females would have asked about the lieutenant's service out of politeness and been delighted to move on to expressions of gallantry. But by turning aside the subject of her real interest, the man had just squandered his opportunity to make a favourable impression on Temper.

With a wry grimace that seemed to say she'd resigned herself to not receiving the first-hand account of India she'd hoped for, Temper nodded. 'I'm sure all the London ladies will try to make a returning hero feel welcome,' she said politely, her voice, to Giff's practised ear, markedly devoid of the enthusiasm she'd shown earlier.

'I shall not care about the others—as long as *you* are welcoming,' the lieutenant replied, his admiring gaze fixed on Temper.

He couldn't blame the soldier for being awestruck. He still caught his breath each time he saw Temper in one of her new gowns. But if the fellow let his eyes wander from her face down to her bosom, Giff would consider it cause to intervene.

'I'm sure we will all do our best,' Temper said coolly. 'On another matter, I've recently had a letter from my sister in Bath, who tells me she has also met a soldier invalided home from India duty. A Captain Johnnie Trethwell. I know the area in which the troops serve is vast, but do you happen to know him?'

'As a matter of fact, I do. He served, like Mundy, in the Queen's Second Foot. I don't know him personally, having never actually met him, but I have heard of him. He was something of an...oddity.'

'Oh? In what way?'

Giff stiffened, sharing the concern he could hear in Temper's voice. If her beloved sister had been enticed by a bounder, despite the fact that her aunt and friends were chaperoning her, he knew Temper would alert Gregory and have them on the road to Bath by morning.

'He seemed to take to India almost as though he'd been born there. Oh, he amused the ladies at the cantonments, but he never quite fit in among the regiment. Learned to speak the language like a local, liked going off exploring in native dress.'

'But he *is*...a gentleman.'

'I don't think he'd do your sister any harm, if that's what is worrying you. Indeed, always very gallant with the ladies, was Johnnie.'

From the tone of his voice, Giff inferred that Johnnie Trethwell had a rake's reputation, but didn't trifle with innocents.

Looking reassured, Temper said, 'I'm glad to hear it. My sister says he is quite the charmer. However...with India such an exotic and fascinating land, I wonder that you did not also wish to go exploring.'

Lieutenant Masters laughed. 'It is exotic! What with the poisonous critters, dangerous animals, deadly diseases and the heat, life in the cantonments was hard enough. I never had any desire to explore beyond where my duties took me.'

'I do envy you, though. I should love to visit foreign places,' Temper said wistfully.

'You must come out to India, miss. A lovely lady like you—there'd be a hundred officers waiting to snap you up like sugar candy.'

'Oh, I don't want to marry! I'd just like to visit and explore the countryside.'

Lieutenant Masters looked as if to speak, then hesitated. After a forced laugh, he said, 'India contains dangers far beyond what you could ever imagine, miss. It would be a deadly mistake to go adventuring on your own. If you don't wish to live in a cantonment with a husband, you'd be safer to remain in England.'

A shadow fell over Giff, making him turn towards the doorway. A man he didn't recognise loitered there, swaying, his glazed eyes fixed on Temper.

'Damme, you are 's beautiful as y'mama, jes like Lord Theo said,' he slurred. 'Collington, pr'sent me to thish charmer.'

Before Giff could rise to shoo the gentleman

off, Lady Sayleford said in a commanding voice, 'Certainly not. You are inebriated, sir. You will quit this box at once.'

The man shifted his gaze to peer at Lady Sayleford. 'Ol' beldame,' he muttered. 'Wanna meet the Beauty. You, Theo—' He waved a hand, almost oversetting himself. 'C'mon, intr'duce me.'

Murmuring an apology to Lady Sayleford, Lord Theo jumped up and moved past Giff to take the man's arm. 'Wendemere, old chap, you're in no condition to meet a lady. Come along, Lieutenant, let us escort this gentleman to…more suitable entertainment.'

The man pulled at his captive arm. 'A'right, I'll go.' Looking back at Temper with a leer, he said, 'Meet you later, Beauty. Wanna get t'know you *very* well.'

He was gazing blatantly down her bosom as Lord Theo and Lieutenant Masters each took an arm and pulled him out, Giff closing the door behind them, ignoring the other gentlemen trying to gain entry. They could hear Wendemere's drunken protests fading as the two men walked him away.

Temper shuddered. 'I feel that I should go home and bathe immediately. Lady Sayleford, who is Wendemere?'

'No one who need concern you,' the Countess said. 'A younger son with no expectations, Lord Alfred Wendemere is a gamester, drunkard, womaniser and general embarrassment to his noble family. Indeed, if it weren't for his impressive lineage, he wouldn't be received anywhere. Not a man I would trust to escort you around a dance floor, much less on a stroll through the park.'

'He behaved worse than a randy ensign after six months at sea,' Mrs Moorsby said indignantly. 'Can't she just refuse to know him?'

Lady Sayleford sighed. 'He's the Duke of Maidstone's middle son, so his presence in society is tolerated. But even his family understands why matrons with innocent daughters do not invite him to their events. He usually confines himself to women of the demi-monde—or the more reckless married ladies.'

'So he targeted me because of Mama's reputation,' Temper said flatly.

After a short silence, Lady Sayleford said, 'I'm afraid that's likely. You will have to accept the acquaintance, if he turns up in a sober condition at some respectable entertainment, but nothing more.' She smiled. 'By now, I'm sure you're adept at gracefully turning away invitations to dance or dine from persons you don't wish to know better.'

Temper laughed. 'I'm not sure about graceful, but I can certainly be forceful!'

'And I'll be nearby to make sure he accepts his dismissal,' Giff said, having taken an instant dislike to any man who would approach Temper in such a disgraceful state—to say nothing of staring at her as if she were a harlot! If Lord Theo and the lieutenant hadn't dragged him off, Giff would have been tempted to remove him, not just from the box, but out to the street, where he could administer a quick lesson in what happens to boors who insulted ladies under his escort.

'The play's about to resume, so please, Giff, don't open the door again,' Temper said, interrupting his belligerent thoughts. 'I'd prefer that it remain closed for the intervals as well. I came to enjoy the theatre, not to exchange idle remarks!'

'With Lady Sayleford's leave, I can certainly do that. I should not like to exclude any of her friends, though.'

'My friends all know I dislike chatting during the performance and are unlikely to seek me out. A drawing room is the proper place for conversation, not a theatre box! Besides, we achieve all we need to simply by being present, where Temperance can be seen and admired. Making gentlemen who wish to speak with her wait until later is not a bad thing.'

'The unattainable lady thereby becoming even more fascinating,' Mrs Moorsby said.

'Exactly,' Lady Sayleford replied.

'A closed door it shall be, then,' Giff said, pleased that Lady Sayleford had acquiesced. Though he didn't think Temper needed to become any *more* fascinating, now he wouldn't have to endure watching a steady stream of gentlemen try to impress her. Freed from playing the guard dog, he could relax and simply enjoy the performance—and the simple pleasure of watching an enthralled Temper enjoy it.

Late the following afternoon, Giff made an unannounced stop at Vraux House, hoping to find Temperance. Fortunately, Overton informed him that Miss Lattimar was indeed at home and escorted him into the small parlour.

'Giff, what a pleasant surprise,' she said as she entered. 'Were you expecting to see Gregory? He's paying a visit to the solicitor, as I imagine Overton told you, but should return shortly.'

'Actually, it was you I came to see—thinking I might catch you between calls and shopping excursions,' Giff said, rising as she entered.

'Mrs Moorsby and I made another contribution to the profits of the linen drapers, modistes and bonnet-makers this morning,' Temper said, her smile as warming as sunshine and bright as the yellow gown she wore.

He took a moment to bask in it while she continued, 'One ride at the Promenade Hour was enough for a while and we haven't a large enough acquaintance yet that we do much calling, so you find me here this afternoon. But is something amiss? I didn't think I'd see you again until the Randalls' ball.'

'Nothing amiss, but by chance at my meeting today I learned of something I thought might interest you. Perhaps,' he added with a grin, 'it will make up for your disappointment with the unforthcoming Lieutenant Masters.'

Temper sighed. 'How…selfish of him, to have so vast a knowledge of India and yet be unwilling to share it!'

'To be fair, most ladies probably wouldn't be interested. He likely thought you were just being polite.'

She raised her eyebrows. 'That may be true about "most ladies", but I asked him to share his observations quite pointedly. Several times. If he wasn't able to tell I truly wished to hear them, that doesn't say much for his intelligence.' She sighed. 'More likely, he didn't know what to say to a female with such odd, unmaidenly interests. The stories he normally tells are probably tailored for the ribald enjoyment of an officers' mess. Poor Lieutenant! But you said you had something to make up for that disappointment?'

'Are you familiar with the Travellers Club?'

Her eyes lit. 'Oh, yes! Founded by Castlereagh in 1819, after the opening of Europe at the end of the Napoleonic Wars. A place where gentlemen who have travelled abroad might meet for discussion and to entertain foreign dignitaries. How I wish I might listen in on some of those conversations—or attend the lectures of the Royal Geographical Society. But, alas, they both are open only to men. Who seem, like Lieutenant Masters, to want to keep all the fascinating details to themselves! What about the Travellers Club?'

'Lord Lansdowne—he's currently Lord President of the Council, you know, the man through whom my committee works to funnel information about our reform efforts to the Privy Council—is a long-time member. He's currently hosting a Lieutenant Williamson from the army of the East India Company. Williamson accompanied Alexander Burnes and Henry Pottinger on their surveys up the Indus River, and was initially supposed to speak to the Travellers Club here in London. But after he suffered a relapse of tropical fever, Lansdowne moved him to Trenton Manor, the country property he rents in Highgate Village. Williamson isn't yet recovered enough to return to London and deliver a formal lecture, but he has improved enough to receive company. Lansdowne is hosting a small reception at Trenton Manor tomorrow afternoon, where members of the Travellers Club and other interested persons may meet and chat with Williamson. Lady Lansdowne will offer tea for any ladies who accompany the gentlemen.

Would you like to go with me? When I told him of your special interest, Lansdowne confirmed that you would be welcome to listen in on the conversations with Lieutenant Williams.'

'Oh, Giff!' Temper cried, leaping up. He thought for a moment she might fling herself at him and, sucking in a breath in mingled alarm and anticipation, braced himself to resist the wave of sensation an embrace would generate.

But at the last moment she skidded to a halt, her cheeks colouring. Dropping her arms back to her sides, she said, 'As my enthusiasm in jumping out of my chair indicates, yes, I would love to go! Lansdowne will let me listen in? Imagine, being able to speak to someone who has actually travelled by *dak* and elephant, seen tigers and leopards, dusty villages and a maharaja's palace! Thank you so much for thinking of me.'

He smiled, delighted to have been able to bring such a look of joy to her face. He found himself wishing he could offer something every day that would make her so dazzlingly happy.

'Mrs Moorsby will accompany us, of course— she can enjoy tea with the other ladies while I attend Williamson's discussion. Might I ask Miss Henley, too? I think she would enjoy the talk—or at the very least, a chance to ride out of London.'

'I believe Lady Henley and Lady Lansdowne

are friends, so she may already be planning to attend. The park at Trenton Manor is said to be very fine, with lovely views down towards London. If the weather is pleasant, I imagine the ladies will stroll around the park while the gentleman talk with Lieutenant Williamson.'

'Can you stay for tea now and tell me more?'

'Regrettably, I must return to the House. More meetings. But I wanted to let you know about the opportunity, so you would have time to prepare.'

'Then I mustn't keep you,' she said, rising from her chair. 'I cannot wait until tomorrow! I'll send Miss Henley a note, inviting her to ride with us, if her mother is not attending. And let Mrs Moorsby know, of course. What time will you call for me?'

'It's not far to Highgate. Leaving Vraux House at noon should be sufficient.'

'I'll be ready,' she promised as she walked with him to the door. 'Thank you again, Giff. It…it means a great deal to me that you take my plans and dreams seriously. Everyone else seems to think them just foolish, childish fantasies.'

He might not think voyaging the world wise and suspected that, in the end, marriage would win out over exploration, but he didn't question her passion for her dream or her commitment to achieving it. 'I've always taken your plans seriously.'

She grinned. 'Perhaps by the time I meet the

requirement of having voyaged at least five hundred miles from London and back, the Travellers Club will be ready to admit lady members!'

Laughing, he let Overton show him out.

Chapter Eleven

But as it happened, Temper's maid came to inform her Giff waited below, not at noon, but just after ten the next morning. Horrified that she must have mistaken the time for their excursion, she rushed down to the parlour.

'I'm so sorry, Giff!' she cried, halting just inside the threshold as Newell turned from where he'd been pacing in front of the mantel. 'I can change my gown in a trice. I must have truly been in alt, to have got the hour so wrong!'

'No, you didn't mistake it. We weren't to leave until noon, but I just found out there will be a preliminary hearing on the anti-slavery bill this afternoon. Apparently the drafting team completed a revision last night and want the other members to read it and comment. It's not imperative that I be there—this isn't a final vote, but...'

'Of course you must be there,' Temper said at once, recognising the pull of conflicting loyalties in him—the duty he'd pledged to protect her and his responsibilities to his committee. 'Our coachman will have no trouble finding Trenton Manor and, in the middle of the day, we don't need a gentleman to escort us. Miss Henley will be travelling with her mother, but Mrs Moorsby and I will be perfectly safe going on our own.'

He looked at her anxiously. 'Are you sure? I shall regret missing the reception, but I could on no account let *you* miss it. Not after having offered you so perfect a treat! Truly, if you do not feel comfortable driving to Highgate alone, I will accompany you as planned.'

'I'm sorry you will miss the reception, too—' more disappointed than she would let him know that she wouldn't be able to share the experience with him '—but your presence at the committee meeting is far more important. With several footmen and the coachman to watch over us, we shall be fine. You tend to your important work.'

He studied her face. 'You are sure?'

She smiled at him. 'Absolutely. And I promise to take careful mental notes, so I may regale you with wonderful stories of the Hindu Kush!'

'Thank you for understanding,' he said quietly. 'Most ladies would be put out at having a gentleman cancel on them at the last minute. My mother would have a fit of the vapours.'

'You clearly don't know the right ladies,' she

teased, wanting to bring the smile back to his face. 'Besides, I intend to sail the Indus myself, some day. Compared with that, an afternoon jaunt to a village barely outside London is no more hazardous than a walk in our back garden.'

To her delight, he seized her hand and kissed it. He probably knew as well as she it wasn't wise, but she revelled in the thrill of it just the same. 'Thank you, Temper,' he said again, releasing her fingers. 'I shall hold you to your promise of giving me a full account. Perhaps tonight?'

'Go on to your committee,' she told him. 'I need to go decide which of my gowns makes me look most like a lady explorer!'

Late that afternoon, her mind afire with Lieutenant Williamson's captivating descriptions of his India travels, Temperance walked with Miss Henley towards the outer edge of the garden surrounding Trenton Manor. The impromptu event had attracted a larger number of guests than she'd anticipated, both gentlemen interested in listening to the Lieutenant—to her surprise, Lord Theo among their number—and ladies and gentlemen who gathered on the terrace to take tea and stroll through the garden. Too enthused after the end of the Lieutenant's presentation to want to descend from the plane of high adventure into the mundane world of London society, she'd slipped her arm through her friend's and marched her off.

'Sorry to steal you away from returning to your mama,' she said when, after traversing several circuitous paths, they'd reached the outermost walk.

'No need for apologies,' Miss Henley said. 'I could tell you were bursting to discuss Lieutenant Williamson's stories and wouldn't be able to abide chatting about everyday society events with Mama's friends.'

Temper smiled. 'Although I shall have to be careful. Lady Henley allows me your company because you've led her to believe I will attract potential suitors for you to impress. Bad enough that I just refused all offers to have any gentlemen escort us. If she discovers that I've dragged you beyond where we might expect to encounter any, she will probably curtail our friendship forthwith.'

Miss Henley laughed. 'We'll return and you may begin attracting that entourage, soon enough. I, too, wanted some time to talk about what we just heard. What a fascinating land India is and how vividly Lieutenant Williamson describes it! Though I appreciate the beauties of our own country, too. This view, for instance.' She pointed towards the vista of London, spread below them in the far distance beyond the broad swathe of meadow to the south.

'Beautiful, yes,' Temper agreed. 'But oh, do

you not long to view for yourself the forests he described bordering the Ganges River? Imagine, banyan trees, their crowns wide as a town house, supported by not just a thick trunk, but by aerial roots anchored into the soil, or dangling like chains? Or stands of bamboo, the trunks narrow and straight as fishing poles, growing so thickly together that a man cannot walk through them?'

'Exotic indeed!' Miss Henley agreed. 'And his description of the Himalayan country—the vast, huge mountains, wild, lonely, almost mystical glens full of rising mist!'

For the next half-hour, they strolled along the outer pathway, both recalling parts of the Lieutenant's stories and descriptions they'd found particularly compelling. Turning back towards the house, Temper said, 'I suppose I must make myself stop contemplating the thrills of foreign lands and rejoin the company. But before we return, tell me this—was the Lieutenant's account fascinating enough to tempt you into travelling with me?'

Miss Henley laughed. 'I'm still not sure I'm that brave. Hearing about exotic places and visiting them in person are two different matters! I was quite enthralled to listen and thought it very kind of Lord Lansdowne to arrange for us to be seated in the alcove adjacent to the library, where we could hear the discussion, but still be apart from the gentlemen.'

Temper smiled wryly. 'Though Lord Lansdowne didn't say so directly, I rather suspect that it was only because Mr Newell had intervened in advance that seats were arranged for us where the ladies might listen to the talk. I owe Giff a good deal of thanks. Otherwise, I would have made the drive here to be afforded nothing more exciting than the opportunity to curtsy to the Lieutenant when Lansdowne presented him to the ladies.'

'And had instead to suffer through conversation about society people and events—while surrounded by an entourage of eager gentlemen,' Miss Henley said, a twinkle in her eye.

'An entourage of eager gentlemen? Let me be the first to join their ranks.'

Temper and Miss Henley turned towards the sound of the masculine voice, to see Lord Theo striding towards them. 'Ladies,' he said, bowing as he reached them. 'I've spent the last ten minutes trying to find you! This garden is like a maze! When Lady Henley decided to stroll and did not see you, she became worried that you might have been lost. I was fortunate enough to have been given the task of bringing you back to her. If I might offer each of you an arm?'

'How kind of you.' Blushing, Miss Henley laid her hand on his sleeve.

Temper sighed. 'Much as I'd prefer to continue discussing the fine points of Lieutenant Williamson's talk, I suppose it is time to return.' With regret, she, too, laid her hand on Lord Theo's arm.

Listening with half an ear to his banter with Miss Henley, as they turned the corner to start down the next pathway, Temper spied a sculptured stone that made her start with delight.

'Is something wrong, Miss Lattimar?' Lord Theo asked.

Dropping his arm, she hurried forward. 'Oh, it *is* what I suspected!' Turning back to them, she said, 'It's a temple carving—in Sanskrit, I believe. Papa has several that are similar.'

'Yes, I believe Landsdowne is a collector,' Lord Theo said.

Temper ran her fingers reverently over the rows of symbols. 'Ah, that I knew enough to read the stories you could tell,' she murmured.

Realising her companions were waiting for her, she reluctantly pulled herself away—only to exclaim again when they came upon another stone a few moments later.

And so it continued as they proceeded down the pathway, along which their host had displayed a number of carved stones, some containing simply symbols, others adorned with bas-reliefs of plants and animals. Her companions slowed their pace,

Temper grateful for their indulgence, but wishing she had far longer to inspect them.

After passing by several far too quickly, arrested by a stone with particularly interesting carving, Temper couldn't resist the desire to linger. She trailed her fingers over the vivid rendering of birds and foliage, thrilled to have this tangible glimpse of the world she longed to explore.

In similar fashion, the Lieutenant's words had given her a tantalising glimpse of her cherished goal, fulfilled. His account fired from dream back to pressing desire the longing she'd felt since her early teens to experience the excitement, and, yes, even danger, of travelling somewhere wholly unfamiliar, where every day brought unusual sights and new revelations.

Bless Giff, who not only appreciated her desire to seek out the exotic, but had gone to some trouble to give her this opportunity to vicariously experience it.

The Lieutenant had mentioned that the wealthy of the Punjab decorated themselves and their ladies with finely worked gold jewellery inset with gemstones, often in fanciful shapes and patterns. Might her papa be interested in collecting something like that?

More likely he'd prefer to acquire weapons from the area, swords and daggers being a particular interest. The wild tribesmen of the northwestern frontier were armed with intricately engraved daggers and large, curved swords—*salwars*, Williamson said they were called. She was almost certain that Papa would be interested in obtaining some fine examples of those.

Still musing about which articles he'd prefer, she glanced up from the stone to discover herself alone. Realising the others must have turned on to the next pathway, she hurried to catch up.

As she rounded the corner, she almost collided with an approaching figure. About to apologise, she recognised the newcomer as Lord Alfred Wendemere and the regrets she'd meant to offer died on her lips.

'Well, well, look who I ran into,' he said—looking indeed, as, after a quick glance at her face, his gaze came back to linger at her bosom. 'Returning from a tryst, were you? Collington told me you were attending this gathering—to listen to some rubbishing lecture, he said, though I'm sure he was joking me.'

With the proximity of their near-collision, she could smell the brandy on him. Craning her neck, she could see no one else on this section of pathway. She must have drifted further behind Lord Theo and Miss Henley than she'd realised.

A ripple of dismay going through her, she took a step backwards, fighting the onset of panic.

But she didn't mean to let Wendemere sense her unease. 'Lord Alfred,' she said, giving him a cool nod. 'I did indeed attend the lecture and took a stroll to ponder some of the speaker's points. But now, if you'll excuse me, I must return to my friends.'

'Oh, but I won't excuse you,' he said, giving her an insolent grin and stepping forward, so they once again stood only a foot apart. 'If you were *pondering*, it must have been to decide which man you'd meet with in the shrubbery next. Why not me?'

Mind racing, Temper considered her options. Lord Theo and Miss Henley were out of sight, the voices from the terrace still a distant hum. If she cried out, she wasn't sure they would hear her—or be near enough to intervene.

'I'll consider letting you go—after you give me a kiss as a forfeit,' he continued. 'I bet you're giving that watchdog Newell a good deal more. Stringing him along with tastes of your person, just as your mother does all those men sniffing around her, like hounds following a bitch in heat!'

'If you choose to be crude and insulting, I have nothing further to say to you. Remove yourself from my path, please.'

'And what if I don't please?' He reached, grabbing her wrist. 'What if what pleases me is to have a little taste of what you're giving Newell?'

Despite her vow to remain unmoved, she felt her pulse accelerate as his look, his tone, jerked at the bonds imprisoning memories of that other time and place. *The sour scent of spirits, his arms forcing her down, his body following to pin her to the ground...*

A sudden wave of panic filled her, flooding her with an urgent desire to pick up her skirts and flee. Wendemere tightened his grip and pulled her towards him.

'Struggle if you like. Pretend you don't want it, when we both know you do. A prime little piece like you, the exact image of your slut of a mother. Resisting me will make the taking all the sweeter.'

In his hot, greedy gaze she read lust, excitement—and the need to dominate. He *wanted* her to struggle and cry out. To be afraid.

Desperately she tried to beat back that fear. Struggle and he might immediately try to subdue her. Though she was no longer an unprepared, innocent fifteen-year-old girl, her brothers having taught her how to defend herself, she didn't think she was strong enough to overpower him with a single punch—or fast enough, hampered by her ridiculously full skirts, to outrun him.

What could she do, then? *Never show fear or weakness*, her mother's words echoed in her head. Surely, with her reputation, Mama had faced foxed and threatening men before. What would she do, confronted now by Wendemere?

Temper had no doubt Mama would act as if she were entirely nonplussed by the situation. As if she'd faced threatening, demanding men before—and used their lust to bend them to her will. So that she, not they, were in control, the man inevitably ending up doing *her* bidding.

Could Temper manage that? She wasn't sure, but better to attempt it than to give in to panic and cede control to Wendemere. No matter how this ended, it would happen as *she* directed.

Sudden fury coursed through her, bolstering her courage and hardening her resolve. How dare he presume to dismiss her—and her mother—as mere toys for his amusement? Designed only for the physical uses he had for them, bound to submit to his lusts?

Instead of whimpering or struggling, as he clearly expected, she relaxed her arm in his grip. 'Really?' she said, infusing her voice with irritation and faint disdain. 'You want to show yourself a "man" by manhandling me? How very *tedious* of you!'

Whatever reaction he'd expected, that wasn't it. He looked surprised for a moment before retightening his grip. 'Don't try to distract me. Whores always want it and you're just a whore like your mother!'

'Perhaps, but I don't want it now. Not if you're going to be boorish as well as boring, wanting me to *struggle*, as if dalliance were some sort of wrestling match! And hardly a *match*—you must outweigh me by several stone! What sort of equal contest is that? If this were a schoolyard, the boys would laugh you out of it.'

She'd thrown him off his script. Before he could recover, she gave an exasperated sigh. 'If you are so uncertain of your prowess that you don't believe you can win a kiss without *forcing* it on me, go ahead, but honestly, I had hoped for better from you. Or—' she paused, giving him a seductive look from under her lashes '—you could *rise* to a challenge to prove your manliness.'

Still fighting the urge to flee, she held his gaze, using every ounce of will to remain looking bored, faintly disdainful—and in command.

She could see the indecision in him, his confusion. His need to cow and overmaster her compromised by her impatient, slightly contemptuous attitude and absence of fear.

'What challenge?' he said after a moment.

'As I said, a wrestling match would be unequal. Why not a contest to test your mettle, in which we are more evenly matched?'

'What sort of contest?'

She batted her eyes at him and laughed. 'Not

that sort—yet. First, you need to prove to me you have the…stamina I require. Race me. In the park, tomorrow morning. You on your favourite mount—of the equine variety—and me on mine. If you win, you get your kiss—and whatever else you desire. Wherever you desire it—though I trust it will be a place where we can fully enjoy the encounter, not—' she wrinkled her nose in distaste 'some rubbishing *bench* in a windy park. And if you lose, you will never approach me again without my express leave.'

'You propose a *horse* race?'

'I do. It's so similar to what you want, isn't it? The building excitement, the speed, your heart pounding, the rush of breath. The ultimate fulfilment.'

He laughed and licked his lips. 'Trying to increase my anticipation?'

'Anticipation always increases desire, does it not?'

'And all I need do is beat you in a horse race?'

'But fairly. No tricks. So the race will be in Hyde Park and there will be witnesses. Accept the more *manly* challenge—' she forced herself to lean closer and use her free hand to touch his lips 'and you may gain…everything you wish.'

Deliberately, with neither speed nor haste, she withdrew her arm from his slackened grip. 'Tomorrow morning, eight of the clock,' she said and turned to walk away. Feeling the pulse pound in her head, still having to resist the instinct to take to her heels, she forced herself to move at a decorous pace.

Behind her, she heard him laugh. 'Tomorrow, then.'

Her relief, when it appeared he wasn't going to follow and try to force her into submission here and now, sent such a rush of sensation through her that she felt faint. She knew she was not equal, yet, to returning to the terrace and chatting as if nothing had happened, nor did she wish to appear before the other guests while she was still so dizzy and depleted, still fighting down the vestiges of panic. As the voices from the terrace grew louder, she switched pathways to skirt around its outside edge and walked instead towards the house, until she came to a side entry door.

With a footman's help, she found the lady's retiring room—mercifully deserted—where, in blessed solitude, she was violently ill. Some time later, after recovering herself, she rinsed her mouth, washed her face and straightened her gown. Giving her mama a silent thanks, she waited until her hands no longer trembled, then headed back to the terrace.

She would collect Mrs Moorsby and, after a quiet word to Miss Henley and Lord Theo, pay her respects to her host and hostess, and return to London.

She had a race to prepare for—and, hopefully, a mount with a sore hoof that was now fully healed.

Chapter Twelve

The next morning, Giff sat in his office in the committee room at Parliament, the draft of the anti-slavery bill lying unseen on the table before him, while he read for a second time the letter he'd just received from his mother.

Dropping it, he wiped a hand across his face, his stomach churning with a familiar mix of resentment, the slow burn of anger, an ache of hurt—and a touch of guilt. Damn it, the work he was doing in Parliament *was* important and required all of his attention, especially now, when they were at a crucial point in pressing forward the passage of two major reform bills. Why did his mother have to choose this moment to increase the urgency of her harangues?

Before he could decide what to reply, if he replied, one of his fellow members walked into the room.

'Jolly fine morning,' Thomas Thetford said,

giving Giff a slap on the back, entirely insensitive to the cloud of irritation enveloping him. 'My, that chit you've been squiring about for your godmother—she's as much a hoyden as you've said. Going to race in the park! And with Lord Alfred Wendemere!' He chuckled. 'Looking magnificent, of course, but you allow the girl a looser rein than I would.'

It took a moment for the words to penetrate Giff's abstraction—and once they did, he couldn't believe he'd heard correctly. 'What did you say?'

Thetford peered down at him. 'Lost in perusing the draft, were you? Brilliant piece of writing.'

'Yes, yes,' he returned impatiently, 'but what was it you said about racing this morning?'

'In Hyde Park,' Thetford returned. 'Not me. I was in Pendergrew's tilbury. Meant to walk here this morning—lovely day—but he saw me and took me up.'

'About Miss Lattimar!'

'Ah, yes. Saw the Lattimar girl by Hyde Park Corner, challenging Wendemere. Impromptu match, I suppose, since I doubt you'd have encouraged it.'

'Certainly not!' Giff returned, indignant. 'One would rather shoot Wendemere than permit him to ride with an innocent maid.'

'Won't comment on the "innocent" part. Looked like she was leading him on, to me. But they were about to race for certain.' Thetford shook his head. 'In high fettle, she was. Looked like one of the Furies, about to deliver vengeance!'

'It'll be nothing to what I'll deliver, if she's come to any harm,' Giff muttered, rising. 'Just for the record,' he told Thetford as he shrugged into his coat, 'I didn't know and I don't approve.'

Nearly at a run, he left the buildings, fetched his mount from the stables and set off to Hyde Park as quickly as the throng of handcarts, barrows, wagons and pedestrians going about their morning errands allowed, curbing his fury and anxiety with difficulty as he went.

Heedless, careless, unthinking! he fumed. Not just of her reputation—teasing Wendemere, for the devil's sake!—but of her very safety! And here he'd thought she'd finally matured beyond her childhood wildness.

Granted, she was an accomplished rider, but if that reprobate caught her alone, especially as he'd believe she had encouraged him…

He bit down an oath and urged his mount faster.

Once through the gates of Hyde Park, he spurred the horse to a gallop, heading down Rotten Row, the most likely venue for a race. Sure enough, as he neared Kensington Gardens, he saw Temper, mounted on her gelding Arion. At least, he thought, blowing out a breath of relief, she was surrounded by a small entourage—not alone with Wendemere. Who, he noted as he slowed his mount to a walk to approach them, was nowhere to be seen.

'I knew you rode well, but that was magnificent,' a female he recognised as Miss Henley was saying.

The gentleman nodding at her words was Lord Theo. 'Indeed it was,' he said and laughed. 'Wendemere looked as shocked as he was disgruntled to have been bested—though it was a near-run thing. If your mount hadn't summoned that last burst of speed, I believe he would have beaten you.'

'Had Arion not been recovering from a sore hoof, it wouldn't have even been close,' Temper said, smiling—until she noticed Giff approaching and her whole body stiffened.

'How neatly you dispensed with the annoyance of dealing with him,' Miss Henley said.

'Masterful,' Lord Theo seconded. 'Having agreed before all of us that, should he lose, he would never approach you again, he'll not be able to go back on his word—not if he wants to hang on to the precarious foothold that remains to him in the *ton*.'

'Even his friends would snub him if he cheated on a wager,' Miss Henley said.

Just before he reached them, two riders on side-saddle halted beside the group, trailed by a groom. The Misses Avery, Giff saw—and, despite his pique, he nearly had to smile at the expression of distaste that crossed Temper's face before she schooled her countenance into a polite smile.

'What's this—a wager?' Miss Avery said. 'Not with Lord Alfred, whom we just passed, looking to be in a tearing rage!'

'Miss Avery, Miss Mary,' Lord Theo said, 'good morning to you.'

'And to you, Lord Theo. How pleasant to encounter you this morning!' She gave the Marquess's son a charming smile before offering a tiny nod to Temper and Miss Henley. 'And you, too, ladies.

'But you must tell me, Miss Lattimar,' she persisted, turning to address Temper. 'Did you truly make a wager with Lord Alfred? How...shocking! You are even more outrageous than I thought.'

'Indeed,' Temper replied coolly—but the militant spark in her eye told Giff she was working hard to curb her annoyance. 'I expect I can be far more outrageous than you thought.'

'So what were the terms? Come, you must tell me.'

'Really, Jane,' Miss Mary protested, looking embarrassed by her sister's persistence.

'She might as well, Mary,' she replied, brushing off her sister. 'After all, Lord Alfred will surely bandy them abroad. The news will be all over the *ton* by this afternoon.'

'I'm sure it will,' Miss Henley said, irony in her voice. 'But I doubt Lord Alfred will be telling the story.'

Just then, the rest of party noticed his approach—or rather, Miss Avery did. 'Mr Newell,' she trilled, giving him the same coquettish smile she'd turned on Collington. 'Come to collect your naughty charge? I don't envy you, trying to keep a lady as…spirited as Miss Lattimar in line!'

'I'm sure curbing a spirit—or a tongue—would be impossible for you,' Temper said sweetly. 'Come to hurry me home, Mr Newell?' she said, her guarded tone telling him she was preparing for a confrontation.

His momentary humour over her riposte to the Avery girl evaporated as he recalled the very real confrontation that must come. 'Yes. Mrs Moorsby is waiting for you.'

Miss Avery laughed. 'I imagine her poor chaperon is *always* awaiting her return from some scrape or other! We will leave you to your task, Mr Newell. Miss Lattimar.'

With a dismissive nod to Temper, she turned back to Collington. 'Would you care to join my sister and I for another turn around Rotten Row, Lord Theo? It's such a lovely morning!'

Lord Theo looked less than enthusiastic about

accompanying the sisters, Giff thought, but there was hardly any way he could refuse Miss Avery without being rude. 'I'd be delighted.'

'Shall we go, then?' Miss Avery said, signalling her horse to start.

'Thank you for meeting me,' Temper said to Miss Henley as the others trotted off. 'Newell, have you time for me to see Miss Henley home?'

Seeming to perceive the tension between the two of them, Miss Henley shook her head. 'No need for an escort, Miss Lattimar. I have my groom. Shall I see you at the Witherspoons' dinner and musicale tomorrow?'

'Mrs Moorsby hasn't informed me of our plans, but probably.'

'Good day to both of you, then,' Miss Henley said. 'And bravo, well done, Miss Lattimar!' With a mischievous smile that rendered her plain face almost pretty, she signalled her groom and set off.

As soon as they were out of earshot, Giff dropped his cheerful demeanour. 'Merciful Heavens, Temper, what in the world were you about?'

Before he could launch into full rhetorical flow, Temper held up a hand. 'Enough, Giff! I know you want to ring a peal over me, but wait until we get back to Vraux House. I'd rather the whole of London didn't hear you abusing me.'

He pressed his lips together for a moment, her

calm paradoxically increasing his fury and annoyance. 'Until Vraux House, then.'

In any event, the streets were now so crowded that riding side by side to carry on a conversation would have been impossible. With difficulty, Giff contained the anger and the questions, biding his time until they reached the privacy of Vraux House.

Some ten minutes later, they arrived and turned their horses over to the groom. Once they were in the house, Giff could restrain himself no more.

'Good Heavens, Temper, what were you thinking?' he demanded as soon as they'd crossed the threshold into the front parlour. 'I know you don't care about, indeed want to *encourage*, the image of yourself as fast and unreliable—but Wendemere? You can be sure that by this afternoon, the Avery chit will have spread the news throughout London that you wagered with the most amoral, dissolute man in the entire *ton*! Whatever possessed you to do such a crack-brained thing?'

She recoiled a little under his vehemence, then raised her chin. 'If you must know, he caught me in the shrubbery at Trenton Manor yesterday. He wanted… Well, I suppose you know what he wanted. I…put him off by challenging him to the race. The terms, as you heard, being that, if he lost, he would leave me alone. And lose he did.

So why are you taking me to task? Having the snide Miss Avery spread whispers confirming the image the *ton* has of me anyway, thereby scaring off any true gentleman, should help me accomplish my goal of ending this unwanted Season more speedily. I'll not apologise for either of those achievements!'

Though Giff heard her, he was having a hard time getting past the appalling image of Temper all alone, trapped in the garden in the grip of a doubtless drunken Wendemere—whose only moral principle was gratifying his own desires. 'You were caught alone in the garden with him? How did you get him to agree to a race—instead of taking what he wanted then and there?'

'By telling him if he insisted, I'd comply, but think the worse of him. And by implying, if he won on *my* terms, he'd get more than a kiss. One can always count on a man to be ruled more by lust than logic. And to feel himself superior to a woman in any pursuit he considers "manly". Like horsemanship.'

'But you took a ridiculous chance! With Arion ailing, how could you be so sure of beating him?'

'I concede, it was hardly a perfect scheme, but it was the best I could come up with in the heat of the…situation. And I admit, I was more than a little uncertain of the outcome. Under normal circumstances, I trust Arion to fly like the west wind he's named for, but after his recent injury, there was a chance I'd have to fulfil the challenge on a job horse—and count on superior riding skill to make up for whatever the mount lacked. Huggins confirmed that racing wouldn't hurt the hoof, but warned Arion might favour it and lack his normal speed. Fortunately, even less than his normal speed was good enough.'

'Still, you took a ridiculous risk. And where was Mrs Moorsby? How *could* you have been foolish enough to walk alone with Wendemere in the garden to begin with?' he demanded, anger over what she might have brought down on herself swamping the relief that she'd survived it, safe and unharmed.

'I didn't go off with him alone,' she snapped back impatiently. 'Miss Henley and I were walking together, discussing Lieutenant Williamson's talk—and how wonderful that was, Giff, you can only imagine! Lady Henley sent Lord Theo to fetch us, but we passed by some marvellous carved Sanskrit stones on the way back, and I... lingered to study them. How was I to know Wendemere would turn up?'

'If it hadn't been Wendemere, it could have been someone else. Good L— heavens, Temperance, with your reputation, you should know better than to let yourself be caught alone anywhere! What were you thinking?'

'Actually, at the moment he accosted me,' she said, her voice gruff, 'I was thinking how much I needed to thank you for giving me such a treat. If I'd known you were going to rake me over the coals so...unhandsomely, I might have had s-second thoughts...'

Her voice breaking a little, with one quick, impatient gesture she swiped at the tears beginning to track down her cheeks.

His anger evaporated. Negligent she'd been, perhaps—but also brave and fierce. Instead of dissolving in tears, or offering what would have probably been a futile resistance at being restrained and threatened, she'd devised an ingenious plan to escape and had implemented it, knowing her tools to win the wager were compromised. All without any assistance.

He couldn't remember ever seeing fierce, rebellious Temper in tears. Unable to stop himself, he reached over and drew her into his arms. 'I'm so sorry,' he said softly into her hair. 'It must have been terrifying.'

He heard the muffled sob she suppressed, sensed the trembling she could not and felt even worse for having harangued her. He was grateful that she'd accepted the comfort he'd felt compelled to offer her.

Fortunately, she pushed him away before desire could reassert itself.

'It was…daunting,' she admitted. 'I think this time it shall be Gregory's brandy instead of tea.'

Ah, Temper—frightened, desperately seeking escape—but ever defiant. As she went to the sideboard and poured them both a glass, he said, 'I expect you've earned a portion of spirits. And you are right—I shouldn't have scolded you. If anyone deserves blame, it's me, for abandoning you. Had I accompanied you to Trenton Manor, you wouldn't have ended up walking in that garden alone—and Wendemere wouldn't have dared accost you. I failed you and Lady Sayleford, not providing the protection I promised.'

'Nonsense, Giff, you mustn't blame yourself! Heavens, you can't dog my every step! I won't apologise for the race, for I think that disposed of the problem of Wendemere quite tidily. He won't dare approach me in public with his disgusting innuendoes, lest he lose face even among his dissolute friends. But you are right—I shouldn't walk alone anywhere, in London or the countryside. I shall take great care never to forget that again, for though he might be compelled to avoid me in public, I doubt Wendemere would pass up an opportunity to take his revenge should he catch me alone. And I can't count on tricking him again.'

'Thank heaven for that! My apologies, too, for being so churlish, a mood for which—' he gave her a wry grin '—you aren't *entirely* responsible.'

He accepted the glass and took a deep drink. 'I've been needing this all morning.'

'Indeed?' she said, tilting her head at him enquiringly. 'Something incited your wrath *before* you discovered me playing the hoyden? Did the draft bill not go well?'

He heaved a sigh. 'No, the wording of the bill is excellent and we're moving forward with it.'

'Bad news from Fensworth, then?' She looked up at him, concern and sympathy in her face. Drat, did she have to be perceptive as well as fierce and brave?

'Just another letter from Mama.' He shrugged, trying to mitigate his anger, unease and the impending doom of duty. 'More of the usual haranguing about funds, only more so. Maybe… maybe I ought to take you up on your offer to review the eligible females and recommend one you think might suit. I may not like everyone pressing me to find a rich bride, but even I admit Mama is right. I've been a man grown for some time, and ought to curtail my "private pleasures"—' he grimaced at his mother's dismissive description of not just his personal enjoyments, but of the work he was trying to do '—and assume responsibility for assuring my own finances. As she pointed out, I will not inherit the estate and the drain of my "increasingly expensive upkeep" robs my father and brother Robert of funds they need to invest in repairs, improvements and supplies.'

She was silent a moment. 'That's a rather harsh assessment. Does your mama have no conception of how important the work you do in Parliament is?'

He shook his head, not able to conceal all the hurt. 'I don't think she knows—or cares. Her focus is, as always, on Robert, the heir.'

'As it always has been?' Temper said softly.

He shrugged. 'He has an important task. Working with Papa to manage the estate and keep it as profitable as possible. Dropping prices for grain since the end of the wars has affected producers as well as workers. It's been several years since Papa has been able to afford to let Mama rent a house here for the Season. I know she resents my living in town, when the estate lacks the funds for her even to come to London to acquire the gowns and bonnets she loves. To her great chagrin, she's forced to make do with garments made up by the village seamstress from the fashion plates she supplies.'

'An unforgivable offence,' Temper said drily.

Giff grinned wryly, Temper's understanding pouring a soothing balm over his anger and irritation. 'It is, to her. Here I am, surrounded by theatres, shops, friends and entertainments, to say nothing of the pleasures of flesh, while she is stuck in the middle of marsh and fenland, with hardly enough funds to purchase new gowns to impress the neighbourhood.'

Temper shook her head and, after a brief hesitation, reached out to press his hand. Her turn to offer sympathy and, grateful, he squeezed her fingers in return. And held on, his chest swelling with a mix of affection and the delicious sensual pleasure evoked by the feel of her hand in his.

With her seated near him, her understanding gaze fixed on him, the sweet satin softness of her palm against his heightening all his senses, he felt more energised and fully alive than he had in weeks.

But then desire flamed hotter, firing him with the urge to lean down and kiss her. As if scalded, he sat back and jerked his hand free.

She rubbed at hers, as if she'd felt that sudden heat, too. It was a moment before she said, her voice a little unsteady, 'Sounds like your mama has two admirable sons. It's a shame she doesn't seem to recognise it.'

Had his mother ever appreciated him? Giff couldn't remember a time when he wasn't the second choice, the afterthought walking behind her, tugging at her skirts, while she showered all her attention on Robert. Pushing away the painful memories, he shrugged. 'One gets used to it.'

'Does one ever get used to being ignored? Un-dervalued?' she asked softly.

She was thinking of her relationship with her father—and how she was treated by the *ton*, Giff knew. Whatever sense of being overlooked he'd felt with his mother was nothing compared to the void between her and Lord Vraux. He, at least, had society's respect and a sense of doing impor-tant work as a standing Member of Parliament. Whereas she'd been labelled a wanton by many in the *ton* who'd never even met her. *Looked like she was leading him on to me*, Thetford had said.

Before he could think how to respond, she shook her head, as if dismissing the unhappy re-flections. 'So, you think you might be ready to yield to your mama's promptings and find a rich wife? Though we must find you one who has more qualities than just a fat purse. A thrifty household manager, a gifted conversationalist and skilled hostess would be on the list, I think. At least a modicum of beauty and a good dose of common sense.'

Even discussing the matter grated on him. 'Ac-cording to Mama, the financial situation is dire enough that I don't have time to look for a para-gon. A female with a fat dowry and no qualms about accepting a marriage of convenience is all I require.'

After a moment's hesitation, she said, 'You don't want a wife who's fallen in love with you?'

He grimaced. 'Since it's highly unlikely I'm going to fall in love with Miss Fat Purse, no. It would be…awkward, dealing with the excess of emotion, tears and tantrums that would ensue. I've had my fill of those, dealing with my mother all these years. Fortunately, I'm not in need of an heir, though I suppose, if she really wants them, I would be willing to give my wife children.'

'So, someone who is rich—and would be happy enough to allow you to continue your pleasant association with the muslin company?'

Hearing it stated so baldly, he had to laugh. 'Ah, Temper, trust you to reduce matters to their essentials.'

She smiled back. 'It's easier to proceed if one goes to the nub of the matter. If you require so little of a wife, Giff, why not marry me? I'm certainly rich enough, you could continue your exploits among the demi-monde with my blessing and, as long as you promise to set aside enough of my dowry to allow me to travel, I'd call it a fair bargain.'

A brilliant smile broke out on her face. 'In fact, the more I think about it, the more perfect the idea becomes! We've known each other for ever, so there wouldn't be the awkwardness of dealing with a near-stranger. We both understand what we each want and need. It could be a perfect partnership, Giff! What do you say?'

Chapter Thirteen

Marry Temper? Desire her as he did, Giff had never given the notion more than a passing thought, believing she saw him—until recently, anyway—only as her older brother's friend. She possessed few of the characteristics she'd just mentioned as desirable in a politician's wife. But then, he'd stated only two requirements for a wife—that she have money and no inclination to hang about him, demanding attention. Temper certainly met both of those qualifications.

But...*marry* Temper? Could he really take her as his wife...and keep his distance? Permission to dally among the muslin company wasn't a very attractive proposition when he considered the pleasure he might enjoy at home—with Temper in his bed.

In fact, between being preoccupied with squiring Temper and his duties in Parliament, he hadn't visited the ladies in weeks.

'You would marry me if I let you go your own way?' he asked, probing at the matter tentatively, like poking a nest you think, but are not quite sure, the wasps have abandoned. 'And what of... intimate matters?'

Her face colouring, she looked away, not meeting his eyes. 'A *marriage blanc* would be a requirement.'

Giff stared at her, perplexed and, he admitted, the male in him a little affronted. He knew she was attracted to him. The air fairly buzzed with sensual tension when they were near each other, and he knew he hadn't imagined the zing of contact when he touched her of late. So...why this reluctance to take the attraction further?

Maybe a lifetime of watching the disdain with which her mother had been treated for indulging *her* desires made Temper determined to repress her own. Or the distaste for the undeserved comments—like those of Thetford—and unsolicited advances—like those of Wendemere—to which her unjustified reputation subjected her made her want to deny the passionate nature he, and any man with breath in his body, sensed in her.

Whatever the reason, despite the fact that he was her brother's best friend, if he actually had a husband's rights to her body, he couldn't think of anything *less* convenient and more designed to drive a man crazy than being married to Temper, having promised not to touch her.

And then there were the exploits she'd probably embroil herself in, here and abroad. He could hardly devote the necessary time and energy to his responsibilities in Parliament if he had to keep one eye always on Temper, rescuing her from her impulsive starts and protecting her from men seeking to take advantage. Lord help the hapless man permanently saddled with the task of controlling *her*!

Still, she'd made him a generous offer and he didn't want to hurt her feelings. Choosing his words with care, he said, 'That's a tempting proposal, Temper, and I do appreciate it. But—'

'—you'd rather not saddle yourself with a handful like me?' she said gruffly, still not meeting his eyes. 'I understand. You really do deserve a better wife, Giff. Someone with those talents and attributes I just mentioned. A woman you would be eager, rather than resigned, to marry. I suppose you'll just have to put your mama off a while longer while I help you look for this paragon. I just thought for a moment the bargain might work—fulfilling your need for funds and mine for freedom. We're friends who respect and trust each other. At least, I hope you feel that way about me.'

'You know I do,' he said, conflicted. It would be madness to accept her proposal under the terms she'd set, but he knew his refusal must hurt. And foolish as it was, the idea of claiming Temper as his wife, once broached, had an insidious appeal…

She gave him a swift, strained smile. 'You were probably my best hope of attaining my desires speedily. Once Miss Avery finishes spreading the word of my exploit with Wendemere, I shouldn't have much trouble discouraging respectable gentleman. Doubtless, I'll be able to end the Season unwed—but I will still have to endure the whole Season. And even after that, there's no guarantee Papa will release any funds to me. Whereas, if I married someone who sympathised with my hopes and was willing to let me to pursue my dreams, I might not have to spend the rest of my life in England, alone and…miserable.'

She looked so woebegone, Giff felt even worse. But before he could commit the idiocy of reconsidering, she shook her head again. 'Heavens, listen to what a poor, pathetic creature I sound! No, Giff, you're right to hold out for a proper wife, not saddle yourself with a hoyden whose chequered reputation—and impulsive behaviour—would make her a millstone around the neck of a rising politician. We won't speak of it again.'

He agreed completely with her assessment— so why did the conclusion make him feel so… unsatisfied? 'Very well, we'll speak of it no more,' he said at last.

'I've taken you away from your duties long

enough,' she said briskly, gathering up their glasses and rising to take them back to the sideboard. 'Thank you for riding to my rescue—even though it proved unnecessary. I shall *try* to be more circumspect and avoid situations that require your intervention.'

'I'd appreciate that,' he said, rising as well, 'since I'm likely to be called on the carpet by my godmother for this event. Though the *ton* may only learn about the race through Hyde Park, being Lady Sayleford, she's sure to discover the whole story. And then chastise me for not being present at Trenton Manor to have averted the situation—even while she applauds your ingenuity.'

She brightened at the compliment, making him feel better about having just disappointed her. 'I would be gratified if she considered the solution "ingenious" rather than "madcap".'

She walked him to the door. 'Goodbye, Giff. I hope your committee meetings go well.'

Giving her a bow, he walked out, heading to the hackney stand to engage a jarvey to return to Parliament. Relieved to be returning with their relationship unchanged, but still…unsettled.

Would she really end up alone and miserable?

He'd always thought she would eventually find some compatible gentleman and yield to the practicality of marriage. Based on her last comments, she was nowhere close to reaching that conclusion.

Still, his major concern was making sure she ended the Season unharmed, whether or not she ended it engaged. It wasn't his responsibility to see that she ended up happy.

But she was such a fierce, bright, compelling spirit, he couldn't help wanting her to be.

The next evening, Gifford looked down the length of the dinner table and suppressed a groan. Apparently Lady Witherspoon was a friend of the late Lady Chilford—and had heard the tale about Temperance that the woman's daughter, Miss Avery, had doubtless whispered to every of member of society she'd encountered since that ill-fated race the previous morning.

Temperance and Mrs Moorsby had been seated in the middle of the long table, surrounded by dowagers who must be the hostess's friends or relations and two elderly gentlemen. No young or single men sat within three chairs of them.

Temper herself had given him an ironic lift of her brow as they took their places, indicating she was well aware of the significance of her placement.

Glancing down at her now, he had to suppress a grin. From the relish with which she was bedazzling the elderly gentleman beside her, she was amused by their hostess's manoeuvre. After all, her desire not to marry was so singular, the woman couldn't be blamed for failing to recognise that she'd delighted, rather than slighted, Temper by placing her far away from eligible gentlemen.

Delighted, however, he was not. To his great annoyance, he had ended up with Miss Avery for a dinner partner.

As dinner progressed, matters only worsened. With society's richest matrimonial prize, Lord Solsworth, seated on Miss Avery's other side, he'd hoped to avoid becoming the sole focus of her attention. But, impervious to the glare the Countess of Agremont kept directing towards her son, Solsworth sidestepped Miss Avery's every conversational opening and devoted himself to the married lady on his other side.

Leaving Giff the only eligible gentleman on whom Miss Avery could work her charms.

In the few moments when Miss Avery turned from him to accord the bare minimum of polite comments to the gentleman on her other side, Giff watched Solsworth. The duke's heir hadn't seen Temper since the race, Giff knew, but he'd undoubtedly heard all the salacious stories. Giff couldn't tell from the glances the man occasionally directed towards Temper whether he'd been intrigued, or disgusted, by the accounts.

As soon as the ladies left them to their brandy, however, Solsworth turned to him. 'I understand

Miss Lattimar bested Wendemere in a race in Hyde Park?'

He stiffened, waiting for the criticism to come. 'She did.'

'And you knew of this race beforehand?'

'Most assuredly not! Else I would have put a stop to it—though I would have had no doubts she would win. She's an excellent horsewoman.'

Solsworth nodded. 'I'm relieved to hear it. I would otherwise have to re-evaluate my good opinion of you. No true gentleman would have allowed a lady to meet that reprobate Wendemere unaccompanied! I've heard he's been pressing his lewd attentions on her. Can't say I'm happy she decided to take matters in her own hands to dispense with him, but the results were certainly impressive. If the scum dares approach her now, he'll lose the few remaining friends he has.'

Giff sighed. 'You'll hardly be the only member of society to disapprove her methods.'

Solsworth laughed shortly. 'Every beldame in London I've encountered since yesterday has condemned her. Including, of course, my mother.' He grimaced. '*She* would pair me up with the eldest Avery girl who, for all that she is lovely and well dowered, makes me feel like the last mouse fleeing the larder, running smack into the cat.'

'She does…press too hard,' Giff agreed. 'Although no thanks to you for giving me any help during dinner.'

'Sorry, old man,' Solsworth replied, his grin unrepentant. 'But when one is touted as the richest matrimonial prize in London—' he rolled his eyes '—one must protect oneself.'

'Understood,' Giff said. Having apparently discovered what he needed to, Solsworth turned to address their host, leaving Giff alone with his thoughts.

As he'd suspected, the duke's heir didn't intend to be swayed by the disapproval of his formidable mother. Did he mean to court Temper openly, or simply remain an admirer?

Solsworth was a bit young to think of marriage—but a woman like Temper didn't come along very often. He appeared to be strong-willed and confident enough to earn her respect, and intelligent enough to try diplomacy to dissuade her from rash actions, rather than incite her rebellion by forbidding them. If he did pursue her, it wouldn't be for her fortune, of which he had no need, but only because he couldn't resist the beautiful, unconventional essence of her.

If he succeeded in winning her affection, it would be accounted a brilliant match for her.

Why could Giff not feel more enthusiastic about it?

Perhaps because he doubted the wife of a duke's

heir would be permitted to roam the world, collecting treasures and having adventures. Could Temper be satisfied with being mistress over a vast ducal empire in England?

Giff didn't think so. And chided himself for feeling relieved.

But then, who *would* make a better husband for the uniqueness that was Temper? Giff wasn't sure. He just knew he hadn't yet met a man he thought would be equal to the job.

Giff's respite ended when the gentlemen rejoined the ladies. While Solsworth, to his mingled relief and unease, made a beeline for Temper, Miss Avery sought him out, first bringing him tea and then asking if he would take a turn about the room with her.

As there was no polite way to refuse, he suppressed a sigh and offered his arm. Somehow this evening, he needed to diplomatically convey that she was wasting her time, attempting to attach him.

Once they were beyond hearing distance of the several groups enjoying their tea, Miss Avery said, 'Have you recovered from the shock of rescuing Miss Lattimar from her latest start?'

Determined not to be drawn into comments that could be construed as either criticism or support, he said blandly, 'She rather rescued herself, I think.'

Miss Avery shook her head. 'She is so bold and beautiful, it's a shame she suffers under the burden of such an impulsive nature. Our situations being somewhat similar, I had hoped we might be friends.'

Biting back the observation that disparaging another female in the presence of other gentlemen was not a tactic likely to win friendship, he'd intended to utter a polite murmur. Then, curious how she could consider their backgrounds anything at all alike, he found himself asking, 'How, similar?'

'She already has a reputation to live down, compromising her ability to make a good match. Whereas, if I do not marry quickly, I may be thrust into a situation of such embarrassing notoriety that my ability to marry at all will be threatened.'

'Indeed? In what way?'

'I probably ought not to say anything…but then, I'm sure I can count on your discretion. As well as, I hope, your sympathy over a poor innocent female finding herself in so difficult a situation.'

Was she trying to elicit his chivalry? Regretting now that he'd invited a confidence, he replied carefully, 'Of course, you can rely on my discretion.' There being no way he was going to guarantee sympathy.

She sighed. 'I imagine you know that my *father*—' she almost spat out the word '—is Viscount Chilford. He's informed the family—in confidence, so I trust you will not repeat this information—that he intends soon to remarry. Which, as it has been two years since we lost my dear mama, I could forgive, even if I cannot understand how he could bring himself to put someone else in her place! I know men have *needs*, but the woman he means to marry is his former mistress, who bore him a child out of wedlock! A low-born former *governess*! The fact that, should he actually commit such a…travesty, my sister and I will be made laughing stocks—'

'Please, Miss Avery, you must say no more,' Giff interrupted, needing to stop her before she uttered anything else to offend him—or embarrass her, once he revealed his connections to the woman she was savaging. 'Viscount Chilford's natural son, Mr Tawny, is a member of my party in Parliament, and a talented gentleman whom I highly respect. Since he also happens to be a close friend of Miss Lattimar's brothers, Christopher and Gregory, I am well aware of your father's plans to marry Mr Tawny's mother. A charming woman I have met on several occasions. I really can't allow you to abuse either of them.'

Her face going white, then red, Miss Avery was

rendered, for once, speechless. After a moment, she said, 'Then I will say no more.'

'Perhaps I'd better return you to our hostess,' Giff said, finally sensing an opening where he might politely but permanently escape the girl's clutches. 'Miss Avery, you are a lovely, highly respected lady who will undoubtedly make a fine match, regardless of who your father marries. But given your desire to wed quickly and with me being too occupied by my Parliamentary duties to consider marriage any time soon, you might do better to bestow the privilege of your attention upon…other gentlemen.'

It took a full moment for the implications of that speech, as diplomatic as he'd been able to make it while still conveying his point, to fully register. Giff could tell when it did, as Miss Avery's already pink cheeks darkened to cherry.

'I see. I had heard that you were in dire need of a rich wife—' She halted, pressing her lips together for a moment before continuing, with a forced smile. 'But I see the rumours were in error—as they so often are. How very awkward! I do apologise.' Though her cheeks remained red, she continued smoothly, 'I hope you won't hold my…unfortunate candour against me, that we can remain friends.'

Her brittle smile didn't reassure him that the feelings she would have towards him in future, after that embarrassing faux pas, would be at all friendly. But happy to grasp any olive branch, he said, 'Of course. It would be my privilege.'

He'd turned to walk her back to the group around her aunt when suddenly she halted. 'Is... is *Miss Lattimar* also aware of my father's intentions?'

'I'm sure she must be. As I mentioned, her brother Christopher is a close friend of Mr Tawny.'

Miss Avery sucked in a deep breath. Giff watched with dismay as the mortification of her expression turned to anger. 'So...she has been *laughing* at me all this time! Pretending to be polite, all the while sniggering behind her hand, knowing of the humiliation that awaits me!'

Alarmed, Giff quickly replied, 'Not at all, Miss Avery! Though she reveres Mr Tawny, given her own...difficult circumstances, I'm sure she would have nothing but understanding for how... distressing the situation has to be for you. I assure you, mockery, or delighting in the misfortune of others, is not in her character.'

'She is female, isn't she?'

Giff was trying to think of some placating response when she shook her head, seeming to master some of the anger and chagrin. 'But then, Miss Lattimar is a most unusual female, isn't she? Are you sure you don't have ambitions in that direction?'

The last thing he wanted was for Miss Avery to circulate *that* rumour. 'Certainly not! Miss Lattimar is my best friend's little sister, which is why I was asked to look after her. Somewhat of a hoyden, I have to admit,' he added, silently begging Temper's pardon for disparaging her to this girl who'd already gone to some lengths to present Temper in the worst possible light. 'And most decidedly *not* the sort of wife a politician would seek, even if he were ready to marry.'

'I don't doubt she would lead you a merry chase,' Miss Avery agreed sweetly. 'Although I've heard she, too, claims to have no interest in marrying.'

Hoping that reinforcing that truth might make a girl who was desperate to marry less inclined to see Temper as a rival—or a target for her malice—Giff replied, 'Unusual as that is, I can confirm the truth of *that* rumour. Miss Lattimar has always had a desire to travel the world—a dream she believes a husband might not view kindly.'

'I expect not. He'd be more likely to relegate her to the country, where she could cause him no embarrassment. And use her dowry to fund portions for their children and improve his estate.'

'Probably,' Giff agreed. 'Though I imagine she will eventually end up wedded, for those reasons and more, she's hoping to delay matrimony—at least until after she's had a chance to travel.'

'I wish her well in her ambitions, then,' Miss Avery said as they approached the tea table. 'I'll let you return to your...unusual charge. And thank you for a most...illuminating conversation.'

'A pleasure, as always, Miss Avery,' Giff said, relinquishing her arm. *A blatant falsehood, that compliment*, he thought as he walked away, conscious of a deep relief at having, he hoped, permanently escaped Miss Avery's matrimonial manoeuvrings.

However, he couldn't help worrying that, despite her fine words, his revelations had deepened Miss Avery's jealous dislike of Temperance Lattimar.

Chapter Fourteen

Three nights later, Temper sat reluctantly in the carriage being driven to a ball being given by Lady Arnold, aunt of the snide Miss Avery. When informed of the invitation, she'd initially protested to Mrs Moorsby that she'd rather not attend an event honouring a female she actively disliked, only to discover that not only she and her chaperon, but Lady Sayleford herself, were to attend.

If her imperious sponsor intended to grace the ball with her presence, Temper knew there was no way she could avoid it.

With Lady Sayleford settled in the carriage beside her, Mrs Moorsby on the backward-facing seat beside Giff, her sponsor turned to Temper.

'I realise you are not happy about attending Lady Arnold's ball—and, no, Angela didn't convey your feelings to me. I've heard that Miss Avery has been unpleasant to you on several occasions. However, Lady Arnold is a friend of long standing and I could not slight her by failing to appear—or failing to bring along the young lady I am sponsoring. I understand Miss Avery has made overtures to you, too, Gifford, although I expect a gentleman of your address can sidestep them handily enough, if you choose.'

To Temper's amusement, Giff first looked as surprised as Temper had been—honestly, Lady Sayleford and her sources of information were uncanny!—then grimaced. 'I did choose, and I hope I have "sidestepped" as diplomatically as possible. However, I would not have avoided the ball. Despite her obvious chagrin at my making my, um, lack of interest known, Miss Avery said she hoped we could remain friends.'

'With friends like that, I'd watch my back,' Temper murmured.

Giff smiled wryly. 'I intend to, being no more trusting of her good will than you are. But I encountered her coming out of Hatchard's yesterday and she pressed me to agree that I would be attending tonight's affair. Though most of the time, she grates on my nerves, I have to admit having a little sympathy.'

'Because her father is to remarry?' Temper said. 'I suppose I can sympathise with her desire to be wed and gone before that happens—if she weren't so *blatant* about her need to attach someone. After all, it would be hard for anyone to watch her mother displaced.'

Giff gave a short laugh. 'Impossible, for her. It was all I could do to remain polite, after she began ranting about what an *embarrassment* it will be for Ben's father to marry the "low-born governess" who was his former mistress.'

'She dared to criticise Mrs Tawny?' Temper said indignantly.

'Miss Avery is rather…intemperate,' Lady Sayleford said. 'But she's correct that, on the face of it, the Viscount *is* making a mésalliance. Though Miss Avery may neither know—nor would she probably care—Angelica Tawny was the woman Chilford intended to marry. Only a sudden reversal in the fortunes of the estate he was to inherit and severe pressure from his family to marry an heiress forced him to marry Miss Avery's mother. Nor did he know at the time of his wedding that the woman he loved was carrying their child.'

Temper shook her head. 'You really do know everything about everyone. I think it's marvellous that, after loving each other for so long and so faithfully, they will finally be able to claim the joy they deserve.'

Lady Sayleford nodded. 'As do I—and that is one wedding I shall be delighted to attend. Robert Avery did his duty, but a chilly business it was. There was no pretence of love; I don't think they'd met more than a handful of times before wedding. His family got a much-needed influx of cash for the estate and his bride the guarantee that she would one day become a viscountess.'

'A cold bargain indeed,' Temper said. 'Although I bet it's one her daughter would jump to accept.'

Lady Sayleford nodded. 'I'm afraid the elder daughter possesses the same cold, self-interested viewpoint her mother had. So I would second Miss Lattimar's advice that, if you have…disappointed her, Newell, deal cautiously with Miss Avery.'

'Don't worry, Godmother, I shall be on my guard,' Giff assured her.

Just then the carriage arrived at Lady Arnold's town house, an imposing edifice in Berkeley Square quite as elegant as Lady Sayleford's home. 'Certainly looks as though she comes equipped with a dowry large enough to tempt someone,' Temper remarked as the ladies exited the carriage.

'What a shame she would come with it,' Giff murmured in her ear as they walked in.

After greeting their hostess and her protégées—Miss Avery's brittle smile in response to her curtsy sending a little frisson up her spine—Temper put thoughts of the unpleasant young woman behind her. Freed by Lady Sayleford, who told them that, having put in the obligatory appearance, she intended to leave within the half-hour, her party went off to find more amenable company.

She was delighted to discover Miss Henley and her mother along with Lord Theo and some of his more dissolute friends. As the dancing began, though she never lacked for partners, Temper did notice that some of the more respectable young men who had flocked to her at other social events kept their distance.

Miss Avery had spread her tales well. Once she caught the girl's gaze resting on her—gloating, perhaps?—but as the tale-bearing served Temper's purposes, she was happy to allow Miss Avery her triumph.

Besides, if her satisfaction over diminishing the number of Temper's admirers distracted her from taking retribution against Giff for rebuffing her, it was more than worth it.

Having sent Miss Henley off with Lord Theo, Temper had chosen not to dance this particular set so she might watch Giff take the floor with Lady Constance. Intelligent, lovely, a keen horsewoman, with her father's political connections, she would make Giff an admirable bride.

A notion Temper ought to embrace with more enthusiasm, she'd been telling herself when she noticed Solsworth approaching.

Was the young man as brave as she'd thought?

Or just rebelling against his mama's attempt at control?

'So good to see you this evening, Miss Lattimar,' he said, bowing at he reached her side. 'How is it that you seem to be more beautiful every time I see you?'

'It must be the healthy benefits of racing in the park,' Temper replied drily.

Laughing, Solsworth said, 'I only wish I could have seen it! A nasty piece of work, Lord Alfred. How clever of you to have found a way to exile him.'

'I hope he remains exiled,' Temper said. 'In any event, I shall take care to be well chaperoned everywhere I go.'

Perhaps by mutual design, she'd had no trouble avoiding Miss Avery all evening. But not unexpectedly, with the 'catch of the *ton*' conversing with her, as the set ended and the dancers moved off the floor, Temper saw the girl walking towards them. And automatically stiffened.

'I hope you are all enjoying the evening,' Miss Avery said, addressing herself to the group of dancers now congregated near Temper. 'My aunt has just informed me that the musicians will be taking a short break. With lanterns lit along all the garden paths, it's quite lovely. She recommends that the guests go out and enjoy a bit of fresh air. Mr Newell, perhaps you would escort Lady Constance? And, Lord Theo, why don't you continue to squire Miss Henley?'

With some amusement, Temper waited to see if Miss Avery's good will would extend to pairing *her* off with Solsworth—and wasn't at all surprised to discover it wouldn't.

'I'm afraid your mother has delegated me to ask that you attend her, Lord Solsworth,' Miss Avery said to him with an apologetic smile. 'May I escort you back to her?'

There wasn't much Solsworth could do to refuse, short of calling Miss Avery a liar. Bowing to the inevitable, he gave her a short nod. 'Of course, Miss Avery. I imagine my mother is in dire need. As usual.'

'Miss Lattimar, I'm sure one of the other gentlemen will offer you their escort. You are enjoying the party, too, I trust?'

'Very much, Miss Avery,' Temperance said, having to work to keep the irony from her voice.

'Not as much yet as I hope you will,' Miss Avery answered, with an enigmatic smile. 'Shall we be off, my lord?'

Accepting one of the several offers made after Miss Avery's departure, Temper walked out to the garden, trailed by Mrs Moorsby and a small party of friends. The cool air and the scent of night flowers' bloom *were* refreshing after the closeness and heat of the ball. It wasn't until they heard the musicians begin to tune up did the guests begin to trickle back into the ballroom.

The gardens being extensive and the light thrown by the torches limited, Temper had seen neither Miss Henley nor Giff with their partners during her own walk. Back in the ballroom, she looked about for them, hoping Miss Henley had enjoyed Lord Theo's amusing attentions—and wondering if Giff had found Lady Constance's company as appealing as her credentials to become his wife were impressive.

She ought to be happy for him if he had, she thought without enthusiasm.

Before she could locate either him or Miss Henley, Miss Avery came rushing up. 'Oh, Miss Lattimar, there you are! I'm afraid there's been an accident—nothing serious, but Miss Henley twisted her ankle while walking down one of the garden pathways. I've had her conveyed to a bedchamber, but she refused to let me summon her mama, saying Lady Henley would make too much of a fuss. She asked if you might attend her? If it's not too much of a bother, of course.'

How like Emma Henley to not wish to be a 'bother', Temper thought. 'Of course I'll go up to her. If you'll excuse me, Mrs Moorsby?'

'How kind of you!' Miss Avery said. 'I'd escort you up myself, but—'

'No, you mustn't abandon your guests,' Temper said.

'Thank you for being so understanding! I'll just have a footman show you the way.' After summoning one of the liveried servants hovering at the edge of the ballroom, Miss Avery hurried off.

'I'll go check Miss Henley's ankle,' Temper said to Mrs Moorsby. 'If it is too painful for her to be able to return to the party, I'll come fetch you, so we may find her mother to have her taken home. Tell Mr Newell what happened, when he returns.'

'I certainly will inform him. Poor Miss Henley!'

With a nod to her chaperon, Temper walked off with the footman.

Meanwhile, as he escorted Lady Constance up the garden stairs into the house, a footman stopped and bowed to Giff. 'Mr Newell?'

After his nod, the servant continued, 'I'm to inform you that one of the guests, Miss Henley, has injured her ankle. Miss Lattimar has gone up to attend her and asked that you come assist.'

'Of course! Poor Miss Henley. If you would excuse me, Lady Constance?'

'Naturally. I hope Miss Henley isn't seriously hurt! Do send for me if I can be of any help.'

'Thank you, I will.'

Lady Constance could be a help—in so many ways, Giff thought with a sigh as he followed the footman down the hallway and up the stairs. She had every requirement a rising Member of Parliament could ask for in a wife—beauty, breeding, impressive family connections and a large dowry. In addition, she was well spoken, intelligent and, though she was by no means as blatant as Miss Avery about indicating it, he could tell she found him appealing.

Unfortunately, he felt not a particle of inclination to pursue her. After Temper, she seemed so…placid.

Probably any woman would seem less dynamic in comparison with the erratic blaze of energy that was Temper. But when he married, he needed a wife who was serene, well behaved and diplomatic—not given to the impulsive, potentially disastrous schemes of his best friend's little sister.

Such as that race in the park with Wendemere.

A few minutes later, he reached the upper floor where the bedchambers were located. Indicating the correct door, the footman bowed and walked away.

After rapping softly, Giff walked in. 'Temper? How can I help?'

From somewhere on the far side of the room, he heard Temper answer, 'That's a good question.'

Peering in the dimness of the darkened chamber, he could just make her out, walking back from the adjacent sitting room, carrying a candle. He went over to meet her, glancing around as her approaching light illumined the bed and the armchair by the hearth.

Neither of which was occupied by a young lady with an ailing ankle.

'Where is Miss Henley?'

'I don't know,' Temper said, walking over to place the candlestick on the nightstand beside the bed. 'Mrs Moorsby told you she'd been injured?'

'No, a footman informed me as I was leaving the garden. Has Miss Henley recovered?'

'Since I haven't yet located her, I don't know that, either. Miss Avery had a footman direct *me* here, explaining that Miss Henley had asked for my assistance. Not finding her in the bedchamber, I thought maybe she'd been carried into the sitting room, but she's not there, either. The footman must have been mistaken about which bedchamber she was taken to.'

'Both footmen?'

'Apparently,' Temper said drily. 'I suppose we shall have to go search for her.'

'I suppose. Although it will look a bit strange, should any of the servants discover us creeping about the bedchambers like housebreakers.'

'Better that than leaving poor Emma sitting all

alone in some *other* bedchamber, believing I didn't care enough about her welfare to come help her.'

Then, as if she'd suddenly realised where they were—alone, at night, in the intimacy of a bed-chamber, a mere step away from the bed, Temper froze. 'We should probably go in search…now,' she murmured, her voice unsteady.

Her jasmine scent filled his nostrils and he could feel the heat of her nearness. The light from the candle outlined her profile, the round of her bare shoulder above the full sleeves of the gown, the voluptuous curve of her breast.

Desire, thick, hot, fierce, rose in his body, clogging his throat so he couldn't croak out an answer. All he could think was how close she was, how beautiful…how much he wanted to pull her down on to that bed and kiss her.

But to do so would be a betrayal—of her trust and their friendship. Forcing his hands to remain at his sides, he cleared his throat. 'Y-yes,' he stuttered. 'We'd better go rescue Miss Henley.'

With a nod, Temper walked past him to the door and turned the handle—only to discover the door would not open. She pulled harder, but to no avail.

'What's wrong?' Giff asked.

She turned to him, her expression gone blank. 'I believe it's locked.'

'Locked!' he echoed. 'Why would anyone…?'

His voice trailed off as the events flashed through his mind. Miss Avery requesting that Temper assist an injured Miss Henley—a request she knew Temper wouldn't refuse. Two different footmen, each conveying them to the same— wrong—bedchamber.

Miss Avery, who believed Temper had been mocking her. She must be furious that Temper still captured the masculine attention she craved for herself, despite Miss Avery's attempts to disparage her.

Miss Avery who, despite his attempt at diplomacy, probably felt unpardonably insulted by his failure to respond to her advances.

'It must have been locked behind me as I crossed the chamber towards you,' Giff said, his anger rising at Miss Avery's duplicity. 'However it was managed, we need to find another way out— *now.*'

Temper's grim expression said she understood exactly what was at stake. 'Agreed.'

But before either of them could take a step, they heard the soft snick of a bolt turning in the lock. The door opened—to reveal Lady Arnold, staring at them.

'Mr Newell…and Miss Lattimar!' Lady Arnold cried, her cheeks going crimson. 'Despite your reputation, when Jane whispered that she'd seen you sneaking up the stairs, I couldn't believe you would be so brazen as to indulge yourself with… with a *clandestine rendezvous* in *my* house! How could you abuse my hospitality so?'

'We did not come upstairs "to indulge in a clandestine rendezvous",' Giff interjected, trying to contain his fury. 'Your niece summoned both of us separately to come attend to Miss Henley, whom she said had injured her ankle.'

'And if that is so, where is Miss Henley?'

'A good question,' Temper muttered, her face an inscrutable mask.

Before Giff could answer that, a hubbub of voices approached from the stairway. A bevy of guests hurried over to stand behind Lady Arnold, their expressions ranging from shock to outrage to blatant prurient interest.

'You see how I found them,' Lady Arnold said, turning to address the group. 'Virtually *embracing* in the seclusion of this chamber, behaviour so licentious I should not have believed it had I not seen it with my own eyes. Never have I been so deceived and humiliated!'

Turning back to Giff and Temper, she made an imperious gesture. 'You will both leave my house *this instant*!'

A figure wriggled through the goggling spectators to halt by the doorway. 'Miss Lattimar!' Mrs Moorsby cried. 'Are you quite all right?'

'Very well pleasured, probably,' someone in the crowd muttered, eliciting an outburst of laughter.

'This is all a terrible mistake,' Giff felt compelled to say, although he knew explanations would likely prove useless. He and Temper had been found alone together in a bedchamber. No one in society would care how or why they had ended up there.

Temper was completely and irretrievably ruined. And there was only one thing to be done about it.

'I am not interested in excuses, young man,' Lady Arnold snapped. '*You* should be ashamed of yourself, too. Such rakish behaviour! Now, I believe I ordered you both to leave.'

'We're finished here, Giff,' Temper murmured. Stepping past him to the doorway, she scanned the crowd, meeting the expressions of curiosity, horror and condemnation with a defiant gaze before addressing herself to her chaperon, her voice level and controlled.

'I'm quite ready to leave, Mrs Moorsby. Mr Newell, it's probably best that Mrs Moorsby and I return without you. Thank you for your escort and we will see you later.'

'None the less, I'll see you both to your carriage.'

Though he was almost spitting with fury, he had to admire the magnificence that was Temper. Facing the censorious crowd like an imperious goddess, refusing to offer any explanation, daring with splendid indifference for them to think the worst of her. She let nothing of the chagrin and outrage she must be feeling show on her face or in her manner.

If he could have found Miss Avery—conspicuously absent from the onlookers—he'd have been hard pressed not to seize her by the throat and throttle the life out of her devious body.

Moving into the hallway, she halted to make Lady Arnold a curtsy. 'Thank you for your hospitality, Lady Arnold. What a shame you possess so despicable a niece.'

'You haven't even the decency to look embarrassed,' Lady Arnold cried after her as the crowd parted to let them through.

Chapter Fifteen

Two days later, Giff paced the parlour in Vraux House, having just asked, and received, Lord Vraux's permission to ask for Temper's hand. Resigned to the necessity of proposing to her, though angry and regretful that he'd been manoeuvred into it, he was still conscious that repressed deep within was a wild stir of excitement at the notion of marrying Temper.

His nervousness increased as the door opened and Temper walked in—looking beautiful, defiant and as nervous as he was.

'Well, Jane Avery's spite has landed us in a fine pickle,' she said gruffly. 'I am so sorry, Giff.'

'None of your doing. Unfortunately, she's as damnably clever as she is malicious.'

'You shouldn't feel obligated to offer for me,' she said, looking up at him earnestly. 'There are many who would consider you prudent rather than irresponsible for refusing to marry a lady of my chequered reputation. Especially after we've both tried so hard to circulate a more accurate version of the events.'

Giff laughed shortly. 'Telling everyone we'd been summoned to Miss Henley's aide, with the footmen mistaking the chamber? It was kind of Miss Henley to offer to play along with that fiction.'

'Yes, after discovering Miss Avery had kept her chatting in the ballroom until she was sure her scheme achieved its result, Emma was happy to try to help. Granted, few in society want to believe the truth, not when Lady Arnold's version is so much more salacious.'

For a moment, Temper's sombre face cleared, and she laughed. 'Although it is almost worth dealing with this imbroglio, to have witnessed the horrified expression on her face when she opened that door.'

'"Indulging in behaviour so licentious she wouldn't have believed it, had she not seen it with her own eyes,"' Giff quoted, not nearly so amused.

'Despite her distraught niece having warned her what was taking place,' Temper added drily.

'Oh, yes, her niece. Who later said, Lady Sayleford reported to me, that she knew you were capable of such wickedness—' *damn the witch, getting in that last jab* '—but was shocked and appalled that she'd been so mistaken about my character.'

'She did manage to smear both of us quite effectively,' Temper agreed. 'Once again, knowing that most of society *also* believe I'm "capable of such wickedness" removes any obligation a gentleman might normally feel to propose.'

'I don't much care what *society* thinks. But what of Geoffrey, or Christopher? How could I look your brothers in the eye, knowing the *ton* believes I compromised you and that I'd evaded responsibility for my actions? To say nothing of my colleagues in the House. No matter how wild your reputation, you are still gently born. It's unthinkable for anyone who calls himself a gentleman to compromise such a lady and refuse to marry her.'

'You feel that your personal honour is at stake.'

'Exactly.'

She sighed. 'I was afraid of that. Miss Avery chose her revenge well, thinking to punish us both by trapping us in a marriage neither of us wanted. You're *sure* I cannot persuade you not to let yourself be trapped?'

For a moment, he felt a brief flare of hope that he might avoid a union about which he had such wildly conflicted feelings—resentment, anger, trepidation, resignation and that sneaky little flare of excitement.

But about one thing he felt no conflict at all. Regardless of what either of them wanted, marriage was the only way to salvage her honour—and his.

He shook his head. 'No, Temper, I cannot. Having obtained your father's approval,' he said, slipping to one knee before her, 'I must ask if you would do me the honour of becoming my wife.'

She gave him a wry smile. 'I suppose I should be gratified that you are doing the asking this time. After you turned me down so definitely. I have to admit, that did sting a little.'

Regret needled him. 'I'm sorry. I didn't mean to slight you, but—'

She waved him to silence. 'I know you didn't. Although a marriage of convenience would serve us both, I'm hardly the sort of wife you'd have chosen.'

'Perhaps not in everything, but I couldn't find a stronger, braver lady.'

'Because I didn't crumble under society's disapproval? Why should I? I've lived with it most of my life.' She sighed. 'Do get up. If you simply can't persuade yourself not to offer for me, we can at least turn our union into a fitting counterstrike to Jane Avery's triumph. She thinks she's forcing us into a marriage neither of us want, having no idea I've already proposed to you once.'

'The best way to thwart someone who wishes you ill is to appear delighted by the situation they engineered to confound you?'

'Exactly. I imagine she thinks my husband will take over my fortune and try to force me to become a conventional, obedient wife. And that you will be vexed and bedevilled for ever by wedding the one woman in London least likely to become the skilful political hostess you need. Well, I do apologise for that! But…if you can agree to the terms I offered when I proposed to you earlier, we might both end up with most of what we want.'

'For you, control over part of your fortune so you may travel the world as you wish?'

'Yes. With you welcome to use the rest to support your efforts in Parliament. While you are also free to…pursue pleasure wherever you please.'

Since the infuriating moment when he realised how Jane Avery had tricked them, he had thought of little else but the terms Temper had offered before—and still hadn't been able to decide one way or the other how he felt about them.

'I can't deny that having an influx of funds to finally put an end to my financial difficulties will be welcome. I also know you've always dreamed of travelling. But, much as I'd like you to be happy, I… I'm not comfortable with the idea of you journeying to the wilds of India and the Orient with only hired guides and a small entourage to protect you. I suppose I could give up my work in Parliament to accompany you, but I know I'd resent—'

'Goodness, no, Giff, you can't even *think* of

doing such a thing!' she exclaimed, looking appalled. 'You've found your calling and a vital and important one it is! I could never allow you to abandon Parliament to chase after me to foreign lands, places you've never had any interest in visiting.'

'Could you agree to not go running off until more extensive preparations can be made? So we may equip a support party large and well armed enough that I won't have to lie awake every night, worrying that you've been attacked by bandits or worse?' He heaved a sigh. 'I suppose there's no way to guarantee against shipwreck or disease.'

Her expression softened. 'Dear Giff. I can't think of any other man who would trouble himself about my happiness, especially as what I must do to secure it is so outlandish. If you promise to let me travel, eventually, then I agree to wait until we can arrange the "extensive" preparations you think necessary.'

'Thank you.' That concession would relieve some of his worries. About the rest—

Before he could decide how to word the more delicate part of his concern, Temper, being Temper, came straight to the point. 'You aren't particularly interested in…having heirs, are you? When you talked of marriage earlier, you said you'd give a wife children if *she* wanted them. Meaning, you are…indifferent to the idea?'

'I don't *need* heirs, having no property or estate to pass down,' he confirmed. 'Are you saying that you'd want the marriage to be…in name only?'

'I don't want to deny you pleasure,' she said quickly, not meeting his gaze. 'I know how much you enjoy the ladies and would be perfectly happy to allow you to continue amusing yourself with them as you please.'

For a man being forced into a marriage he didn't want, having his prospective wife offer him free rein to pursue other women would normally be a welcome concession—he supposed. But would being able to experience passion with other women make him any more able to resist the desire he felt for Temper?

He wasn't at all sure it would. And if he were honest, the prospect of luring Temper into making their marriage complete excited him far more than the idea of pursuing mindless pleasure. And if he couldn't convince her…maybe he'd better equip her to travel as speedy as possible so he might send the temptation she represented far, far away.

Though life would seem much…duller without the zest of wondering what outrageous thing she would do next.

As if reading his thoughts, she said, 'You'll have your work in Parliament to occupy you—meetings and consultations and persuading the recalcitrant to your point of view. It will be so time-consuming and exhausting, you'll have no time to miss your undutiful, wandering wife.'

'Will my undutiful wife miss me?'

Pinking a little, she looked away. 'I shall always miss the friend who gave up so much to give me my heart's desire. The first man ever to treat my dream as a serious intent, rather than a little girl's foolish imaginings.'

'I hardly think of you as a little girl. Nor have I for some time.'

She looked at him and that potent, wordless sensual connection hummed between them again. He still couldn't understand her reluctance to act on it—on an attraction he knew, with *absolute* certainty, to be mutual.

If he'd pulled her down on to the bed that night at Lady Arnold's, she wouldn't have resisted him. He was almost sure she would have responded with all the passion he could wish for.

Almost sure.

When he focused from those thoughts to look back at her, the fraught moment had passed. She was once again tense, guarded, as if poised to flee.

Maybe not quite so sure.

'Would you accept my proposal if I want more than a *marriage blanc*?'

She shook her head. 'I… I don't think I could.'

As puzzled as he was frustrated by that affirmation, Giff wanted to demand some further explanation. But her averted gaze and wary stance made it patently clear she had no wish to discuss the matter. Indeed, she looked so unexpectedly... fragile, he couldn't press her.

In time, he hoped, she would trust him enough to reveal the reasons for her reluctance to embrace the passion between them. Maybe then he'd get the chance to persuade her into changing her mind.

Time they would have, for marry they must. And if swearing not to touch her was the price for winning her acceptance, he had no choice but to pay it.

Gently, he took her chin, raising her face so she had to look into his eyes. 'Then a *marriage blanc* it shall be. Never doubt that I want you, Temper. But never worry that I will ask of you anything you are not willing to give.'

She gave him a little nod, a fine glaze of tears sheening her eyes. 'Thank you for being so... understanding, Giff. Though I apologise again that you're not getting the skilled political wife you deserve, if you can accept those terms for our marriage, then, yes, I accept your proposal.'

A bargain of wedlock meant to last a lifetime should be sealed with a kiss—even if it had to be a chaste one. Never breaking her gaze, he slowly lowered his head. Looking at the same time both wary—and wanting—she didn't try to avoid his lips.

Ah, how soft hers were! Restraining the immediate surge of desire that demanded he press harder, deeper, probe with his tongue to explore the taste of her, he made himself remain motionless, his hands the barest touch at her shoulders, his lips brushing hers in the lightest of caresses.

With a little sigh, she let his mouth linger.

Fortunately for his rapidly unravelling self-control, after a few moments of sweet torture, she broke the kiss and stepped away. But the fact that she had permitted that touch—that he could sense she was holding herself under as strict a control as he was not to respond any further—gave him hope.

Maybe he just needed to convince her that passion could uplift and delight as well as shame and degrade.

And he'd have a lifetime to persuade her of that.

'Shall we go announce the engagement to your family?'

She nodded, her cheeks still a little pink—and the pulse at her throat still beating erratically. 'Before we do, I have one other request. I received a letter from Pru this morning. It seems she has met the gentleman she wants to marry! That soldier I told you about.'

Giff searched his memory. 'Captain Johnnie Trethwell—late of Her Majesty's Second Foot, invalided home from India?' At her nod, he continued, 'Gregory mentioned she's written him about the man, as well. Not exactly the landed gentleman I thought she was seeking.'

Temper laughed wryly. 'It seems neither of us will end up as we envisioned. Me, who never intended to wed, getting married, while instead of a sober country squire, Pru's giving her hand to the scapegrace youngest son of the late Marquess of Barkeley. Though she did say in her letter that his aunt, Lady Woodlings, intends to settle some money on him, so he won't be coming to her completely pockets-to-let. In any event, they're on their way to London now with Aunt Gussie, to secure Papa's permission and to arrange for a special licence, so they may be wed as quickly as possible. Would...would you be willing to obtain a special licence, too, that we might be wed at the same time?'

He hadn't expected she would want the marriage being forced on them celebrated with a calling of banns followed by a public wedding at St George's, Hanover Square. 'You'd prefer a small private ceremony, with just immediate family and friends?'

'Wouldn't you?'

'Yes. I'll write to inform my father of our intentions—not that I need his permission to marry, though he'd have no reason to withhold it. I doubt he'll wish to leave Fensworth long enough to attend the wedding. Though Mama may celebrate the loss of my expense by arranging a trip here so she may use that quarterly allowance I'll no longer need to have new gowns made up,' he added, trying to keep his voice light and disguise with humour the bitter truth that his parents had only ever seen him as a drain on their resources. 'Enough of that. I can't think of anything more appropriate, than having two sisters who have rarely been apart stand up together on their wedding day.'

She smiled and pressed his hand. 'Thank you, Giff. I will so appreciate having her beside me when I take…take this step into the unknown.'

He brought her fingers to his lips for a brief kiss before releasing them. 'Remember, you may be losing Pru as friend and confidante, but you will always have me.'

She nodded quickly. 'Yes. I'll always have you…as my greatest friend. If you'll wait here, I'll go find Mama and Gregory.'

At that, she walked out, leaving him staring after her.

Her greatest friend. Much as he wanted to protect her and let her be happy, could he marry her and live with being only that?

Chapter Sixteen

'Goodness!' Johnnie Trethwell exclaimed, looking from Temperance to her mother back to a beaming Prudence, whom he had just ushered into the parlour at Vraux House on a sunny afternoon two days later. 'One of you alone is dazzling, but the three of you together is almost more than a man can take in!'

He was certainly charming, this rogue who was to be her brother-in-law, Temperance thought as she and her mother made their curtsies, while Captain Trethwell went on to shake Gregory's hand.

'We're trying not to overwhelm you, Captain,' Temperance said. 'It's just the three of us now, but Christopher and Ellie will be joining us for dinner, along with Gifford Newell.'

'And Papa…?' Pru asked.

'I wouldn't count on Vraux making an appearance,' their mother said drily. She hesitated, an uncertain look crossing her face before she walked over to give her newly returned daughter a hug.

Which, Temper was pleased to note, Pru not only tolerated, but returned with equal warmth. Perhaps her sister's time away had given her a new understanding and tolerance for their mother.

But then, radiant happiness did have the splendid effect of expanding to encompass everything around one.

Once her mother stepped back, Temper took her place. 'My turn! Welcome home, sister dear! How I've missed you!'

'And I, you,' Pru said, hugging her back fiercely.

'Oh, I don't know,' Temper said, stepping away. 'I think you've found a more than adequate replacement.'

She thought she'd accepted when she sent her sister off to Bath that the person who'd been closest to her in all the world would never fill that role again. But the ache in her chest at voicing that truth told her that, though her head might have recognised the fact, her heart was only now beginning to face it.

You'll always have me, Giff had told her. The memory both comforted…and disturbed her.

'I must go hunt down Lord Vraux,' Captain Trethwell was saying. 'As I mean to become a member of this family with all possible speed, I'll want his consent at once, so I may head off to Doctors' Commons and go about obtaining a special licence.'

'I'll take you up,' Gregory said. 'He's in his library, cataloguing. As usual.'

'Excellent,' the captain replied. 'I have a number of questions to ask him about his collections.'

Gregory shrugged. 'You may ask. I can't guarantee you'll get any answers.'

'While your fiancé confronts the dragon,' Temper said to her sister, 'why don't we have some tea? You can tell us all about your sojourn in Bath—before Aunt Gussie joins us and you have to censor your account.'

'Mama, shall we have tea sent to your sitting room?' Pru asked, looking at her mother with an affection Temper hadn't seen her display in years.

Nor had that lady either. Pru's request prompted a brilliant smile from Lady Vraux, tears glittering in the corners of her eyes as she nodded her assent.

'I should like that very much. Welcome home, my precious daughter.'

And so the three women walked up to Lady Vraux's boudoir, Pru still radiant with a happiness that caused a deep pang of melancholy—and foreboding—in Temper's breast. Not that she resented her sister's joy—indeed, she was thrilled that Pru had found the man, and the life, she wanted.

While Temper had no misgivings about the

character of the man she was to marry, she wasn't sure what she was getting herself into.

'Isn't he wonderful?' Pru said as they took their seats around their mother's divan.

'Certainly a handsome devil,' Lady Vraux said, giving her daughter a knowing smile. 'I shall have no worries about you sleeping well at night in your nuptial bed. At least, not for the part of it you sleep.'

'I am so looking forward to that,' Pru confirmed, a naughty twinkle in her eye. 'Stolen kisses on a riding trail are one thing—but to have the luxury of time and the comfort of a bed!'

Laughing, Temper covered her ears. 'No licentious details, please! But do tell us *everything* about your captain and how he convinced you he would be much better for you than that gentleman farmer you always said you wanted.'

And so, over tea, Pru explained how her attempts to be the perfect society maiden, undercut by the reputation that followed her to Bath, were eventually abandoned in the face of society's hypocrisy—and the realisation that her high-born, titled suitor was a much lesser man than the untitled adventurer who had freed her to be who she truly was. 'I even managed to create a scandal—and insult the most highly placed social arbiter in Bath!' she said with a laugh as she finished her tale. 'I discovered that I am much more like you than I imagined, Mama.'

Her humour fading, she took her mother's hand. 'Will you forgive me? I've been…awful to you, the last year or so.'

Lady Vraux shook her head. 'Nothing to forgive. Without having the least intention of doing so, I made the path difficult—for you and Temper. That you both will marry well and be happy is the best present each of you could ever give me.'

Pru's eyes widened. '*Both* marry well?' Whirling to face Temper, she said, 'What have you been keeping from me?'

'Nothing! The matter was only settled two days ago.' Temper forced a smile. 'You'll recall that before you left, I threatened to create a little scandal of my own? You weren't the only sister who managed it. Only I inadvertently dragged Giff into mine. As it…appeared he'd compromised me, he, of course, insisted on doing the honourable thing.'

'Now you must give *me* all the details,' her twin said.

Once she'd finished, though her sister exclaimed angrily over the duplicity of Miss Avery, she ended by saying, 'You know, Temper, I think Giff will make you an excellent husband. You know and trust him, and what's even more important, he knows and trusts you. He won't be expecting marriage to change you into a conventional, biddable wife who will be content with just managing his house and raising his children.'

Temper shifted uncomfortably, aware of her mother's thoughtful gaze fixed on her. 'He knows what he's getting, that's for certain. Though if it hadn't been for the scandal, I doubt he'd have offered for me. Aside from wealth, I'm hardly the sort of wife a rising politician would choose.'

'Why not?' Pru replied. 'You are lovely, intelligent and far more knowledgeable about what is going on in the country—and the world at large—than most of the women in society!'

'Thank you, loyal twin. But we both know I am also impatient with fools, far too apt to say whatever I'm thinking, and…and far too restless to remain in England. Though I won't make Giff much of a wife, he *is* probably the best husband for me—if I must have a husband. He's willing to let me travel, so I don't expect we'll spend a great deal of time together after the wedding. In fact,' she ended, brightening at the prospect, 'once I can work out the details of an entourage large enough to satisfy him about my safety, I can drag out of Papa the sort of objects and artefacts he wishes to acquire next and head off in search of them!'

Pru's smile dimmed. 'Oh. About that. I… I haven't yet told you what Johnnie means to do, now that he will be leaving the army.'

'And what will that be?' Lady Vraux asked.

'Use some of your dowry to buy you that horse farm in the country?'

'No. His aunt, Lady Woodlings, and some other backers have invested their funds in a trading company he will own and manage. Using the extensive contacts he's developed after his years in India, he plans to travel there and throughout the Orient and the Magreb, acquiring weapons, objets d'art and artefacts to sell to collectors like Papa. He planned to query Papa today about what he'd like him to look for.' She took a deep breath. 'And I intend to accompany him on his travels.'

While Temper sat frozen, trying to mask her shock and dismay, Lady Vraux laughed and clapped her hands. 'My little Prudence, who has always wanted to settle in some quiet English backwater, will travel the world? How wonderful!'

Prudence gave Temper a searching look, to which Temper hoped she returned a convincing smile. 'Amazing! How oddly our destinies have changed. You, the girl who never thought to leave England's shores, setting off with an adventurer, while I...marry a politician tied to London and Parliament.'

'I'm sorry, Temper,' Pru said softly. 'You'll still be able to travel, won't you? If you want to.'

'Of course I shall travel! Our match is a simple marriage of convenience—not a grand passion, like yours.'

Her mother reached over to touch her hand. 'I would wish a grand passion for you, too, my darling.'

'Oh, Mama, you know me. All the passion I possess is a quick temper,' she replied, trying to ignore the sick feeling in her belly. She'd planned now for years on exploring to fill her father's treasure chests. What would be her purpose now? And where would she go?

'You can always travel with us,' Pru offered.

Temper laughed. 'Not even the most charming and tolerant of gentlemen would be amenable to dragging his new sister-in-law along on his honeymoon! Never fear, I shall come up with…alternate plans. Now, shall we switch to the most important topic? What we shall all wear to the wedding!'

Though her mother gave her another searching glance, Temper was easily able to distract Prudence, whose thoughts never wandered far from her Johnnie, into a lengthy discussion of which styles, colours and fabrics would make her look most beautiful when he claimed her as his bride.

While distracting herself from her misgivings over what, exactly, her own future was going to be.

Less than a week later, Temper stood beside her sister outside the formal drawing room at Vraux

House, where the clergyman, the two bridegrooms and a small company of guests awaited them.

To the surprise of both sisters, their father had announced he would not only attend the nuptials, he intended to give the girls away. And to their amazement, as he met them outside the parlour, immaculately dressed in the formal dress coat he rarely wore, he looked both of them in the eye, murmured, 'As beautiful as your mama', and *kissed* each of them on the cheek.

If she hadn't already been so nervous about what she'd committed herself to do that she was scarcely aware of anything else, Temper might have fainted from the shock.

'You do look beautiful,' Pru murmured.

'We both do,' Temper replied, desperately anxious to get through the next few minutes, when she would be the focus of all eyes and must play the happy bride.

She was hoping her sister's obvious glow of joy, as shimmering as the golden gown she wore, would attract most of the guests' attention. Her own gown, in a style that matched her sister's, with its low, off-the-shoulder neckline, full, gathered sleeves and tiny waist, was in a turquoise-blue silk Mama said matched her eyes.

Then her father gave the footman a nod, he opened the door and they walked into the parlour.

Catching the besotted glance of giddy delight

that passed between Pru and Johnnie as she approached her bridegroom, Temper felt a stab of pure envy. Such bliss, such perfect contentment— and such promise of sensual fulfilment—would never be hers.

But at least she need not fear her bridegroom and could enter this marriage assured that Giff would abide by the terms they'd set. Even if the reality of a marriage of convenience hadn't turned out to be nearly as simple and straightforward as she'd blithely assumed when she'd first suggested one to Giff—was it only a few weeks ago?

In the interim, that inescapable, edgy attraction between them had intensified. She didn't worry that Giff would try to trick or force her into abandoning the restrictions of the *marriage blanc* she'd insisted upon.

But would she?

She sneaked a glance at him now, so tall, solemn—and handsome—as he stood beside the priest. Despite her nervousness, a ripple of desire eddied in her belly as she recalled the tenderness with which he'd kissed her after she'd accepted his proposal.

As the swirl of heated sensation rushed through her at the velvet-soft touch of his lips brushing hers, she'd had to force herself to remain immobile…lest she press herself against his heat and hardness, or pull his head down to extend the kiss.

Each time he touched her, arousing those volatile sensations, she was tempted to let down her guard and allow him to take her into a deeper intimacy—an intimacy she wasn't at all sure she could tolerate. Each time, once away from his disturbing presence, when she thought about allowing attraction to progress towards its natural end, the cold revulsion she kept locked away threatened to break through. No, she didn't dare risk it.

Then she was at Giff's side, his warm hand covering her cold one, sending another of those sensual shocks through her. The soft air, heated by the amassed candles and guest-filled room, wafted to her the scent of shaving soap and virile male.

She tried to ignore it, needing to muster all her scattered wits to focus on making the correct answers to the questions being posed by the priest, lest the guests notice how completely panic-stricken she was beneath an outward mask of calm. Or realise what a shocking contrast the two couples presented—one ecstatic, the other coolly reserved.

In another few minutes, she would become what she'd never expected to be—a wife. And now, too late, she wasn't at all sure that had been a wise idea.

Standing before the priest and the assembled guests, Giff envied his prospective new brother-in-law the sense of eager anticipation about his upcoming nuptials he'd displayed since the moment they'd been introduced at the welcome dinner at Vraux House a week ago.

Gazing now at the man's expression, his delight in the bride he was about to acquire patently obvious, Giff felt, like a cold rock in his stomach, the contrast between Trethwell's exuberant happiness and his own misgivings—which he could only hope he'd buried deep enough to conceal.

He'd tried to respond with appropriate enthusiasm when Trethwell had congratulated him at that dinner on winning the hand of Pru's sister. 'They are astoundingly similar, at least in looks,' he'd said. 'My Prudence is a bit softer and sweeter. Your Temperance, she tells me, is a firebrand!' Giving him a wink, he added, 'I hope you've been conserving your strength. If the twins are alike in every way, you're going to need every bit of your endurance for the honeymoon.'

He'd need to conserve his strength for the honeymoon, all right, he thought, suppressing a sigh. Enough strength to keep desire under tight control, once the beautiful woman now standing beside him, repeating the ancient words of the wedding ceremony, belonged to him completely, his to take with the full permission of the law and the church.

Just not with hers.

Before he knew it, the vows were completed,

the clergyman put away his prayer book and led the two couples off to an anteroom to sign the parish register.

He was married now. To Temperance Lattimar. The beguiling, bewitching, exasperating, unpredictable woman he desired, respected and never, except in some quickly repressed erotic daydream, ever expected to wed.

Once out of sight of the assembled guests, the smile she'd fixed on her face faltered, giving him a glimpse of anxiety, confusion—and surely it wasn't *fear* he read there!

His own misgivings instantly submerged by concern for her, once they'd affixed their signatures—Temper writing in a firm, quiet hand despite the turmoil he'd glimpsed in her eyes—he caught her arm, retaining her before she could follow the others back into the parlour.

'Let's take a moment before we rejoin the assembly,' he murmured.

She exhaled a shaky breath. 'Yes, let's. I need to…muster my composure.'

Tenderness, laced with a bit of amusement, tempered his concern. 'Temperance Lattimar, *discomposed*? I would never have believed it.'

'Well, I've never been married before, either,' she snapped back with more of her usual zest.

He lifted her chin so she had to look into her eyes. 'I may be your…husband now—and it takes me aback to say the word, too—but I'm still Giff, the man you've known since you pitched a rock at my head when you were six. You can still count on me to watch out for you. You can trust me to keep my promises.'

She stared into his eyes for a long moment before nodding. 'I know,' she whispered. 'But can I trust myself?'

Before Giff could wonder what she meant by that enigmatic utterance, Overton entered the anteroom. 'Mr Newell, a rider has just arrived with an urgent message for you. I've allowed him into the parlour with the guests, so he might deliver it immediately.'

'Of course. Temperance?'

As she took his arm to walk back to the parlour, Giff wondered what could have prompted someone to dispatch a rider to him with an urgent message. Not from Parliament—a runner on foot would have been sufficient for that. So it must be from Fensworth. Sent with speed and urgency, it couldn't be good news.

Though all his family had been in good health last he heard from them, disease could strike—and kill—with speed and suddenness. Setting his lips in a grim line, Giff approached the mud-spattered rider.

'You have a message for me?'

Engaged in gulping down a glass of punch, the

dispatch rider choked to a stop. 'Yes, sir,' he said, holding out the folded paper.

Breaking the seal, Giff scanned the document. The noise of the room, the conversation of the guests, even the concerned presence of Temper beside him, faded into the background as he read it through a second time.

'What is it, Giff?' Gregory asked, coming over to halt beside him. 'You've gone as white as that parchment!'

Giff looked up at his friend, the news so unbelievable, he still couldn't take it in. 'There's been an accident. My father and Robert have put every penny they could scrounge into building more steam engines to drain water from the lowest areas around the fens. Two— No,' he corrected, looking at the date on the letter, 'three days ago, Robert was driving them in his gig to inspect the latest project when one of the carriage wheels caught in the mud under the standing water from the previous day's rains. The horse panicked and bolted. The gig slammed through the railing at the top of a wooden bridge and went over, ending upside down in the stream below. Trapping Father and Robert.' He swallowed hard. 'They drowned. Both of them.'

'Oh, Giff, I'm so sorry,' Temper murmured, pressing his hand.

'This way, Gifford.' Through the roaring in his

ears, the eerie sense of unreality that suffused him, he heard Lady Sayleford's voice. 'Give them some room, please, ladies and gentlemen,' she continued, her hand on his arm as she led him out of the parlour.

'Brandy,' she ordered the butler who followed after them, before pushing Giff towards a sofa in a room he vaguely noted was the family's private back parlour. 'Sit here, catch your breath.'

'Admit the Lattimar brothers,' she told Overton as he returned from the sideboard with a brimming glass, 'but no one else. Temperance, help him with that.'

Temper put her hand up to reinforce Giff's trembling one, until the hot burn of the brandy down his throat steadied him.

Temper's brothers entered, their faces grave. 'Gregory told me what happened, Giff,' Christopher said. 'I'm so very sorry.'

'What can we do to help?' Temper asked, cradling his fingers around the whisky glass. 'You'll want to go to Fensworth as soon as possible.'

'Yes. I must prepare to leave at once. My mother…the solicitor says she was so distraught when they broke the news, they had to dose her with laudanum. She'll be devastated. She doted on Robert.'

'She has another, equally capable son,' Temper said stoutly.

He managed a grim smile. 'Not that she ever seemed aware of it.'

'She will be now,' Lady Sayleford said gently. 'You'll want your new wife to accompany you. Plan on taking my carriage for the first stage; you can arrange for post chaises for the rest.'

He nodded distractedly. 'Yes, I'll have Temper and her maid travel later, but I must ride now, so I can reach Fensworth as quickly as possible.' Turning to Christopher, he said, 'I'll send you my notes on the factory bill. Can you take over attending the hearings for me?'

'Of course. I'll send you reports, since we don't know how long you'll need to be...away.'

Gregory froze, his eyes widening. 'Hell and damnation—excuse me, ladies! Giff won't be coming back to Parliament, Christopher. At least, not to the House. Behold, before you, the new Earl—and Countess—of Fensworth!'

Chapter Seventeen

Returning late the next morning from a flurry of shopping for appropriate garments—the last time she'd lost a relation close enough to require the wearing of mourning having occurred when she was thirteen—Temper began directing her maid to organise and pack the few articles of clothing she currently possessed that were suitable to wear on the trip into Lincolnshire.

While she was engaged at that task, Overton came in to inform her that Lady Sayleford was awaiting her in the downstairs parlour.

Curious what Giff's godmother might require of her—and surprised the Dowager Countess had called on *her*, rather than sending her a note requesting that she present herself in Grosvenor Square—she quickly tucked back the stray strands of hair that had escaped her careless coiffure and hurried down to the parlour.

'Lady Sayleford,' she said, curtsying as she entered. 'What can I do for you? Would you like tea?'

'No tea, thank you. I came to see if there was anything I could do to assist your departure,' the Countess said, rising to return Temper's curtsy. 'Although you know,' she said as she resumed her seat, 'I should now curtsy first. You outrank me, the Fensworth Earldom predating the Sayleford honours by a century.'

Temper laughed ruefully. 'I'm afraid it's going to take some adjusting. Within a space of twenty-four hours, I've gone from being "Miss Lattimar" to "Mrs Newell" to "Countess of Fensworth". When the shopkeepers "miladyed" me this morning, I kept looking around to see which titled female had arrived.'

'How is Gifford doing?'

'Honestly, I don't know. I haven't seen much of him. After the guests left the reception yesterday, he went off with Gregory to expedite the transfer of my dowry funds to his bank, then back to his lodgings to pack up the rest of his things. Our decision to marry having been…accelerated by events, we'd not yet had time to decide where to set up our own household. Giff intended to stay here at Vraux House in the interim.'

'Not much of a wedding night,' Lady Sayleford observed.

'No,' Temper answered shortly, not about to reveal that the doors between their adjoining bed-chambers had remained closed.

'I'm glad that he'll be able to tap some funds immediately.' The Countess shook her head. 'Poor Gifford has been coping on a pittance for years. Now, suddenly, he'll have all the expense of managing an estate.'

'If the transition from commoner to countess was—disorienting—for me, it has to be so much worse for him. Saddled now with the responsibility for the care and upkeep of an inheritance he knows hardly anything about.'

'I never approved of how his parents focused all their attention on his brother, virtually ignoring my godson. He should have been taught about the estate from childhood. After all, with his brother having not yet married and produced another heir, Gifford was next in line. His father shouldn't have left him in ignorance about how things stood.'

'It never seemed to me that either parent valued him as they ought.'

'No. It's going to be a difficult adjustment for him, taking up duties for which he has been given no adequate preparation. Having those new duties compel him to leave London at such a crucial moment, with the factory bill he's been working so hard for soon to come to a vote. Then, once he can return, having to find his place among an entirely different set of political associates in the Lords.'

She paused. 'He will need help and support, my dear. Which makes me thankful that he managed to wed you before this happened.'

Temper gave a rueful laugh. 'I shall do everything I can to lighten his burden, certainly. But I can't help thinking that if he had become the Earl of Fensworth before the...contretemps with Miss Avery...he would have been so besieged by matchmaking mamas and eager maidens of quality, he would have ended up marrying a woman much better suited to becoming a politician's wife and a countess than I am.'

'I'm not so sure about that, my dear,' Lady Sayleford said with a smile. 'Gifford would look for more than just "suitable" qualities in a wife. So I hope you will be...gentle with him. He's in love with you, you know.'

'In love with—!' Temper echoed, astounded. 'Lady Sayleford, I am certain you are mistaken! He still sees me as the troublesome little sister of his best friend. A madcap whose disreputable exploits dragged him into a situation that, according to his overly fine sense of honour, could only be resolved by marriage.'

'You are a bit too prone to act or speak before you think,' Lady Sayleford acknowledged. 'But you also possess courage, intelligence, compassion and a fierce independence, traits that will endure and will make you a valuable wife and a worthy countess. And I assure you, though of course he hasn't realised it yet, Gifford does, in fact, love you. Why else would he have gone to so much trouble to ensure you had a Season? Or have kept so close a watch over you? Or so quickly decided that the only answer to Miss Avery's treachery was to marry you at once?'

Chuckling softly, she shook her head. 'So I repeat, be gentle with Gifford. He is worthy of your loyalty and your deepest consideration. Now,' she said, rising, 'I'll return you to your packing. My coachman is prepared to leave as soon as you are ready.'

Still flabbergasted, Temper rose as well. 'Remember,' Lady Sayleford said, pressing her hand as she walked out. 'The key to your happiness— and his—lies in your own hands. And I must say, I've never sponsored a more entertaining debut.'

Scarcely knowing what to reply to those parting words, Temper merely curtsied as the Countess made her departure. Sinking back on to the sofa, she stared into the distance, trying to wrap her mind around what she'd just been told.

Gifford Newell—no, the Earl of Fensworth— was *in love* with her? She simply couldn't credit it. She knew he desired her. She was pretty sure he *liked* her and she was certain that she amused and entertained him. But…love her?

If anyone other than Lady Sayleford had uttered such nonsense, she would have laughed in her face. But…the omnipotent *Lady Sayleford*, who knew everything about everyone?

Still, Gifford Newell was her godson. Perhaps her fondness for him had skewed her perceptions.

But what if she was right…if Giff truly had fallen in love with her…? Even though he didn't know it yet?

Putting her hands to her aching temples, Temper shook her head. She wouldn't, couldn't think about that possibility now. She was still struggling to comprehend all the implications of going in a few short hours from a maid to a politician's wife to the wife of a peer.

Whatever else he was or might be, Gifford had been first and foremost her friend. A friend who had been saddled with a heavy burden he'd not been trained to handle, had had the new calling he'd come to love snatched away from him and was dealing with the shock of losing almost his entire family in one blow.

Her first task, as both wife and friend, was to help him weather those catastrophes.

The question of love, and what she was going to do about the ever-increasing pull of passion between them, would have to wait.

A week later, after several days travelling in a series of jolting hired vehicles, Temper's carriage halted in front of Fensworth House. With a solid central block flanked by two wings, all constructed of Elizabethan brick, it had a timeless quality...though the grey skies reflected in the thousand panes of the mullioned glass windows gave it a look of fatigue and sadness, too.

Small wonder, when it had lost both master and heir at a blow.

Wondering where the new master might be, Temper let the post boy hand her down and walked up the entry steps, her maid trailing behind.

She had to knock twice before the door was answered—by what looked to be a housemaid. Who froze, gazing awestruck at Temper's fashionable cloak and bonnet, before hurriedly dropping a curtsy. 'Can I help you, ma'am?'

With the butler nowhere in sight, Temper concluded that Fensworth didn't often receive callers. 'I'm... Lady Fensworth,' she said, still finding it hard to identify herself by that name. 'Is Lord Fensworth at home?'

Her eyes widening, the girl took a step back. 'Oh!' she breathed, once again staring at Temper. 'You be the wild beauty Master Gifford up and married!'

So that was the staff's assessment of the younger son's bride. Suppressing a wry smile at that frank assessment, Temper realised that her first job would be to demonstrate to the staff that, however wild a bride they might think her, she meant to be the unquestioned mistress of the house.

A quick gaze around the hall solidified that intention. Knowing that the estate had been purse-pinched for years, she'd expected the furnishings might be somewhat shabby and they were—the aged window hangings needed replacing, the carpet was worn and the furniture dated from the last century. But poverty was no excuse for the layer of dust sitting atop the mahogany hall table, or the grit she felt under the soles of her travelling boots.

Either Giff's mother had been too absorbed in her own concerns to bother about housekeeping—or the staff thought the 'wild beauty' who had unexpectedly become their mistress would be too ignorant to properly run a household.

Before she could decide how to proceed, a tall, stooped man in the garb of a butler approached from a door opening on to one of the wings. 'You may go, Maisie,' he said to the maid, who bobbed another curtsy and scurried off.

Turning to Temper, he bowed. 'You must be the new Lady Fensworth. Welcome to Fensworth House, your ladyship. I'm Mixton, the butler.'

'Thank you, Mixton. Is his lordship at home now?'

'No, your ladyship. He and the steward left early this morning to inspect the northern fields.

He is usually gone most of the day, sometimes not returning until late evening, but I'll send a groom out to let his lordship know you're here.'

'Thank you—but tell him he need not change his plans. I'll see him whenever he gets home. Now, if you'd have a footman bring up my luggage and send a maid up with hot water, I'd like to be shown to my rooms and settle in. And I'd like you to send the housekeeper up to see me.'

'Of course, your ladyship. Had we known the time of your arrival, I should have mustered all of the staff to welcome you.'

'I'm sure you would have. But the circumstances have been…most unusual, haven't they? Please convey my sincere regrets to the whole staff on your loss. It must have been devastating for all of you.'

A wave of sadness briefly creased the butler's impassive countenance. 'It was…difficult. The late Earl was a good master, and we shall all miss him. Miss them both.'

Especially since they were now saddled with a mistress about whom they knew nothing and a master they knew scarcely any better.

Which, however, was certainly not Giff's fault.

'You will find your new master to be a fine, capable, compassionate man, as well,' she said. 'How is the Dowager Countess?'

'Still laid up in her rooms, your ladyship.'

'Then you needn't notify her of my arrival. I shall have my husband introduce us when it is convenient for them both.'

'Very good. This way, your ladyship.'

Following the butler up the stairs, Temper noted that the head male servant, at least, seemed to know his job. Glancing around at the state of the stairs and the dusty hall furniture she passed on the way to her room, she wasn't sure about the housekeeper.

Her suspicions deepened after she'd been shown into a spacious bedchamber—whose dusty curtains were drawn, whose bed linens had obviously not been aired and which boasted an equally dusty hearth on which no fire had been laid.

The staff might not have known exactly when she would arrive, but there was no excuse for not having properly prepared a room for her. Temper frowned, girding herself for the confrontation to come.

The housekeeper was either too old to do her job properly, incompetent—or perhaps so loyal to Giff's mother, she fiercely resented her replacement? Or thought, with her former mistress prostrate with grief and the new mistress a 'wild beauty' with no knowledge of how to properly run a house, she might get away with neglecting her duties?

Whatever the cause, the slovenly condition of

the house must be rectified immediately. Giff had enough worries to deal with. At the very least, he deserved to return to a home that was clean, warmed and welcoming.

Half an hour later, a stout middle-aged woman knocked at her door. 'I'm Mrs Hobbs, the house-keeper, your ladyship,' she said, curtsying.

'Good day, Mrs Hobbs. First, let me extend condolences on your loss. I imagine the entire household has been at sixes and sevens, and I do sympathise. However, I must tell you candidly that what I have seen of the house thus far has been… disappointing. I may be young, but I assure you, I have been thoroughly trained in how to maintain a gentleman's establishment. And Fensworth is not just a gentleman's establishment—it is the home of an earl! There is no excuse for the state of neglect I have observed.'

The woman's face paled, then reddened. 'We… We've never had funds enough to properly staff—'

'Funding will be no problem now. Send to the village for extra staff, if you must. But before my husband returns today, I expect all the floors in the public areas to have been swept, all the furniture dusted and polished, and a fire laid in any room his lordship might be expected to occupy. By the end of the week, I expect every room in the house to have been thoroughly cleaned, the linens aired and pressed, the window hangings taken down and brushed, and all the windows themselves washed. I will add any additional requirements I notice when you give me a tour of the house. What have you planned to serve his lordship for dinner tonight?'

'We— Cook doesn't prepare a formal meal. As his lordship usually comes in so late, we just send up a tray of cold meats and cheeses.'

Incensed that they would treat Giff so shabbily, Temper shook her head. Obviously, his mother's slighting assessment of her younger son had been communicated—openly or subtly—to the staff. Temper meant to ensure that evaluation was changed forthwith.

'Henceforth,' she said in icy tones, pinning the woman with a glare, 'you will ensure that the cook prepares the Earl *of Fensworth* a proper meal every evening and have it ready to be served in the dining room. If he chooses to have a tray in his room, that will be his lordship's decision.'

'Y-yes, your ladyship,' the woman stuttered.

'My husband may not have been brought up to be the Earl—but Earl he is. I expect him to be served, and his home to be run, in a manner befitting his rank. If you and your staff are not capable of meeting that standard, I shall find staff who can. I trust I've made myself clear?'

'Y-yes, your ladyship,' Mrs Hobbs stammered again.

'Good. Later this afternoon, after I've rested, I would like that tour of the house. Also a list of the menus Cook proposes to serve for the next week. You may go now.'

Curtsying, the housekeeper turned and fled.

Temper went over to the window to pull open the curtains, coughing at the cloud of dust disturbed by their movement. At least the window had a pleasant view over the park. Sighing, she sank down on the sofa.

She might have made an enemy of the housekeeper, but there was no remedy for it. The woman needed to know that Temper was taking the reins and would hold them in a firm grip. If Mrs Hobbs resented the 'outsiders' who had arrived to take over from her beloved master and his heir, she would either get over it, or be replaced.

Besides, dealing with one recalcitrant English housekeeper would be good training for managing the coterie of foreign servants Giff would insist were necessary to protect her, once she began her foreign travels.

Chapter Eighteen

A few hours later, after recording on some stationary she'd found in the library desk the additional items she'd noted during her tour by the housekeeper earlier that afternoon, Temper set the list aside.

Fortunately, it appeared that, for the most part, Fensworth House was in sound condition. There wouldn't be a need for extensive repairs or renovations, and the furnishings, though outdated, were of a superior quality that would reveal itself after they'd been properly cleaned and polished.

To her surprise, once they completed the tour and Temper had gone over a summary of what needed to be done, Mrs Hobbs, who had been wooden-faced throughout the inspection, made her a deep curtsy—and thanked her!

'The Dowager was never much interested in Fensworth, your ladyship,' she confessed. 'We all knew she'd rather be in London. So I'm afraid…

standards slipped. It will be a right pleasure to have the staff and funds to bring this old house back to what it should be.'

So it appeared she would not have to waste time wrangling with the housekeeper—or trying to replace her, Temper thought gratefully.

As she put away her pen, she heard a stirring at the doorway. Looking up, to her surprise, she saw her new husband striding into the library.

'Giff!' she said delightedly, genuinely glad to see him despite the disturbing sensual response he aroused, just by walking into the room. 'I didn't expect you to return this early. Mixton said you're usually out quite late.'

'I couldn't stay away and let servants welcome you to your new home,' he said, coming over to her, arms outstretched—before he lowered them and halted awkwardly a pace away. 'I'm so glad you're here,' he said simply.

Scanning his face, she thought with a shock that she'd never seen Giff so drawn and weary. 'You look so tired and thin!' she exclaimed, her heart flooded with such sadness and compassion for him that, abandoning the restraint she'd promised herself to exercise, she rose and walked into his arms.

As he hugged her tightly, she could almost feel his body vibrate with grief and sadness and a tension she understood only too well—a sense of being pulled out of his familiar world into a place and duties almost as foreign to him as it was to her. For long moments, she let him hold her, hoping to transfer to him her warmth, support and affection.

Finally, he let her go. 'I should go up and change. I'm still smelling of horse, although at least my boots aren't muddy this time. And you've already begun setting things to rights, I see. Such a flurry of sweeping and polishing and cleaning I passed as I walked in! I suppose Mama has been too…cast down to look after things and I've been so preoccupied with the estate, I simply haven't had time to deal with the house.'

'That, dear sir, is why you have a wife. Mama might have been infamous among the *ton*, but she was a capital housekeeper and she taught Pru and me well.'

'It will be a relief to come home and not find everything dark and grimy,' he confessed. 'Have you ordered dinner as well? Meals have been… haphazard of late.'

'You shall have a proper dinner tonight! And every night hereafter. Shall we invite your mama to share it?'

'I doubt she'll leave her room, but we shall ask her. Once I've washed and changed, I'll take you in to meet her.'

Temper blew out a breath. 'Oh, dear. I can only

imagine what her friends in London have told her about me. About us.'

'She knows all about the scandal, that's for sure. Amid the flood of weeping that began the moment I walked in, the only thing she said was that she hoped I wouldn't create here any scandals as tawdry as the one in London.'

Though Giff gave her a rueful smile, she could tell by the hurt in his eyes how much that comment had stung. Furious on his behalf, she had a hard time restraining the acid comment that jumped to her lips. 'I allow your mother a great deal of latitude, given her loss,' she said after a moment, 'but even so, that was…unkind.'

'Probably, but about what I expected. The prodigal son come home to displace her beloved Robert? I couldn't hope to be greeted with open arms.' He sighed. 'I don't mind, really. I'm used to it by now. All I shall insist upon is that she treat you with respect.'

Oh, he minds, she thought, holding on to her temper with an effort. How could a mother be so oblivious to the worth of her son? Well, that was another thing Temper was determined to change.

'It's not your fault you had to replace her "beloved Robert",' Temper retorted. 'And if she and your father hadn't been so…short-sighted, you would have been far better prepared to step into his shoes. But enough of that. We shall have a good dinner, and I will do my best to amuse you.'

That drew a genuine smile. 'I could use some amusement. Although I'm not so sure how good the dinner will be.'

'It had better be excellent, or we'll be looking for a new cook.'

He chuckled. 'My little termagant. Have I told you yet how glad I am you are here?'

'You have,' she said, smiling at him fondly. 'We'll see if your "wild bride" can stir things up at Fensworth as effectively as she did in London. Let me change for dinner and then I'll be ready to meet your redoubtable mother.'

Giff tapped her nose with his finger. 'I'll see you shortly, then.'

Watching him walk out, Temper frowned. If the Dowager Countess thought grief over her losses would allow her to get away with abusing Giff any further, she was about to discover otherwise. And probably get an earful of plain speaking into the bargain.

A short time later, Giff walked Temper upstairs to his mother's rooms. 'She still occupies what should be the Countess's suite. I hadn't the heart to insist she vacate the rooms.'

'Are you occupying the Earl's suite?' she asked,

more than a little nervous to know exactly where Giff intended to sleep.

'No, I've gone back to my old room—just down the hall from the one you have. Which is the prettiest of the guest bedchambers.'

Relieved to know he didn't sleep in a room adjacent to her own, she nodded. 'There will be time enough to change the living arrangements.'

Giff sighed. 'Yes. That's one battle I didn't want to have to fight yet.' Pausing before an imposing chamber door located at the centre of the bedchamber wing, he said, 'This is it. Are you ready?'

Her anger over his mother's shabby treatment of him still smouldering, Temper gave him an encouraging smile. 'Remember, you married a hoyden who possesses not a particle of conventional maidenly deference and lets no one intimidate her. I shall have no trouble dealing with your mama.'

He smiled down at her. 'I don't suppose you will. And for the first time, if I had to wager on the outcome, I wouldn't bet on my mother keeping the upper hand.'

They entered a room with shuttered windows and a mantel draped in black. As her eyes adjusted to the dimness, Temper made out the figure of a woman reclining against the pillows of a massive four-poster bed, a handkerchief clutched in her hand as she stared sightlessly ahead of her.

No matter how much Temper resented the woman for her treatment of Giff, she had to admit the Dowager had good cause to grieve.

'We won't disturb you for long, Mama,' Giff said, walking with Temper to his mother's bedside. 'But I wanted to present to you my wife, who arrived this afternoon from London. Mama, this is Temperance.'

The Dowager glanced over, her faintly contemptuous gaze looking Temper up and down. 'So you're Felicia's daughter. You certainly have the look of her. And her propensity for scandal, apparently. If only Gifford had used his time in London more profitably.'

Squeezing Giff's hand to forestall his reply, Temper said pleasantly, 'Scandals have a way of being magnified out of all proportion. And Gifford has used his time in London most profitably, indeed. As I'm sure you know, he's a leading member of the group of Parliamentarians who are forging legislation that will make the most significant changes in the way the country has been governed since the Magna Carta. He's now turning that same intensity and attention to detail to mastering the requirements of managing Fensworth— after having received very little preparation for the task! You must be very proud of his achievements. I know Lady Sayleford is and so am I.'

The Dowager regarded Temper with some hostility. 'Impertinent chit, aren't you?'

'Forthright, certainly. I know you aren't feeling yourself yet, but we did want you to know we'd be delighted if you could join us for dinner.'

'Join you for—!' the Countess exclaimed, her eyes widening. 'I am by no means ready yet to leave my rooms!'

'I am sorry to hear it. You must let me know if there is anything I or the staff can do to make you more comfortable,' Temper replied.

'So eager to wrest control from my hands?' she said bitterly.

'Not at all, Countess. Only doing what must be done. We won't intrude upon you any further now, but I hope to visit you again soon.'

As the Dowager made no response to that, Temper dipped her a curtsy. 'Goodnight, Lady Fensworth.'

She could feel the anger vibrating in Giff as she took his arm. But he merely inclined his head and said, 'Goodnight, Mama.'

Giff blew out a breath as they walked back down the stairs. 'That didn't go too badly, I suppose. Though I wish you had let me tell her in no uncertain terms that I will not allow her to insult you.' Then he laughed. 'Not that she was able to intimidate you one little bit. Bravo, Temper!'

She chuckled. 'That was just the first round. I do sympathise with her loss, but whether your mama likes it or not, you are master here now. Sooner or later she will have to acknowledge that. Or maybe not,' Temper added thoughtfully, an alternative solution suddenly occurring to her.

'Enough about my mother,' Giff said as they walked into the dining room. 'Ah, what a delicious aroma! I'm ready to tuck into the best dinner that's been served me since I left London.'

'I certainly hope so,' Temper said as he held out the chair for her.

'Thank you again, Temper,' he said as he took his own seat. 'I'm sure the meal will taste as delicious as it smells. After dinner, though, I'm afraid I must study the estate books and then look over some agricultural journals I had sent out from London. Will you be too disappointed if I abandon you? I expect you are tired after your journey and will be longing for your bed. You...you needn't lock your bedchamber door. I intend to honour all the promises I made you.'

Her greatest worry alleviated—for the moment—Temper felt a swell of relief and gratitude. 'Thank *you*, Giff. I am tired. You don't need to entertain me, you know. Concentrate on your duties. And if there is anything I can do to help, please tell me.'

'You're already making a difference,' he said,

motioning towards the gleaming silver, shining crystal and the array of dishes being brought in by the footmen. 'How could I ask you for anything more?'

So he wouldn't be asking for...that, Temper thought, unease stirring in her belly. In spite of this temporary reprieve, with her new husband no longer simply 'Mr Newell' but now 'the Earl of Fensworth', the terms of their marriage would inevitably have to change.

How much of a respite would she get before she must steel herself to perform *that* duty?

Deciding there was no time like the present to settle matters with the Dowager—who, if left to her own devices, would probably immure herself in her rooms in deepest mourning for years—after bidding Giff goodnight, Temper went up to knock on the door of the Countess's suite.

The door was answered by a dour-faced maid. Not waiting to give the Dowager time to refuse her, Temper walked past the woman and over to the bed.

Looking startled, Lady Fensworth turned to Temper and frowned. 'What are you doing here?'

'I wanted to see if there was anything I could bring you before I retire,' she said pleasantly.

'You could return me to my solitude.'

'And so I shall. Once we...understand each other a bit better.'

'Understand each other?' the Dowager repeated. 'All you need to understand is—'

'I imagine your London friends keep you updated on the latest gossip,' Temper broke in.

Exhaling an exasperated sigh, Lady Fensworth said, 'Of what interest to me is idle gossip?'

Declining to answer that comment, Temper said, 'You might want to leaven whatever you've heard about me—or my marriage to your son—with the knowledge that Lady Sayleford agreed to sponsor my debut, supported both of us through the fiasco at Lady's Arnold ball—I'm sure you've heard both sides of that story—and was present at our wedding. She loaned her own carriage and staff to bring me here. So I would weigh any... negative assessments of my character against the fact of her steadfast support and her blessing on our marriage.'

'Well, Gifford is her godchild. She would be bound to support him.'

'There isn't another high-ranking lady of the *ton* who knows more about what goes on in society than Lady Sayleford. You would agree?'

The Dowager nodded reluctantly.

'And Lady Sayleford has never given her backing to anyone who does not meet her exacting standards—has she?'

Lady Fensworth remained silent for a moment. 'Not to my knowledge,' she allowed at last.

'Exactly. In any event, what you think of me isn't of great concern. But I would ask you to remember that although Gifford wasn't your favoured son, he *is* still your son. The staff need to know that you support, rather than resent, his becoming the Earl. As head of this household, they take their cues from you.'

'That boy has been nothing but trouble since he was born!' she burst out. 'The birth itself was… difficult. I was recovering for months and, after that… I was never able to bear another child. Four babies I lost before their time, three precious daughters and another beautiful son.'

Shocked, Temper sat in silence. So that explained the Countess's animosity, she thought, compassion welling up for the woman. Her heartache and resentment of Giff were as deep as they were unreasonable.

'I've never lost a child,' Temper said softly. 'I can't imagine such devastation. But surely you recognise that it wasn't Gifford's fault?'

The Countess sighed. 'I suppose I do…in my head. But every time I looked at him as he was growing up, all I saw was the faces of those little dead babes.'

'Which is why you sent him away to school and

left him there. Why it's so difficult for you to accept him here, now.'

'He represents everything that has been taken from me!' she cried. 'First the babies and now my beloved husband and s-son!'

'It must be hard,' Temper acknowledged, trying to summon up as much sympathy as she could—a difficult task, since this woman had cheated Giff out of the mother's love that should be a child's birthright, for tragedies over which he'd had no control. 'Giff tells me you love London. Your son may have married a woman your informers claimed is "infamous", but she is also very wealthy. If it is too painful for you to watch someone else take Robert's place, why don't you lease a house in London? Live there for as much of the year as you wish, visit friends, go to the theatre, shop for whatever you like. It may help to ease your grief, if you don't have to wake up every morning here, immediately remembering they are gone and feeling again that crushing loss.'

For a long time, the Countess remained silent. 'There might be something to what you propose,' she said at last. 'I do love London. Not that I could even contemplate going to balls or entertainments or the theatre.'

'Not yet, of course. But you would have friends to call on you and invite you to quiet dinners, walks or drives in the park, shopping and all the resources of a great city. Distractions only from your grief, I grant. But distractions have their uses.'

Lady Fensworth turned her head to gaze at Temper. 'Lady Sayleford approved of you, did she? Perhaps… I am beginning to see why. Very well, I will…consider what you've proposed.'

'That's all I ask. And now I will leave you in peace.'

Temper walked out, closing the door softly behind her, her heart grieving for the tragedies that had ruined an innocent little boy's youth and robbed his mother of loving a son who was so deserving of it.

Maybe, if the Dowager were able to get away and clear her mind, she would find it in her heart to love Giff now.

At the very least, Temper hoped she would take herself off where her contemptuous indifference wouldn't continue to unfairly wound the man Temper cared about so deeply.

Chapter Nineteen

Two weeks later, the bone-weary new Earl of Fensworth turned his spent horse over to a groom and walked back towards Fensworth House. The day he'd stood in the parlour in Vraux House and discovered that tragedy had overtaken his family seemed a lifetime ago, he thought as he trudged towards the entry. His only worry then, how to continue with his life and work with as little disturbance as possible after having taken an irresistible bride he must none the less resist. He laughed without humour. How much simpler life had been!

The last weeks had been a never-ending blur of packing, travelling, consultations with bankers, solicitors, estate agents, farm managers, housekeepers, tenants and the doctors who tended his still-ailing mother.

The one, unexpected bright spot in the long dark agony had been Temper. His new wife had proved herself tireless, industrious and surprisingly capable in doing all she could to assist him. Fortunately, by the time he took to his bed in the wee hours, he was so exhausted both mentally and physically that he fell asleep before he could be tempted by the knowledge that his beautiful wife reposed in a chamber just a short walk down the hall.

As he gradually gained mastery of the thousand estate details he had to learn, the merciful boon of those long hours of work would disappear. But for now, with everything else he had to deal with, he was heartily grateful not to have to wrestle with restraining his desire for her.

And then his heart leapt, pulling him from his tired reflections, as he spotted Temper approaching down the drive.

'Here,' she said, holding out a welcome mug of ale as she reached him. Craning her neck towards the stables, she continued, 'I hope the groom has something equally reviving for your horse, or I may have to charge you with animal neglect. The poor nag looks done up.'

'Yes, I told Hoarly to give him an extra ration. We rode the entire southern border today and, though the river level has gone down somewhat, it's pretty heavy going, with the sucking mud of the verges and the pools of standing water. I'd take you there, but the riding is still dangerous.'

'The two failed steam pumps haven't been repaired yet?'

The ones his father and brother had been going to investigate the morning they drowned. 'Not yet. After inspecting them, I agreed with Randolph that we should reinstall the windmill devices on top, so we may get some pumping use from them until we can bring in some steam mechanics from Lincoln. Our local wheelwright, wainwright, farrier and blacksmith have all had a go, trying to fix them, with no luck.'

'You trust Randolph's advice?'

He took a swig of ale before responding. 'I guess I have to. He's been the estate agent here for twenty years and certainly knows the place far better than I do. I've not really lived here since I was sent away to school at age six.'

He brushed away the memory, still hurtful after all these years, that after a modicum of education at Eton, his elder brother had been summoned back home to be tutored by clerics, his father considering the education of his heir in the running of his estate more important than a stint at university. Even more important, Giff knew, he'd wanted his eldest son with him.

Unlike the second son, who languished alone at school, unless a classmate like Gregory invited him home for holidays and term breaks.

He resurfaced from those bitter memories to

find Temper gazing at him. 'You are intelligent, grasp things quickly and have a strong sense of responsibility,' she said, gripping his hand. 'You will master the details you need to run the estate. You've already made a splendid beginning.'

He clutched her fingers, savouring the contact, inhaling the lovely spicy scent of her. 'I appreciate the encouragement.' He laughed ruefully. 'So many of the staff have been...sceptical of my abilities.'

'How could they not be, when you weren't brought up to run this place and have spent so much of your life away that they don't really know you? Once they see what a splendid job you are doing, they will come to admire and rely on you, as they did on your father and brother.'

'I certainly hope so.'

'I know so,' she said, gently withdrawing her fingers. 'Now that you're back, are you feeling the same attachment to Fensworth that your brother and father had?'

'I never felt it as a boy—I suppose I resented too much being excluded. But it does grow on you, this sense of the land. Even more, the responsibility of knowing that how well you manage it will impact the lives of nearly a hundred souls. Though I still intend to continue my work in Parliament, I will spend much more time here in future than I have in recent years.'

'As the master, you must. Now, if Randolph is so competent, why hasn't he had the estate employ a mechanic who knows how to rebuild and maintain the steam engines? You have, what, fifteen of these pumping machines to prevent flooding and keep the fields dry and arable?'

'Oh, the usual answer—money. Not enough to hire permanent staff, Randolph said when I asked him.'

If the draining had been completed and successfully maintained, the tragedy that took his kinsmen's lives might have been avoided. And he would be back in Parliament, listening to testimony, crafting legislation, engaged in spirited discussions about things he knew well and about which he cared passionately—rather than in this remote area near the Wash, struggling to deal with agricultural issues about which he knew so little.

'Well, money will no longer be a problem, will it? I saw several pretty little cottages when I walked the perimeter of the high ground yesterday. With steady work and a nice thatched house, you might be able to lure one of the Lincoln mechanics to remain at Fensworth.'

'A good suggestion,' he said, once again grateful for the no-nonsense, practical advice she continued to dispense. 'How wise I was to marry a rich woman.'

She chuckled. 'Well, at least you derived one benefit from wedding a hoyden.'

As he looked down at her dancing eyes and lovely face, despite his fatigue, the repressed desire came flooding back. Along with an unexpectedly strong surge of tenderness.

With his free hand, he caught hers again and brought it to his lips. 'I've received more benefits than I can count. For which I am more grateful than I can express.'

Sadness shadowed her eyes. 'Nothing can make up for the loss of your family. Whatever assistance I can offer, you know I'm happy to give.'

'And how useful it has been! Whipping the negligent housekeeper into shape, co-ordinating with the vicar to plan the funerals, organising the staff to receive condolences from the neighbours, keeping my mother supplied with doctors to tend her—even hiring your own post chaises to travel here, while I selfishly rode all the way from London.'

'Burdened with such worry and grief, I couldn't have stood being cooped up in a carriage either,' she said.

Although it wasn't just grief and worry that had compelled him to ride the long miles into Lincolnshire alone. With his emotions raw—grief, frustration at having to leave Parliament with his work undone, deep misgivings about the unknown duties awaiting him at Fensworth—and his strength at a low ebb, he wasn't sure he could have travelled for days with Temper in a closed carriage and still managed to resist his desire for her.

Just as he now worked himself to exhaustion, to make sure temptation didn't overwhelm him some lonely evening.

'No worried frowns,' she said, making him sigh as she smoothed her fingers along his forehead. 'See what a very capable explorer I shall make?'

'Capable indeed,' he had to admit, stifling a pang of protest. He didn't *want* her to head off for parts unknown.

How quickly he'd grown accustomed to seeing her every day, to relying on the assistance she offered in a calm, capable manner he wouldn't have previously believed possible for impetuous Temperance Lattimar.

The impulsive child truly had grown into a competent manager, as well as desirable woman. And unlike his mother, who required the ministrations of various maids and dressers and a series of social engagements to keep her entertained, since their arrival, Temper had required almost no attention from him.

She cared for herself with the minimum help from a single maid. Rather than remain indoors to be waited on by the household staff when he was gone for long hours, riding about the estate, she rode out herself in all weathers to bring him a basket of meat and ale. When he did remain at the manor, occupied with the estate books, being tutored by Randolph about seeds, planting, crop rotation and harvests, or reading about the myriad agricultural topics of which he knew so little, not once had she interrupted him, demanding that he curtail his work to devote some time to her.

In the odd moments he'd found himself free and gone in search of her, he'd found her reading in the library. Or riding out, always with a groom he insisted accompany her—an impediment he'd worried the impatient Temper might try to evade. To which, at his apology for curtailing the speed at which he knew she preferred to ride, she'd replied simply, 'With all you have on your plate, you don't need to worry about me falling into a canal or being thrown into the mud.'

He didn't have much experience with women— other than with demi-reps in the bedroom—but he guessed that such independent self-reliance was rare among females.

He knew his mother had never exhibited a trace of it.

The more he was with her, the more she impressed him. And the stronger grew the feeling that he didn't want her to leave and trek about the world for months at a time, without him.

'I hope you're not meaning to desert me for some exotic place quite yet,' he replied at last.

'Of course not! I won't leave Fensworth until you feel you have a firm handle on the duties you must perform here. Even after I return to London, it will be some time before I'm ready to travel.' She gave him a smile that didn't quite succeed. 'With Prudence and her soldier having taken over the mission that was to have framed my explorations, I must first decide where—and how—I wish to travel. And then there will be all that entourage-building you're so concerned about.'

'I've almost finished the essentials of what I need to do for the estate. Once the last pumps are working again, nothing else requires immediate attention. The crops are in, all the repairs and supplies needed by the tenants are being addressed and the household supplies not provided locally have been ordered from Lincoln or London.'

'You intend to go back to London soon, then?' she asked, looking surprised.

'Yes. In the last day or so, when I finally had enough time to think about something other than estate business, I realised that, though everyone has been addressing me as Earl, I don't legally hold that title yet. I won't until the Committee on Privileges reviews the documentation proving I am the legal heir and issues a writ of summons to the Lords. A process I expect will take some time. Until then, I'm plain Mr Newell and can legally remain in the House of Commons. If the summons is delayed long enough, I might actually see the factory bill to passage before I have to give up my seat and move to the Lords.'

'How satisfying that would be to see it through!' she exclaimed, looking delighted for him.

'The most satisfying thought I've had since I read that courier's message in London, another lifetime ago. Now,' he said, holding open for her the side door they'd just reached, 'I must go up and bathe before I drip mud all over the floors you just made the housekeeper polish. I think I can spare the time tonight to join you for dinner, if you'd like.'

'I would like that! Besides…' her smile faded and she looked suddenly…nervous and uncertain '…I, too, have something I've been putting off, that we really need to discuss.'

'That sounds ominous,' he said, watching her expression with concern.

She sighed. ''I know. I'll see you at dinner.'

Whatever it was she wished to talk about, Temperance did not bring up anything serious at dinner. Instead, fortified by a bottle of his father's best claret she'd had the butler bring up from the cellars, she kept him chatting with a series of questions about the myriad details he'd been learning about the estate.

After dining, with Giff declining to remain and

consume his port in solitary splendour, he accompanied Temper into the small sitting room, where a snug fire burned on the hearth.

He poured himself a glass of spirits and joined her on the sofa.

'I've been so busy, I've not had time to introduce you to the rest of the families in the county. When we return next, we'll need to give a ball, so everyone can meet the new Countess.'

Temper laughed and shook her head. 'Me—a countess!'

'No more incredible than me becoming the Earl. Who would have thought it?' He sighed. 'Certainly not my mother.'

'Is she feeling any better? I've had the doctor summoned whenever she calls for him and send in whatever her maid says she requires, but I haven't forced my company on her.'

'I looked in on her briefly tonight.' He gave a short laugh. 'She even seemed...rather happy to see me, although that would be such a novel occurrence, I might just have imagined it.'

'Perhaps she's beginning to realise that, though she may have lost a son, she has another just as competent—and worthy of her love.'

'I wouldn't go that far,' he said wryly. 'But you have been working your magic again, haven't you? She told me you'd suggested she might want to relocate to London, where she wouldn't be...

surrounded by so many unhappy memories. She actually asked if there would be funds to support such a move.'

'I hope you assured her there would be!'

'I did. Fortunately, though the estate operated with barely a profit these last few years, Father was not forced to go into debt. There are no mortgages or loans to repay, so with the infusion of my rich wife's dowry, the Fensworth finances are finally on an even keel again.'

'I could visit her and encourage her intention of going to London. Perhaps add that if she cannot master her grief, her health will certainly suffer and neither her late husband nor her beloved elder son would have wanted that. That in London, where she isn't daily reminded of their loss, she would have a better chance to heal.'

'So she wouldn't have to see me here, in Robert's place.'

'I could tactfully remind her of that, too,' Temper said drily.

He laughed. 'Temper, tactful? You may turn into a politician's wife yet!'

Her smile at that rejoinder was tentative and, from her suddenly tense and hesitant manner, he sensed that she was about to bring up whatever was concerning her. Tensing himself in apprehension, he waited.

'It's the matter of my becoming your wife that we need to discuss.'

'Thus far, I think you've done a marvellous job.'

'At part of it, I suppose.' She took a deep breath. 'With the shock of the news and the flurry of preparations to leave London, it wasn't until the long carriage ride to Fensworth that the full implications of your changed status occurred to me. No longer a private individual, a simple politician, but the holder of an ancient title and a vast property. Which must be handed down to an heir. Since my arrival, despite all the busyness, I've… I've thought of little else.'

Was she implying she might consider amending the terms of their *marriage blanc*? Tamping down a thrill of hope, he said, 'Naturally, the estate will be handed down to an heir. I have cousins.'

'Yes, but surely you would prefer to pass your inheritance down to…a son of your own.'

He swallowed hard against a rising tide of excitement and arousal. 'Does that mean…you are considering a change in our…intimate relationship?'

She nodded. 'I think I must.'

Hands trembling, he set down his glass. 'Are you sure you want to do this?'

She shrugged. 'You are responsible for the estate. As your wife, I am responsible, not just for the household, but for the succession. Try as I have to convince myself otherwise, that's a fact.'

With everything he desired almost within reach, Giff had to restrain himself from leaping up and dancing around the room. 'Are you *sure* you're sure?'

She nodded.

The fatigue of the last few weeks forgotten, Giff leaned towards her. As she angled her head up, he leaned down and kissed her.

Slow and easy, he cautioned himself, trying to hold back the rampaging desire. *She may now be willing, but she's still an innocent maid.* He shouldn't try to sweep her straight from a single chaste kiss to complete union, probably not even in a single night.

But the touch of her lips was so intoxicating, he had to have more. Slowly, he deepened the kiss, until, as he gently probed at her lips with his tongue, she parted them. He moved within, licking and sampling, drunk on the taste of her. And when, with a little sigh, she moved her tongue to meet his, thought was paralysed entirely and need seized control.

He kissed her with ever-increasing urgency, trailing his fingertips over the satin of her bare throat, her silken shoulders, tracing the edge of her low bodice. And then he had to touch her, cup the full, voluptuous roundness of her breasts.

One hand on her chin to hold her mouth to his, he skimmed the other down her arm and under her breast. Though she probably wore too thick a covering of chemise and stays to be able to feel the full effect, he had to rub his thumb over the nipple.

But at the first glancing touch, she stiffened and pulled away. 'S-sorry, Giff,' she gasped. 'But I—I am too tired to start anew tonight. Forgive me?'

Though he wanted to weep and snarl with frustration, there was only one answer. 'Of course, sweeting. It's been a long day. Go to bed and get some rest.'

She gave him a tremulous smile. 'Thank you, Giff.' Rising quickly, she practically ran out of the room.

Chapter Twenty

Back in the safely of her chamber, Temper closed the door and leaned against it, trembling as the panic slowly subsided.

It was her duty to give Giff an heir. She knew that. For the past few weeks, she'd been working up the courage to act upon that knowledge. And tonight, she had fully intended to allow him to claim all the rights of a husband.

But then he'd touched her *there*—and she just couldn't.

She stumbled over to the bed and sat on the edge. She was tired, just as she'd told Giff. Maybe tomorrow, after she'd rested, it would be easier.

But even as she whispered those comforting words, the sense of panic, of being barely able to breathe, descended again. *The dead weight of him crushing her, his harsh ragged breaths, the searing pain.*

Shuddering, she forced away the memories.

Despite all those weeks of trying to prepare herself, she didn't know if she could go through with it tomorrow, either. Or the next day or the next. No matter how competently she might be fulfilling the other duties of a wife, she couldn't *do* this.

Marrying Giff had been a dreadful mistake.

What was she to do about it?

All she knew was, after what had happened tonight, she couldn't remain at Fensworth and deal with him now. The ease of being with Giff, the satisfaction of helping him cope with the problems that had been dumped in his lap, the teasing, intoxicating, sensual thrill of his physical nearness—all of that had lured her into inviting him to begin something tonight that she hadn't been able to finish. She needed to get away from his disturbing, brain-numbing presence, so she could think clearly and decide what to do next.

She stood, waiting for her heartbeat to slow before she rang the bell to summon the maid who would help her prepare for bed.

Tomorrow she'd tell Giff she was returning to London.

And so, the next morning, after having barely slept, Temper rose early, needing to talk with Giff before he rode out with the estate agent. Sitting in the breakfast room, her ear perked for the sound of his footsteps, she toyed with a cup of coffee, her stomach too queasy to tolerate food.

Fortunately, a letter the maid brought to her last night, delivered to Fensworth by a servant returning late from the village, gave her a perfect excuse to implement the course of action she'd already decided upon.

Then the sound of bootsteps in the hallway reached her. She put a hand to her throat, conscious of the sudden acceleration of her pulse.

'Temper!' Giff said, halting in surprise when he saw her. 'What are you doing up so early?'

She curved her lips into a smile, hoping it didn't look as forced as it felt. 'I wanted to catch you before you rode out. I… I've had a letter from Pru. She and Johnnie are about to leave on their first voyage. Since I don't know when I might see them again, I want to return to London and bid them goodbye.'

'Of course,' Giff said, walking over to pour himself some coffee. 'It will be ten days or so before I can leave, but you needn't delay. When do you think you'll be ready to go?'

'Today.' At the surprise on his face, she added hastily, 'I must leave immediately, or I shall miss them. And I don't have much to pack. We departed London in such haste, only a few of the new mourning gowns I'd commissioned were completed. All the rest should be awaiting me in London.'

'Today!' he repeated, shaking his head. 'I wish you didn't have to leave so soon. But I wouldn't want you to miss saying goodbye to Pru.'

'Thank you for understanding, Giff. I'll leave you to your breakfast,' she said, rising from her chair, 'and go start my packing.'

He caught her hand as she walked by him, stopping her flight. 'The packing shouldn't take you long to do?'

When she continued to look away, not meeting his gaze, he sighed. 'I'm sorry about last night, Temper. I was…too hasty. I didn't mean to…frighten you. I promise, when I rejoin you in London, I'll do better.'

Ah, but could she? Or would it be better for her to repudiate her responsibilities, take a draft on her bank and begin provisioning a voyage—somewhere, anywhere—immediately, so there was no awkward reunion in London?

She'd figure that out after she got to back to Vraux House.

'You've nothing to apologise for,' she said. *This whole debacle is my fault, not his.* 'I'll…see you in London, then.' *Maybe.* 'Goodbye, Giff.'

Gently pulling her hand from his grip, she hurried out of the breakfast room.

* * *

A week later, Temper mounted the entry stairs at Vraux House, having just bid farewell to her sister and her new husband as they left on their maiden voyage. She couldn't help feeling an overwhelming envy of them for setting out on the adventure she'd always dreamed would be hers.

And for looking so happy in their marriage when she'd made such a hash of her own.

On the drive back to London, through the days and nights since, she'd done little but agonise over what to do about her dilemma. Insist on adhering to the original terms of their bargain, despite Giff's change in status? Flee to the West Indies? Force herself to do her duty, whatever the consequences?

The options kept going around and around in her head. Giff would be returning to London soon and she still had no idea which one she should choose.

As she crossed the second-floor landing, heading for the next flight up to her chamber, she noticed the library door was open, her father at his desk within. Acting on impulse, she checked in mid-stride and turned to enter his inner sanctum.

Unusually, he looked up as she walked in. 'Temperance?' he said, as if not sure he'd recognised her.

'Yes, it's me, Papa,' she said, coming over to stand by his desk.

'I gave you away to be married, didn't I? Where is your husband?'

'Gifford is still at Fensworth, settling matters at the estate. He'll be returning to London soon.'

Her father nodded. 'Good. He should be nearby, where he can protect you.'

Emboldened by her own desperation, she said, 'Is that why you married Mama? To protect her?'

At first she thought, as he had when she'd questioned him before, that he would simply not answer. Then, at length, he nodded. 'I knew her family would force her to marry money. Viscount Loxley wanted her. He was a bad man, he would have hurt her and she is so lovely—a treasure that must be safeguarded. Like you and Prudence. I couldn't give her—other things—she needed, but I could keep her safe and let her choose the men she wanted.'

'So…you loved her?'

He shrugged, as if the word didn't have any meaning for him. 'I could protect and support her.'

And wasn't that love, of a sort? Perhaps the only sort of which her father was capable? One couldn't expect of someone more than they had the resources to give.

'Did you ever tell her that?'

Lord Vraux shook his head. 'Why would I?'

Temper sighed, feeling a wave of sympathy for her father—and her mother. The world of emotion was foreign to him and trying to talk about it resulted in a conversation about as revealing as if she'd been questioning him in English and he responding in Urdu.

Before she could say anything else, he'd turned his attention back to the object on his desk—an illustrated medieval manuscript, its luminous blues, yellows and reds gleaming in the light.

Knowing he'd already forgotten her existence, Temper walked from the room.

Love came in many different shapes and varieties. The stilted, limited variety her father had given her mother hadn't been enough for her—yet it was probably all Vraux had to offer.

Would a limited marriage be enough for her—or for Giff?

Especially if, as Lady Sayleford claimed, he truly loved her? She'd not yet forced herself to fully examine how she felt about that possibility. How deeply her own feelings were engaged towards him.

She couldn't begin to consider those questions until she determined what she meant to do about the more immediate problem of whether, or how, she could live with him.

She told herself that he had agreed to her terms before they wed. He did have cousins to step into his shoes, safeguard the estate and carry on the family name, without needing heirs of his own body. The fact that he was now an earl shouldn't change anything.

But a small voice inside kept whispering that she, who prided herself on courage, was really just being a coward. That Giff was valiantly shouldering broad new responsibilities—while she was failing him in the only duty that counted for a peer's wife. Especially if he loved her, she owed him more.

She owed him an heir.

When he joined her in London, she would have to do better.

In the late afternoon a week later, with more than a little trepidation, Gifford Newell walked up the stairs to Vraux House.

'Lord Fensworth!' Overton said in surprise as he opened to door to him, a smile creasing his normally impassive face. 'Welcome back to London! Her ladyship is in the garden. Shall I tell her I'll bring tea to the front parlour? Or…would you prefer her to meet you in your rooms?'

As most newlyweds would? Giff thought, biting back an ironic smile at Overton's discreet phrasing. 'I'll need to wash off the dust of the road. You can tell my wife that I'll be in my rooms.'

Thus giving her the choice. Would she come

up to him? Or send a footman to say she'd prefer to meet him downstairs for tea?

It probably depended on just how badly he had frightened her. For there was no escaping the conclusion that it had to have been his rather limited advances—and not so limited display of ardour—that had sent her fleeing back to the safety of London.

He sighed as he trotted up the stairs. If her sojourn back home had convinced her they must revert to the original restrictions she'd imposed on their marriage, he had no right to protest. He'd given his word, after all.

It wasn't fair, just because an earldom had fallen out of the sky to settle on his shoulders, to expect Temper to change something that, for reasons he hadn't yet been able to determine, she had felt so strongly about she'd hinged her whole acceptance of his proposal on them.

And so, if he had to, he must live with them. And hope that, in time, he might discover enough of the reasons behind her reluctance to help mitigate the constant state of frustrated arousal that bedevilled him.

Just in case, Giff dismissed his valet as soon as the man brought him hot water and towels, telling him he intended to rest after his long journey and would call him when he was ready to dress.

Unlike Overton, Miles permitted himself a grin before bowing himself out with a cheeky 'Enjoy your *rest*, sir.'

It appeared everyone in the household expected he would be disporting himself with his new wife. Except, probably, his new wife.

Resigning himself to the fact that he was going to feel rather foolish when he called Miles back, if she *didn't* come to his rooms, he had just wiped his dripping face when he heard a light footstep pause outside his door. Then a knock, and Temper's voice calling, 'Giff, may I come in?'

The half-arousal he'd been fighting for the last hour, knowing he would soon see her again, hardened instantly. Through a suddenly dry throat, he croaked out, 'Of course.'

He mustn't assume, just because she was joining him, that she was ready to give intimacy another chance. She would know as well as he what the whole household expected of a newlywed couple's reunion, and wouldn't want the staff speculating about the state of their marriage.

Patience, he urged himself, his hands trembling as he replaced the towel and turned to greet her.

She was walking towards him, looking so lovely and so welcoming that his chest tightened. With her golden hair and warm smile, she was like sunshine filling the cold and lonely void of a heart that had never received the affection it craved from the family that had been supposed to love him—and hadn't.

To his deep satisfaction, she allowed him to embrace her. *Thank you, Lord, that I didn't frighten her away completely*, he thought as he held her, breathing in the sorely missed jasmine scent of her. Whenever restraint was required, he would master it to keep her here, in his arms, where she belonged. Where he needed her. Even if this was all he would ever have of her.

When she pulled back, mastering the urge to hold on, he let her go. 'How stunning you look! I'd forgotten how beautiful you are.'

She laughed—seeming, to his infinite relief, to have regained the ease in his presence that had been so notably lacking their last morning at Fensworth. 'In ten days? And you're just being gallant. I look like a hag in black!'

'Nothing you wear in any colour could ever make you look remotely like a hag,' he retorted. 'Shall I have tea sent up? Or…would you rather take it in the parlour, after I've made myself decent?'

'I…thought we might remain here. And possibly become even more…indecent.'

His pulse rate accelerated so violently, he felt dizzy. 'You're giving me that chance…to do better?'

She nodded, looking nervous, but determined. 'I'd give us both that chance.'

Almost too afraid to breathe, Giff walked over to her, cradled her chin in his hands and leaned down to kiss her, hoping that first contact conveyed all the tenderness and respect and awe he felt for her, while muting the need.

To his great delight, she opened her mouth to him, inviting the invasion of his tongue. His arms went around her, pulling her closer, as his tongue played with hers, light strokes and parries that deepened and intensified.

Then, when she pulled his shirt from his trousers and ran her hands up the bare skin of his chest, he could wait no longer. Every sense exulting, he lifted her, carried her to the bed and laid her gently back against the pillows.

She settled back and, without any further preliminaries, started drawing her skirts up towards her waist. Startled out of his sensual haze, he stopped her hand—and looked into her face.

A face that was set, resolute—and devoid of any trace of desire.

Inwardly cursing, he sat down beside her and smoothed her skirts back down to her ankles.

'You look like one of those Christian martyrs, tied to the stake and waiting for the lions to be released. What sort of beast do you think I am?'

She attempted a smile. 'I know you won't…
ravish me.'

He tried to contain the frustration, disappointment—and hurt. 'I have my pride, too. If my touch
is so…repugnant, I certainly won't force it on you.'

'No, it's not that! Surely you can tell that I find
you…attractive.'

'Then what is it?' he demanded. She flinched
and he made himself soften his tone. 'I'm just
a simple male, Temper. I don't understand and I
want to.'

She shook her head, tears starting at the corner
of her eyes. 'I should never have married you. If
I'd known you were going to inherit…'

'What, unworthy me, becoming Earl?' he
snapped, devastated that she might share his mother's opinion of his abilities after all.

Her eyes widened. 'You *unworthy*? How could
you believe I think that? It's quite the opposite,
really. You deserve to have married a lady of impeccable reputation. Someone better. Someone…
whole.'

He stared at her. 'I have no idea what you're
talking about.'

With a deep sigh, she swiped at the tear that
had started to slide down her cheek. 'I suppose
you deserve the truth. So I will…tell you what I've
never revealed to anyone. But you must promise

never to breathe a word of it to another living soul. Absolutely *no one*. Do you promise?'

'Of course! Though I can't imagine any sin you could confess worthy of the distress it's obviously causing you.'

'How about the fact that I'm not really a maid?' she spat back bitterly. 'That I've been…used.'

Chapter Twenty-One

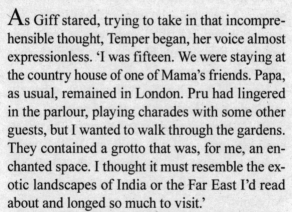

As Giff stared, trying to take in that incomprehensible thought, Temper began, her voice almost expressionless. 'I was fifteen. We were staying at the country house of one of Mama's friends. Papa, as usual, remained in London. Pru had lingered in the parlour, playing charades with some other guests, but I wanted to walk through the gardens. They contained a grotto that was, for me, an enchanted space. I thought it must resemble the exotic landscapes of India or the Far East I'd read about and longed so much to visit.'

She paused and he waited, sick about what he knew must be coming, anxious to know the whole story, though knowing he mustn't rush her.

'I was sitting on a bench, listening to the splash of water in the fountain, when I suddenly realised I wasn't alone. A man stood at the grotto's entrance, watching me. I later learned that he'd attempted to force his attentions on Mama and been slapped for his efforts, dismissed and told never to return. So when he came upon me he was angry… and aroused.'

She blew out a breath. 'The short of it is, he… forced himself on me. Growing up as I did, I suppose I should have guessed what he intended, but I didn't. Not until he'd pinned me on the ground under him and dragged up my skirts. He was so heavy, I could hardly breathe! I fought him, but it was too late, I had no leverage and he was too strong. Afterwards, he went off and I just…lay there. Stunned. Horrified, disbelieving, that a perfect day under a sunny blue sky could have turned into such a nightmare.'

He could have howled with outrage at her anguished tone. 'And you never told anyone?'

'No,' She laughed shortly. 'Of course, he threatened me, saying if I said anything, he'd claim I'd invited his advances. That since, by then, I already looked so much like Mama, everyone would believe him.'

'The bastard!' Giff exploded. 'Surely you knew your family—'

She held up a hand. 'I did. Even at fifteen, I knew what he claimed was false. That I was *not* responsible and had done nothing to encourage him. But I felt so…soiled. I couldn't tell anyone. Pru would have been horrified. Gregory might have tried to call him out. And at learning that one of her rejected lovers had… Mama would have been devastated.'

She turned her face away from his gaze. 'I wanted to run away and hide for ever, but I knew I couldn't. So I tore my gown in several more places—he'd already ripped my bodice—and rubbed in more dirt. I went back and told them I'd fallen out of a tree. I could tell Pru thought it odd, because though I'd always loved climbing trees, I never lost my balance. The others just laughed— or scolded. Up in the chamber assigned to me, I stripped off the gown and soaked in a tub, made the maid bring me more and more hot water, but… I couldn't make myself feel clean. I've never really felt clean, ever since. Before my maid could attempt to repair the dress, I took it to the woods and burned it.' She turned her pained, devastated face to his. 'And now you know the whole of it.'

'Who was it?' Whoever he was, wherever he was, Giff would seek him out—and make him pay.

She shook her head. 'It doesn't matter. He's dead now, anyway—killed in a stupid wager, racing curricles at night. I actually felt cheated when I heard. For weeks after the…incident, I'd teased Christopher into helping me practise with a pistol, telling myself some day I'd shoot him and that would finally put an end to it. But…it has never truly ended.'

Giff swiped a hand over his face, furious, appalled and aching for her pain. He didn't know what to say. Words of comfort were meaningless in the face of the outrage perpetrated against her.

'If what I've just told you makes you feel... differently towards me, I'll understand.'

'Feel differently?' he echoed, uncomprehending.

'Because I'm not the pure maid you thought me. I'm...spoiled.'

Aghast, he said, 'You think I'd *turn away* from you, because—'

She nodded, scattering the tears now dripping down her cheeks. With a savage oath, he grabbed her and pulled her into his arms.

Where she clung to him and wept.

He whispered soothing noises into her hair and held her close while his heart ached and rage burned...because he knew there was nothing he could do to right the wrong done to her.

Finally, the flow of tears slowed and she pushed away from him. 'Sorry,' she muttered.

'You've nothing to be sorry for,' he replied, catching her chin and making her look at him, so she would see and believe the absolute truth of what he was about to say. 'But you're right—I do think differently about you now. I always knew you were strong and courageous, but I had no idea how strong and brave. That at fifteen, scarcely more than child, you bore the whole weight of this horrendous tragedy on your shoulders, alone. To protect those you loved. I don't know how you found the fortitude. I wish there were some way I could wipe the horror from your memory, but I can't. I will do whatever I can, however, anything I can, to make it more…bearable.'

'Thank you,' she whispered. 'I *do* find you attractive, which is why I've been so beastly, seeming to lead you on, then retreating. I was so afraid that if…if I let you go further, it would unleash all those ugly memories and…and I'd scream, or fight you, and I couldn't bear that. But I know now, I must risk it and become fully your wife. You have the responsibility of the Earldom and need to provide it with an heir. And… I've never known a better man, or one I trusted more.'

He smiled. 'I'm relieved to know you trust me. Do you also believe I would never hurt you?'

Again, that little nod.

'And I never will. There will never be anything between us that you don't want. *Want*—not just endure. There's nothing I crave more than to make you fully my wife, but I will only do so when— if—*you* desire it as much as I do.'

She looked troubled. 'I'm not sure I will ever truly desire…that.'

Holding up a hand to stay her from interrupting, he continued, 'Forget about the Earldom and its heirs. That's not important. What occurs between a man and a woman should be beautiful, not ugly. A mutual giving and taking only of pleasure. It will be that way between us, when you are ready. If you are ready. Not before. Never before.'

While she looked at him wonderingly, Giff managed a grin. 'I won't promise not to try to tempt you...but I will never take you. Now, dry your tears, my beautiful, strong, courageous wonder of a wife, and let's go down for tea. It was a long drive and I'm devilishly thirsty.'

Late that night, Giff tiptoed into the bedchamber adjoining his to look down at his sleeping wife. Who, God be praised, after they'd gone down to join the rest of her family, had seemed much lighter and freer than when she'd left Fensworth. As if an intolerable burden had been lifted.

Which, he supposed, it had. He couldn't imagine what it must have cost her, keeping her dreadful secret hidden for so many years.

He hadn't worked out her violator's identity until just a few moments ago, but the bastard who'd raped her must have been Ralph Petersmere. A man of dubious reputation, he'd chased after all the leading beauties of the day, Temper's mother included. Then burned through most of his hapless wife's fortune before dying in the wreck of his curricle during a mad dash across Hounslow Heath, his wager that he could do so in the pitch black of a cloudy, moonless night the talk of the clubs for weeks after the accident.

Had the man not already been dead, Giff would have arm-wrestled Temper to put a bullet through him.

Such sweet innocence, so brutally betrayed, he thought, gently brushing one burnished curl off her forehead. No wonder she reacted so bitterly to all the comments about how much she resembled her mother. His heart contracted again at the pain that miserable excuse for a man had made her endure.

Though he wanted with everything in him to help her heal, he hadn't the remotest idea how to start. Nor was there anyone whose advice he could seek, without risking revealing the secret she'd suffered so much anguish to conceal.

He also knew that unless she did heal, they would never be lovers. Would he be able to stand the frustration of wanting her, knowing he might never have her?

She'd given him permission to slake that frustration elsewhere, of course. But for weeks now, he'd found the idea of intimacy with any other woman…unappealing. He was more than his lusts. And the only woman he really wanted was the fierce, beautiful, unconventional woman he'd married.

As he smiled down at her, an emotion so powerful he could scarcely contain it welled up to immerse him. With sudden, stark clarity, he realised that sometime over the past days or weeks, he had fallen in love with his wife. Simply, completely and absolutely.

He loved Temperance Lattimar with all the fierceness of someone who'd never fully loved, or been loved, before. He would stand by her and protect her and do everything he could to ensure her happiness.

Even if it meant letting her travel abroad without him. Even if it meant never making love to her as he ached to.

But as for the latter, he thought, just barely brushing her lips with one gentle finger, he wasn't ready yet to abandon hope.

After all, she'd admitted she desired him. He would just have to move slowly, tempting her, teasing her, leading her one small step at a time deeper into intimacy. Until she was as ready and eager for that final step as he was.

He wouldn't stop believing that some day, she would be.

But in the meantime, he'd need some respite from the continuous sensual response she sparked in him. Thank heavens he would be spending the next few days with other members of the factory commission out of London, continuing their evidence-gathering at a mill just beyond the city.

While he would spend his evenings working to convince Temper just how complete, pure and perfect a woman she truly was.

The next afternoon, with her husband away at his Parliamentary duties, Temper was reading in her chamber when Overton came up to inform her that Lady Sayleford awaited her in the drawing room below.

Marvelling at the anomaly of that lady calling on her not once, but twice, she quickly put her book away and walked down.

Was she calling to see if Temper had followed her advice about treating her godson gently? Especially since his response to her shocking revelations, Temper couldn't imagine according him anything but gratitude, awe and reverence. In a world where gentlemen could conduct themselves as they chose, but women who didn't meet an inflexible standard for purity were condemned, she couldn't think of another man who would have treated her with such compassion.

Perhaps…perhaps he really did love her.

Certainly, there could be no greater love than attempting to understand the torment she'd suffered after the attack and pledging to do whatever he could to help her finally recover.

And though he'd said he didn't know how he *could* help—he already had. Just knowing she no

longer carried alone the consequences of those terrible events eased the tightness that had sat like a
boulder in her chest for the last seven years.

Perhaps some day, with Giff to lead her, she
might even be able to contemplate the complete
union between a man and a woman with something other than revulsion.

Right now, it was enough to know he *knew* and
had comforted her, rather than rejected her.

Walking into the parlour, she made Lady Sayleford a deep curtsy. 'What's this, another visit?
More deference to a lady who is your senior?' she
teased. 'Although Giff tells me I shall not legally
be Lady Fensworth until after he's summoned to
appear before the Lords.'

'A mere formality,' Lady Sayleford replied.

'To what do I owe the honour of your visit?'

'I'd heard you had both returned to London
and that Gifford meant to continue his work in the
Commons for as long as he is permitted. I hear
he's been learning all he needed to know about
the running of the estate—a task for which, I understand, you provided considerable assistance.
Thank you for that.'

'You are most welcome. I can't imagine why his
father excluded him from the running of it for so
many years. He's more than worthy and capable
of his family's trust and admiration!'

She halted, near tears as she remembered his

compassion and understanding yesterday. And thanked heaven that there was *one* secret in London Lady Sayleford didn't know.

'I'm glad to see you agree with my assessment of his worth. And perhaps are coming to believe you might be the right wife for him after all?'

'I don't know about that yet,' Temper replied with a rueful smile. 'But I am trying.'

Lady Sayleford nodded. 'Good. I imagine, with your sister's husband beginning a trading venture that rendered rather superfluous your plans to travel the world acquiring treasures for your father, you might be feeling as if you've…lost your purpose. I'd like to challenge you to become more involved and knowledgeable about your husband's. To that end, I've brought you a copy of the "Report of the Select Committee on Factory Children's Labour", based on testimony collected by Michael Sadler's Parliamentary committee last year. Though its publication this January was greeted by great public outcry, some in government argued the report was too one-sided and inflammatory. Which is why Gifford and his committee are now conducting further investigations. I thought you would find it…illuminating.'

She held out the heavy volume, which Temper accepted. 'Thank you! I'm sure I shall. Can I offer you tea?'

'No, thank you. I'll leave you to read the report—and think about ways you might help Gifford advance his cause in the short time he'll have before he must take his place in the Lords.'

'I will certainly do so.'

'That's all I ask. Well, I shall leave you to it.' As she walked out, Lady Sayleford paused, her surprisingly fond gaze fixed on Temper's face. 'I can't think of anything that would delight me more than seeing dear Gifford happy. I shall hope for you both to regain your rightful places— together.' After giving Temper's cheek a gentle pat, she walked out.

Temper watched her disappear, once again having to take a deep, shuddering breath to force back tears. Gaining Lady Sayleford's affection as well as her approval was a boon she'd never expected.

Now to follow her good advice. Hefting the heavy report, she headed back up to her bedchamber.

Hours later, Temper awakened from a light doze to see the candle on the table beside her had burned low—and to hear Giff's distinctive step in the hallway outside her bedchamber. When he walked past to his own door, she jumped up and went to open the one between their adjoining chambers.

'Temper!' he said in surprise, halting on the

threshold. 'What are you doing up so late? Is something wrong?'

'Not with me, but certainly within our nation.'

He came to her and she held her breath. Contradictory as it seemed, given the way she had run from him in Fensworth, his nearness now seemed to spark a response in every nerve, more intense than ever—despite the fact that her reluctance to pursue that attraction to its logical end had not abated.

Perhaps it was knowing that *he* knew the truth about her, and would not press her into any intimacy she did not want, that made her so acutely conscious of him—and unafraid to be aroused by him.

Instead of the kiss she expected, however, he merely brushed his lips against her cheek. Conscious of an illogical disappointment, she held up the Factory Commission Report.

'Lady Sayleford lent me this, wanting me to understand more of the work you're doing. I've just finished reading the whole document, and am shocked and appalled! I know it's late and you must be tired, but could you take a few moments to tell me what your new committee is discovering? Are conditions truly as bad as those detailed in this report?'

'Too tired to discuss my great passion? Other

than you, of course,' he added with a smile. 'Of course not.'

'Have you dined?' She followed him to the sofa in the small sitting area shared by the two rooms. 'I wouldn't rouse Overton, but I could rustle about in the kitchen and find you something.'

'Yes, we dined before we returned to London,' he confirmed, placing his lighted candle on the table. 'I'll just pour myself a whisky. Would you like one?'

'Not this time,' she replied, taking a seat. 'So, what has your committee found? I understand Sadler tried unsuccessfully to push through a bill in the last session, based on the evidence in this report. Do you think you will have any more success in this session?'

Bringing his drink with him to the sofa, he took a seat beside her, close enough to cause another delightful shiver to ripple through her. 'Although the current commission thinks some of the claims of the Sadler report to be exaggerated, there is plenty of evidence to confirm many of the abuses it detailed. We expect shortly to finish gathering testimony and a bill has already been drafted.'

'I'm so glad to hear it. Lady Sayleford seemed to think there might be something I could do to help, although I cannot imagine what.'

'If you truly are interested, Lady Maggie, Lyndlington's wife, has a Ladies' Committee that is working with us. Writing letters to newspapers, to owners of mills who are opposing legislation, calling upon their sense of compassion towards the weakest and most powerless among us, the children. Not to mention, pointing out the practical fact that undernourished and fatigued workers will produce an inferior product, the sale of which would eventually damage the factory's reputation and decrease demand for its products.'

'Yes, I can imagine that argument being more effective,' Temper said drily. 'I will send Lady Lyndlington a note tomorrow, asking if I might join her at their next meeting.'

'She would like that,' Giff said, downing the rest of his whisky. 'Did you wait up just to discuss this with me?' At her nod, he said, 'Then I'd better let you get some sleep.'

'I'll bid you goodnight, then.'

Before she could stand, she caught his eyes on her and froze. She felt his gaze, almost as palpable as a touch, travel slowly from her face down her neck to the swell of her breasts. Though he said nothing, she was intensely aware that she sat beside him clad just in a fine linen robe over an even thinner night rail.

She sucked in a breath, half-alarmed, half-eager, as he reached towards her. But he touched only her lips, slowly outlining them with a single fingertip, the pressure almost imperceptible. His gaze holding her mesmerised, he drew his hand back, kissed the fingertip, then brought it back once again to her lips, slightly moistened by its contact with his mouth.

Her breathing growing uneven, she remembered the softness of that mouth, the feel of his tongue against hers, licking, teasing. Heat began to spiral in her belly, while a skittering of sensation sparked below. Seemingly of their own accord, her lips parted.

She waited breathlessly, ready for him to place his mouth where his finger had been—tracing her lips, his tongue delving inside to suckle and caress.

Instead, he kissed her forehead and straightened. 'Goodnight, my sweet wife.'

With that, he walked back to his bedchamber and closed the adjoining door.

Leaving her sitting alone on the sofa, her pulse racing, *need* spiralling in her belly—and not sure whether to be indignant or relieved.

Chapter Twenty-Two

A week later, knowing the session would run late, Giff left Parliament in mid-afternoon, wanting to have tea with his lovely wife.

Better to see her during the day, in the near-public space of a parlour where at any time they might be interrupted, helping him keep a damper on his ardour.

Though Temper was responding to him more and more freely, he still tried not to return to his bedchamber until very late, when the promptings of conscience reined in his desire. It wasn't fair to try to lure her into the intimacy he craved when she was too drowsy to be fully aware of what she was doing.

For when—and he was increasingly confident it would be *when*—he finally made love to her, he wanted their union to be a conscious choice, made while she was in full possession of her faculties.

Not something drifted into in a sleepy haze that she might regret in the cold light of dawn.

The hackney dropped him off and he ran up the steps, telling Overton when the butler admitted him to ask Temper to join him in the small back sitting room and send in tea. He went there to wait for her, setting his gift on the table, filled with the delighted anticipation of seeing her.

A few minutes later, she rushed in, cheeks flushed. 'Giff!' she cried, coming over to give him her hands to kiss. 'What a delightful surprise! Did the session end early?'

'No, it's still going on. Since I doubt we'll break before midnight, I decided to sneak away for tea. And I wanted to give you this. I thought Lady Sayleford might have a copy and she did. She said you might keep this one, with her good wishes.'

'What is it?' she asked, picking up the package.

'Don't open it yet—let's have our tea. I only have time for one cup and then I'll leave you to it.'

So she put it back down and poured him the tea Overton brought in. While he quickly sipped his cup, she asked him about the progress being made in committee, adding in titbits of the responses they'd received from the letters she had been helping to write for the Ladies' Committee she'd recently joined.

A short time later, putting down his cup, Giff

said, 'Having been a good little girl, waiting so patiently, you may now open your present.'

Giving him a look, she slapped his hand before picking up the package. Laughing, he watched expectantly as she removed the wrappings.

'*The Letters and Works of Lady Mary Wortley Montagu,*' Temper read from the title page of the leather-bound volume. 'You thought I would appreciate them?'

'Not the poetry, particularly, but the letters from Turkey. Her husband was the British ambassador to the Ottoman court in Istanbul. Lady Mary made extensive visits to Ottoman women, whose dress, habits and traditions are vividly described—even a trip to a *hammam*! When Lady Sayleford told me about the book, I immediately thought you would find it interesting.'

Her eyes shining with delight, she looked back up at him. 'I shall enjoy it indeed. Thank you, Giff! You are so good to me and I don't deserve it!'

'On the contrary, you deserve all the pampering in the world. And I mean to see you get it.'

And then as he waited hopefully, she set down the book and came over to embrace him. Catching his breath on a sigh, he held her close, drinking in the scent and feel of her, knowing if she wanted the moon, he would try to drag it out of the sky.

Then, surprising him, she tipped his chin down and kissed him.

Not just a quick brush of the lips, either. She licked and suckled his lips, then swept her tongue within and slowly, thoroughly, explored his mouth.

Sweat breaking out on his brow, he made himself pull away.

'It's not fair to kiss a man like that when he has to go back to work,' he chided.

'Just a taste to remind you why you should not arrive home quite so late,' she responded tartly.

Laughing, he walked away, stopping to blow her a kiss from the doorway. 'I hope that's a promise.'

'Come home early and you'll find out,' she shot back.

Ah, yes, he thought, as he took his hat and cane from Overton, more encouraged than ever. He just needed to be patient a little longer and everything he hoped for would be his.

Well, maybe not quite *everything*. But a man would have to be unreasonable to possess the fire and loveliness of Temper and feel himself lacking, because she had not pledged her love, as well.

Once all the barriers she'd erected to protect herself from hurt and shame finally came down, then there would be time enough to try to win her heart as well as her body.

* * *

Later that evening, Temper reclined on the sofa in their shared sitting room, fascinated by the accounts in the book Giff had brought her. He really was too good to her, she thought, closing the volume.

Several times over the past week he'd surprised her with small treats or presents he thought she'd enjoy. In the late evenings, when he finally returned from his Parliament sessions, he'd wake her, giving her the sweetest of goodnight kisses that always left her wanting more…though she'd not yet worked up the courage to press him for it.

And she didn't intend to, not until she was certain she would not suffer a recurrence of the panic that had sent her running from Fensworth.

Of course, she thought with a sigh, she couldn't decide she was ready for more if he persisted in coming to her so late she was only half-awake.

Opening her book again, she had turned to the next chapter when she heard footsteps approaching down the hall—Giff's.

Perhaps he was going to take her up on her challenge that he come home early—and see what happened.

She wasn't sure just how far she dared go, but she meant to push herself to the limits. He'd been so patient with her and he'd waited long enough for his reward.

She heard his quick knock and smiled. Let the encounter begin!

'Hello, Giff,' she said as he entered.

He made her an elaborate bow. 'Here I am. Early, as requested.' Indicating the book on the table beside her, he said, 'Have you been reading all this time?'

'Yes, practically from the moment you left me.'

'Ah, then you must be in need of this.'

Stopping behind where she sat on the sofa, he reached down to rub her neck, then slowly massaged her shoulders, until she almost purred with pleasure. While his ministering fingers did effectively ease the ache in her neck, as they soothed, they also stirred back to glowing sparks the embers of the sensual awareness always glimmering between them.

Wanting, needing his kiss, she leaned back, pulling his head down. Finding the odd upside-down contact stimulating, but not nearly close enough, she broke the kiss and patted the sofa beside her. 'Sit here, please. So I may kiss you properly.'

Chuckling, he complied. 'I was hoping you might kiss me *improperly*.'

He took her in his arms and kissed her again. As his tongue probed at her lips, teasing, not demanding, she opened to him, the shock of sensation making her gasp as his tongue found hers and tangled with it.

Desire intensified as he stroked. Need spiralling through her, wanting to touch more of him, she tugged at his cravat and pulled it off, helped him shrug out of his jacket. She found the bare skin at the V of his shirt, rubbing him with her fingertips as he kissed her harder, deeper.

Slowly he moved his hands lower, from her shoulders down over to the swell of her breasts. This time, rather than stiffening, she moaned and leaned into him as he gently massaged and caressed. And then, as she gasped from the sheer mindless delight of it, he bent and took one rigid nipple in his mouth, suckling her through the thin linen of her night-rail.

She clutched his shoulders, pulling him closer, wanting more, so awash with desire that she whimpered in protest when he moved his mouth away, only to gasp with renewed delight as he moved his mouth to her other breast. Wanting to feel him against the length of her body, she pushed him back until he was half-reclining and slid quickly over him, not wanting to lose the delicious feel of his mouth at her breast—until she encountered the hardness of his erection at her belly.

Shock and a deep, primitive dread made her freeze, desire abruptly dissipating as she shifted away from him. Then, telling herself she *would* master this, she moved her hand down, determined to touch that which she most feared.

He caught her wrist. 'Enough for tonight,' he said, his voice strained.

'But you want me to touch you. Don't you?'

'I do. But *you* don't really want it. I could sense the change in you, from desire to…caution. I won't have you come to me because you think you should. Only when you are truly ready.'

Moving away from her, he kissed her forehead. 'Goodnight, my sweet wife.'

Once again, partly relieved, mostly frustrated, Temper watched her husband walk into his bedchamber, shutting the door behind him.

She rose and took a step towards that closed door. Then hesitated. How wonderful it would be to wake and find herself in his arms. And yet…

Recalling the feel of his hardness against her, she took a shaky breath. Much as she longed to give him everything he desired, she wasn't sure she was quite ready. Yet.

The thought of attempting, and failing, made her shudder. At some point, Giff would have to tire of being aroused, teased and ultimately refused. Swiping away tears of frustration and disappointment, she walked back to her solitary bed.

Two nights later, Temper sat up again, book on her lap, waiting to hear her husband's step ap-

proaching down the hallway. So nervous and un-
decided, she'd had the book open for hours, but
read barely a page.

A remark made by Miss Henley when she'd
brought her friend to meet the other members of
the Ladies' Committee at Lady Maggie's house
this morning had resonated in her brain all day.
After discussing tentative plans for the group to
continue after the anticipated passage of the Factory Act, Emma had gazed around at the group,
a wistful envy in her eyes.

'How lucky you all are,' she'd said quietly.
'Each of you having found good men to protect
and guard you, until that time women have enough
legal rights to protect and guard themselves.'

Agreeing with her compliment, they had all
assured her that a lady as intelligent and accomplished as she was would surely find such a man
for herself, as they had—all through unlikely
paths.

None quite so unlikely as hers, Temper thought.
But she certainly had found a man willing to
guard and protect her. Whom she trusted absolutely never to hurt her.

Wasn't it time to trust that, with him, she might
move past the fear that still bound her?

She'd almost managed it two nights ago. But
then, the memory of that choking sense of suf-
focation, the pressure, the pain, had been vivid

enough to cause the hesitation that had made Giff leave her.

It wouldn't be like that with her husband, she knew. 'A mutual giving and taking of pleasure,' he'd described it. How she wanted that!

Did she want it enough to brave breaking though the barrier?

She remembered how she'd felt after returning that afternoon long ago. How she'd soaked and soaked in the bath and never felt clean.

But Giff knew every degrading thing that had happened to her—and he hadn't looked at her that way. She'd braced herself for him to think less of her, to turn from her in disgust. Instead, he'd held her while she wept and told her he thought her brave and strong.

Maybe…if she were able to face the ugliness, with him to encourage her, she'd be able to let it all go, or most of it. The anguish, disgust and shame. Let it go and feel whole again, clean again, at last.

She'd been ready to face tigers, bandits and disease in pursuit of the exotic and extraordinary in faraway lands. How could she not have enough courage to cast off the shackles of the past and seize the extraordinary she'd found with Giff, right here and now?

As she sat there, considering that possibility, the dread slowly loosened its hold over her. As if the prison of horrific memories in which she'd been locked for so long was finally opening, she felt a sense of lightness emerging. Freeing her from fear. Freeing her to *feel*.

And not just to feel the physical and sensual. With the darkness that had overshadowed her life for so long lessening, she was at last able to see the truth that had been hidden in her heart. The depth and strength of the emotion Giff inspired in her.

The *love* he inspired in her.

She laughed, shaking her head in wonderment. She had probably been in love with Giff for years, blinded to that fact by her dread of physical intimacy and her determination to avoid any entanglement that might push her into it. Realising she didn't just like and admire and respect Giff, she *loved* him, filled her with renewed determination to brave the ugly memories and triumph over them.

Because she wanted to be his, body, heart and soul.

And so she would be, she vowed. Tonight.

So, late that night, abandoning her book, Temper went to her dressing table and dabbed a touch of her favourite jasmine perfume at her throat and wrists. Shrugging off her robe, she pulled the linen night rail over her head and tossed it aside, then slipped back into the robe alone.

Pouring herself a glass of wine for courage, she settled back on the sofa to wait.

Fortunately, before she went mad from the constant veering from anxiety to heated antici-pation and back, she heard the footsteps she'd been waiting for. Her mouth going dry, as her husband walked into the bedroom, she gave him a tremu-lous smile.

'Waiting up for me again?' he asked. 'How fetching you look,' After crossing the room, he bent down to kiss her forehead and halted.

'And how delicious you smell! I'd better give you a goodnight kiss quickly and go, before I'm tempted to devour you.'

She caught his hand. 'Maybe I'm ready to be devoured.'

He froze, and she felt the pulse at his wrist jump.

'Let me show you,' she said.

Rising from the couch, she led him into her bedchamber and pushed him to sit on the bed.

She leaned over and kissed him, opening her mouth to him, then pursuing his tongue with her own. That giddy, now familiar heat began its slow spiral in her belly as he sucked and caressed her tongue.

Murmuring, she moved closer, wanting his hands on her—the hands that had created such wonderful eddies of feeling when he rubbed her back and neck and breasts the other night. But, to her frustration, he made no move to touch her or pull her against him.

Perhaps he wasn't yet sure she wouldn't end up denying him again. Well, time to be more convincing.

She stepped away and, while he watched, let the robe slide from her shoulders. Encouraged by his sharp inhale of breath, his hands clutching at the bed linens, she stood steadily under his gaze, letting him inspect her naked body in the candlelight.

Then, when he still made no move towards her, she stepped back to the bed, unknotted his cravat and pulled it off him. Tugged him out of jacket, then waistcoat, then stripped the shirt over his head. Sighing, she paused to admire his broad shoulders and strong chest.

After bending to pull off his boots, she urged him to stand and plucked open his trouser buttons, the fabric pulled taut by his erection. He let her tug the garment down, stepping out of it once she got it to his ankles.

And then stood motionless as she sucked in a breath, getting her first good look at his arousal. He didn't try to cover himself, letting her stare at his fully erect manhood—while still making no attempt either to pull her against him or on to the bed.

'Don't you want to…do something?' she finally whispered.

'And wake myself from the most wonderful erotic dream I've ever had?' he said. 'Not a chance.'

'Then I suppose your erotic dream woman will have to take matters into her own hands.'

'Oh, I very much hope so.'

He let her urge him down against the pillows, but when she went to straddle him, he stopped her.

'Not yet,' he murmured. 'I've been waiting so very long, I won't last if you start that and I want so much to touch you. Will you let me?'

She nodded and he helped her to lie down in his place.

For an instant, the panic nibbled at her—could she bear it, to lie under him, crushed by his weight?

But she forced it out of mind. This was Giff, her darling Giff, and he would never hurt her.

Following his direction, she stretched out on the bed, acutely conscious of the heat of his body, so magnificently naked and so close to hers. But he didn't lie down atop her in that position of pain and domination she'd so long feared. Instead, he stretched out beside her.

Leaning over her, he kissed her, long and slow and sweet, until the last vestiges of resistance she hadn't quite been able to master dissolved in the liquid heat of his mouth. She arched her back, eager to feel the caress of his clever fingers over and around her breasts, and he responded, both hands going to circle and lift, both thumbs to tease at the nipples. And then, creating a sensation so intense it made her dizzy, he took one nipple in his mouth.

She could hardly bear the wonder of it, his warm wet tongue against aching hardness of her naked flesh. She could feel moisture gathering between her thighs, a pressure building there that had nothing to do with coercion or pain.

He moved down to explore her wetness, moving his fingers over the tender flesh, exerting only exquisite light pressure with his skilled touch, over, around and then, to her amazement, delving inside, sparking even more acute delight.

Only then did he raise himself over her. He withdrew his finger and she felt something thicker, blunter, nudging at the entrance of her body. But there was no unpleasantness, only a marvellous slow glide of his flesh into hers that instinctively made her arch to take him deeper.

It was incredible. It was marvellous. Quickly she learned his rhythm, arching up as he withdrew, feeling the wonderful liquid fullness as he pushed down again, driving himself deeper. The friction of it created a tension within her that seemed to build and build as they moved faster, her body straining to reach some release as the sensations grew more and more intense, until she felt she must shatter.

And then she did, one final thrust launching her into a starburst of pleasure so intense, it paralysed all thought and movement. She heard a cry and knew it must have been ripped from her own throat.

As she sank backwards, gasping for breath, the sensation slowly subsiding, she dimly noted that Giff, too, had gone rigid, crying out, filling her with one last thrust. She wrapped her legs around him, wanting to hold him there for ever in the centre of those powerful vibrations.

But she must have dozed, for when she came to herself, she discovered Giff lying against the pillows, one arm around her, snuggling her against his chest.

'That was marvellous,' she murmured and heard the rumble of his chuckle against her ear.

'I'm so glad to hear that, sweeting, for I'm afraid at the last, I lost any semblance of control.'

'You deserved to. I made you wait long enough for your pleasure.'

He leaned up on one elbow to look down at her, his expression grave.

'Was it long enough? You don't have any regrets?'

'Only that I waited so long. I've never felt so... cherished.'

'And I do cherish you, my darling wife. I admit, I wasn't initially enthusiastic about wedding you, but you turned out to be everything I needed. Everything I could possibly desire.' He laughed. 'I ought to send Miss Avery flowers. Without her ill-intentioned intervention, I might never have claimed the woman I love beyond everything.'

Her eyes widening, she looked up at him. 'You really do love me?' she asked delightedly. 'Lady Sayleford told me you did, but I hardly dared believe it.'

'Did she? When?'

'Oh, weeks ago, before we left for Fensworth. Though she said you didn't know it yet.'

'Wise lady,' he said ruefully. 'She truly does know everything—even before we do.'

'I must have loved you for years, but been too... compromised by what I'd gone through to be able see it.'

It was his turn to look surprised. 'Wait, now. What did you just say?'

'I love you, Gifford Newell.'

He stared down at her, the shock and surprise on his face gradually giving way to a huge grin. 'Say it again.'

'I love you.'

'Again.'

Laughing, she repeated, 'Love you...love you... love you', interspersing each avowal with a kiss. 'If I'm whole now, or almost whole, it's because you believed I was. You've replaced the fears I could not face with memories that are only joyous and beautiful.'

'And what of your dream to travel? Will you give me this bliss, and then leave me?'

'Reading the Sadler report convinced me there are places in England in need as foreign to me as anything beyond our shores. I would do all I could to help you make Fensworth the showplace it should be and bring progress to those needy areas. Now, while you work in the Commons, and after you take your seat in the Lords. I'll even try to become more...diplomatic, so I may preside over your dinner parties.'

'Temper, not saying what she thinks?' he teased.

'I can be discreet. Occasionally. I'll try to be whatever you need me to be.'

'Then be yourself. The child who once amused me, the woman who challenges me, the wife I love. Once the reform legislation passes and I take that seat in the Lords, I could apply to the Foreign Office for an appointment as an ambassador somewhere exotic. Give you chance to write your own "Turkish Letters". I'd like to give you everything you want.'

'Being with you *is* everything I want. Except...

this loving business. All my life I've heard how it makes poets write rhapsodies and people do foolish things. But maybe they are mistaken. Maybe it wasn't quite as wonderful as I thought it was.'

Grinning at the sudden dismay on his face, she said demurely, 'I think you must show me again.'

'Devil,' he said, nibbling her shoulder. 'Now and for ever, gladly.'

* * * * *

MILLS & BOON

Coming next month

HIS CONVENIENT HIGHLAND BRIDE
Janice Preston

Lachlan McNeill couldn't quite believe his good fortune when he first saw his bride, Lady Flora McCrieff, walking up the aisle towards him on her father's arm. Her posture was upright and correct and her figure was… delectable. The tight bodice and sleeves of her wedding gown—her figure tightly laced in accordance with fashion—accentuated her full breasts, slender arms and tiny waist above the wide bell of her skirt. She was tiny, dwarfed by her father's solid, powerful frame, and she barely reached Lachlan's shoulder when they stood side by side in front of the minister. True, he had not yet seen his new bride's face—her figure might be all he could wish for, but was there a nasty surprise lurking yet? Maybe her features were somehow disfigured? Or maybe she was a shrew? Why else had her father refused to let them meet before their wedding day? He'd instead insisted on riding over to Lochmore Castle, Lachlan's new home, to agree the marriage settlements.

Their vows exchanged, Lachlan raised Flora's veil, bracing himself for some kind of abomination. His chest loosened with relief as she stared up at him, her green eyes huge and wary under auburn brows, the freckles that speckled her nose and cheeks stark against the pallor of her skin. His finger caught a loose, silken tendril of coppery-red hair and her face flooded pink, her lower lip trembling, drawing his gaze as the scent of orange blossom wreathed his senses.

She is gorgeous.

Heat sizzled through him, sending blood surging to his loins as he found himself drawn into the green depths of her eyes, his senses in disarray. Then he took her hand to place it on his arm and its delicacy, its softness, its fragility sent waves of doubt crashing through him, sluicing him clean of lustful thoughts as he sucked air into his lungs.

He had never imagined he'd be faced with one so young…so dainty…so captivating…and her beauty and her purity brought into sharp focus his own dirty, sordid past. Next to her he felt a clumsy, uncultured oaf.

What could he and this pampered young lady ever have in common? She might accept his fortune, but could she ever truly accept the man behind the façade? He'd faced rejection over his past before and he'd already decided that the less his wife ever learned about that past, the better.

Continue reading
HIS CONVENIENT HIGHLAND BRIDE
Janice Preston

Available next month
www.millsandboon.co.uk

LET'S TALK
Romance

For exclusive extracts, competitions
and special offers, find us online:

 facebook.com/millsandboon

@MillsandBoon

@MillsandBoonUK

Get in touch on 01413 063232

COMING SOON!

We really hope you enjoyed reading this book. If you're looking for more romance, be sure to head to the shops when new books are available on

Thursday 21st March

To see which titles are coming soon, please visit
millsandboon.co.uk/nextmonth